earth

a novel

book one in the elemental journey series

caroline allen

Winner Of The 2015 Independent Publishers Gold Medal For Best Regional Fiction, Midwest

PRINT ISBN: 978-0-9975824-0-6
EPUB ISBN: 978-0-9975824-1-3
Library of Congress Control Number: 2015900762

III

acknowledgments

A BIG THANK you to my sister Cathy, who helps me hold the truth of who I really am no matter how often I forget. To Elizabeth Mehlin, for her enduring friendship through our mutual creative endeavors. To Jon Sternfeld, who was one of the first people in the book industry to see some worth in this novel. Big hugs and gratitude to Luanne Brown for opening the door for me. To Leah Kohlenberg, whose advice saved Lady Luck's life. To Patricia Wynn Davies in the UK and Krystine Hetel in Massachusetts for reading early versions of this book and providing much-needed feedback. To Judith Laxer, who years ago channeled a message that my short stories might be put together to form a novel—from this, all four novels in the series came to me one night in an epic dream.

Much gratitude to my editor, Caroline Clouse, who has literary guts, creative chops and her finger on the pulse. To the book manager, Ensley Eikenburg, for her literary passion. To the book's designer, Greg Simanson, who never got cross with me for suggesting changes to the wonderful cover. To Polly Buckingham of Stringtown Press. Many of the stories in this novel found their first public audience at readings held by Stringtown in the Pacific Northwest. And a well of gratitude to Carol Santoro, of Santoro's Bookstore, for loving books so much, and for holding a brick-and-mortar space for public fiction readings.

A deep appreciation to all the writing clients I have coached through my business, Art of Storytelling. As I taught you, you taught me. Together we explored much more than just the technicalities of writing. We learned to honor and be guided by our authentic voice.

earth

We had the courage to be open to our vulnerability and to heal through truth and poetry. You are as much a part of my process as I have been of yours.

To my guides and muses, without you, this novel would've never been born, wrestled with and finally brought to publication.

And, finally, to my dead ancestors who showed up whether I wanted them to or not to guide my hand through the writing of this novel. You wanted to tell your story as much as I wanted to tell mine. The poor have a right to be heard, even if their story is a bruised and bloody one.

*This book is dedicated to the earth.
Thank you. I love you. I'm sorry.*

part

i

The Osage were renowned for the lyricism of their rituals. They were known to whisper to every newborn the story of the universe's creation.

chapter 1

I WAS THIRTEEN the day of my awakening. It was a weeding day. The heat stung the skin, boiled the brain. Sweat crawled like slime in crook and neck.

Mother worked the weeds a few rows over. She was small, close to the ground, Mother. Charcoal hair, a cow-milk face, a fairy-tale mother too close to a dirty earth. She worked row after row, hard and fast.

We stood in the massive vegetable garden ringed by posts and barbed wire. Scratchy cornstalks, the crimson suddenness of obese tomatoes, heavy watermelons on bulky vine, green beans in stuttered formation, bulbous onions exposed beneath soil, rows and rows of abrasive leaves and sweating half-grown food. Beyond the garden, a sprawling overgrown forest. Above, a blackbird lumbered through the weighty air. All morning, the sky had looked loaded, heavy with threat.

I bent to pluck a jarring straggler. I bent to pull a stuttered shoot. An arrowhead emerged from the soil. Once upon a time, the Osage peopled this land, sang its legends. I unearthed the silver stone, rubbed the still-sharp tip, worried it between index finger and thumb.

A sudden explosion tore at my body, a colossal clattering. I stood, arched my back, flung arms to the sky. Energy cracked my skull. The force began at my head, began at my feet, soared downward and upward and rammed at my gut. I sunk my boots deep into the marly soil. Eyes flung open.

earth

Roots sprouted from feet, a tuber from spine. Downward crawled the tuber into the soil, down and down, so deep into that rich soil. Inside the flesh of the earth, the tuber sprouted branches. From the branches, tendrils licked the mulch.

I arched, flung my arms skyward. My shoulders became the joints of tree limbs. Mulched forearms grew bark, fingers popped bulbs. Dirt coursed through veins, surged like a shock wave through arteries. I was some sort of massive tree, sprouting down into the soil, rising up toward the sky.

It felt good and right, like a memory, but then something began to go horribly wrong. All around, the earth started tearing up. The flesh of the ground rumbled and quaked. A crevasse, a great splintering, raged across the garden. The trees in the forest splintered and cracked, burst into flames. One of my arms fractured, broke in two as if struck by lightning. All around me in the garden, the crops dried, withered, shrunk. The sound was a low whine, an earth wail. Flocks scattered agony across the blue-black sky.

A white light quivered low and fast across the desecrated soil. Some kind of person was flying across the sky toward me. She blew to a halt in front of me. A woman, a Native woman. The surprise was the color of her: iridescent ruby, gold, sapphire. Her body threw off rainbow waves, a richness that made you want more, that sucked you in so deep. She put her face in mine. The flesh of her cheeks seemed to be swimming with light. Sparks flew from nose, mouth, eyes. Her eyes were so brown, so deep; her robe danced in wind song. She was Osage. I knew it deep in bone and vein.

She opened her mouth to speak. She had come with a message for me. I reached toward her in anticipation.

"Pearl!" I was being shaken. "Pearl!" I flopped, useless. The Native woman was gone. In front of me now, the milky face of my mother. She knelt in the dirt. Those mesmer green eyes. Under her breath, she said, "Not again."

She grabbed beneath my armpits and tried to haul me to my feet. My legs were jelly. "On the pain of Christ, wake up."

I came to. Everything was normal again, whole, the massive garden with its motley vegetables, the forest on the other side of the barbed wire, the sky mottled and gloomy. She shook me, gritted. "Wake up."

"You wake up," I said, low and exhausted, arms filthy with dirt.

chapter 2

I AWOKE THE next morning to a glowing. Outside the open window, the earth twittered in orchestral harmony. It flowered and burst, crackled in blue flame. I could hear, more. I could see, more. Something had happened to me after the vision in the garden. Everything seemed to glow.

The rising sunlight blazed rocks on the windowsill, lit pebbles on the dresser, glittered a crusted boulder in the corner of the hewn wood floor. Not just rocks, but eccentric roots. Rocks and roots and jam jars full of earth. Worms and ants and such. The sunlight turned the earth in my room alive with pulsings, with twitterings. I swallowed the changing color, the changing life within them, their changing form.

When I was little I used to see the earth this way, but as I grew up it went away. When I was little, the world fumed and seethed in multihued palette. The mystery set my belly aglow, tingled my spine. When I was little, I could not discern myself from other living beings. Everything was me. Dog, deer, calf. Sassafras, cottonweed, elm. Stream, lake, river. Every boot entering dog flesh entered my flesh, every knife worrying a joint, worried my joint.

With people it was even worse. Not just Meghan, Mother, Father; not just Jason and Bonnie, *any* person. The nuns at Holy Cross always said, *There but for the grace of God go I.* When I was little, I didn't think that way. When I was little, there was no separation between me and anybody else. When I saw a person, any person, I thought, *There go I. There go I. There go I.*

After Meghan left, life turned a hoary grey. My half-sister had a way of blocking our parents, of taking the first round of heat. After she left, Mother and Father were too difficult to resist, so I gave up. But it wasn't just them. I had to blame Holy Cross, too. Everybody's vision of the earth was just so mean. Each day of my life, each year was a study in distancing. The world gave lessons in learning not to love, learning how to leave, deciphering how to steal and horde and, in the end, understanding how to ignore the earth altogether. At first I resisted. After Meghan left, I let them win. I turned my face away from the land, prayed the feelings would die inside of me. I locked myself up, locked myself down.

A bird alighted on the windowsill. A starling, *runts of the sky*, Father called them. Why was it not with the others? Bands of starlings alighted in trees, hundreds of them, chattering like excited sisters. As I stared at it, I was its wing, its prattling throat, the tail feather. Its pulse was mine. I was filled up with its tiny breath. It didn't have to be some exotic creature; this yellow-beaked runt would do. I saw no difference in it and me.

I reached down and ran my hand along the rag quilt I'd kicked off the bed. It smoldered with old shirts, towels, trousers, textured patterns of our life. Mother's tiny stitches pulsed like erratic heartbeats. I reached for the clutch of pebbles and sassafras root littering the scarred side table. I held the gaggle to my cheek, breathed in muck and musk.

In the kitchen below, farm reports on the distant radio: summer corn up 1.1 percent; hay, potatoes up 2. I could smell the glum grease of bacon, the shady musk of coffee. The screen door banged. Boots on gravel. Truck door creaked, slammed. Engine growled.

Father had gone hunting. Depending on the season, he hunted deer, squirrel, rabbit, quail, wild turkey. He fished bass, crappie, pike, perch, catfish, carp. We lived off the food the land had to give us, forest creatures, garden harvest, flesh and egg of chicken, meat and milk of cow. We would have never survived without what the soil, forest, and river had to give. It was the 1970s. You could still find such spaces then, gullible earth places.

I jumped when my bedroom door creaked open, Mother's white face in the crack.

"Get on up now. We're runnin' late," she said, her eyes so exhausted. She studied my room. She didn't see me seeing her. She could never see how much I saw. She would have cleared that room like a hurricane, like a thunderstorm, if she thought she could get away with it. It was full of too much reminder of dirt. She was so tired of the earth. She was so run down by the land. She wanted town more than anything in the world. She wanted away from the drudgery so bad, she'd do almost anything to make it happen. She stood just outside my doorway and peered in with a face like rot.

We clanked and thumped down the pitted road to the farm. Mother drove the orange truck with rounded fenders and a gear shift on the steering wheel. The farm sat more than a mile from the house. I sat on one of the fenders in the back, feet on old rope. On both sides of the pock-marked dirt road, the acres of thick forest were full that day of mystery and parable, interlocking plots of legend and folklore. The woods sweated summer, and I sweated with it. We buzzed, cackled, cawed. I let my hair be swiped by overhead branches. I let the trees caress me. I reached for the pouch around my neck.

I untied the pouch and took out its gem. Inside, a pearl, but it wasn't like any pearl you saw in books. It was gluey, with a glob like a birthmark. It had lumps. It was misshapen. Ugly. Meghan gave it to me because of my name the night before she disappeared. I didn't know it was a goodbye gift. I would never have accepted it if I knew it was a gift of guilt for leaving me behind.

We used to play a game, Meghan and I. When people leave like that, you cling to the only stories you know, you build up memories into mythology, hang onto their legend for dear life. She'd spent so many years alone with Father as a very little girl. Her real mom had died of breast cancer when she was two. Father didn't meet my mother until Meghan was five. It was three whole years, and she was so little, and she only had Father. I thought about that a lot. How could anyone survive with no one but Father?

Meghan and I played this game where we drew on each other's backs, letters and pictures while the other would guess.

"Come on, guess, for God's sake. What am I drawing?"

"Apple?"

"It's two circles. Two. You're supposed to be the smart one." She kept drawing over and over. She smelled like an overripe peach, like rotting fruit that bruised when you touched it. We had a few pictures that we used all the time: a smiley face, a stick person.

"Table?"

"Two circles? How can that be a table?" She poked me hard. The story of our lives, written in Braille, carved into each other's flesh.

I ran the back of my hand across my snotty nose. We were in her room. Her room was a magic kingdom, Aladdin's cave. Strips of fabric that should never have gone together hung like glorious tapestries from the windows. She'd learned quilting, and then took the front side of a pair of jeans she'd outgrown, and the front side of a T-shirt she liked, and she'd sewn them directly into an old rag quilt, like this empty person was lying on top of her bed. On the bedside table stood one of her doll lamps. She'd asked once for my old dolls, tore off their heads and used them for lamps. If Mother stayed clear of my room because of all the earth, she didn't ever even open Meghan's door.

I wore blue footy pajamas. She had on some Chinese robe she got at the thrift store and sat on the bed beside me. She pushed her fingers hard into my back.

"Stop hurting me!"

"Don't you even know what a circle is?"

"Train?"

"No!" She scratched my arm with her fingernails. That was her favorite trick, leaving blood tracks on your flesh. She was like a cat that would go suddenly mean. I grabbed my arm, scooted away. She had some serious hormones growing in her body, because her fingernails always grew long, sharp, strong.

"It was bike, you idiot. Bike!"

That was the last time I saw her. I spent hours wondering if I'd made her leave, if my stupidity was too much for her when we played the game. The next morning she was gone. Before I knew she was gone, before I knew that she wasn't just at school, before I knew that days would turn into years with no sign of her, I found a small box at the foot of my bed. I opened it, and there was that ugly misshapen pearl on a bed of cotton. There was no note, but I knew it was from her.

Mother maneuvered the truck out of the forest thickness into the light, and parked. I put the pearl back in the pouch, stuffed the memories as hard as I could into that pouch. I looked up to see the farm glittering like a gem. Our farm was a miracle. How had I not seen this before? The barn glowed like a crimson sunset across the way in the field; I watched the cows eat the scrub and weeds and felt how delicious the ground tasted, how full their bellies were, the shack with bent fencing for chickens like a dilapidated castle in some fairy tale, the football field-sized garden sprouted giddy shoots, all babbling in their own eccentric language. The smell of mud and excrement. The guttural accents of livestock. A paradise where shit and stink had no need to hide.

I caught my foot on the rope and fell from the back to the hard-bitten ground. Mother came, stood over me as I blew on my bloodied knee. As a family, we stood over each other a lot. We never touched. It wasn't done.

"I need you to keep your head on straight today. We got a lot of work," she said and made her way to the garden.

Since I could remember, I'd collected the eggs, bottle-fed the calves and then helped Mother work the garden. My hurt knee made it hard to walk, and I wobbled into the cockeyed two-by-fours and bent barbed wire, where we kept the twenty-five chickens and one rooster. The scrawny rooster must've smelled something. He was a mean cuss. He came right at me, pecked me into a corner, wildly flapped his useless wings. He stuck his spur into my burning knee as he climbed my leg, landed square on my back, working his crazy wings the whole time. I swore, swung my arms. His wings tangled in my black chaos of hair. I hollered. He scratched and kneaded, flapped and squawked. I swung my body to throw him off. He sunk a spur deep into the back of my T-shirt, deep into flesh.

Every year, the chickens arrived as chicks in a cardboard box. Dozens of beaks perched upward. A tweeting, a keening. Baby birds begging. Feed me. Three or four were always dead at the bottom of the box, buried beneath the clumsy feet of the others. Mournful of the dead chicks, I'd look up into Father's cracked eyes, and he'd say, "Don't look at me like that. If they can't keep up, they deserve what they get."

The hens glowed and crackled with a fiery luminosity in the dark shed. I didn't know how long this would last, how long yesterday's vision would keep heightening my senses like this. It was painful to see this much. Thousands of small black and white crusty dollops of shit crunched as I walked. Feathers, flesh and excrement sweated up in rancid stench. I reached beneath the warm radiant bellies. The heft of the hens on the back of my hand, the comfort and warmth of the oval eggs in palm. I was filled up by the beauty of it, stacking the brown marvels into the tin pan. On the way back out, that crazy rooster again.

The calves lived behind barbed wire. We raised them for less than a year and slaughtered them for the meat. In a plastic blue bucket, I mixed formula and water with a stick, poured the watery mixture into oversized baby bottles, attached the bottles to metal holders, hung them from a wooden plank affixed to the fence.

Quack and Baby sucked and kneaded the rubber nipples. I stroked the tops of their heads. The scratchy fur of them. The deep pools of their eyes. I watched the drool from their mealy mouths drip and mix with dry dirt.

Instead of the warm soft underbellies of their mothers, the calves got plastic, rubber, metal. And me.

I waddled to the garden gate. My knee burned from falling off the truck; the back of my T-shirt felt wet with blood from the holes the rooster had poked. My hair was a rat's nest from the rooster's wings and my heart hurt. I put my arm through the fence and took the wire off the nail. Mother was bent over the green beans.

I went up and saw the beans were suffering. Mother was trying to figure out what was ailing them. She turned a small green finger in the palm of her gritty hard-knuckled hand.

I reached down and took a different bean in my palm. Something happened. A glow. This time it wasn't only me noticing. The bean pulsed. It appeared to heal. Mother stood up straight now, watching.

"Pearl," she said hard and low. "Go on and get yourself back to the truck."

I felt the bean like it was a friend, or a piece of my flesh. I didn't want to let go.

Mother took my hand, took the bean out of it. Her hands shook. "You've had your fill of this garden this week. Go on back to the truck and wait."

I sat in the bed of the truck and watched the leaves chatter to each other. I had never seen Mother so angry. I didn't understand what happened when I held the bean, and I didn't understand why it'd made Mother so angry. All I could think was she was never going to let me work the garden again. *Telling me I can't go in the garden is like telling me I can't eat, or go to the bathroom. The garden is my body. How could I not be allowed my own body?*

We were back at the house, and I was helping Mother clean the floors when Father returned from hunting. It was summer, there was no school, so I was put to work all day.

Our house was built of thick brick. No wolf could huff it down. A fireplace as big as one wall made from local rock. A river-worn slab of cherry wood for a mantel; on the mantel, rocks. Father collected stones: river rock, forest boulder, chunks of gravel. In the corner, a glassed cupboard protecting the specials: canary gypsum, streaked limonite, black feldspar; in a hidden drawer, a lump of gold. The furniture had holes where stuffing peeked through. The orange shag carpet was torn.

On the wall, glassy-eyed deer heads. Seven severed heads. Twelve- and ten-point bucks. Blank eyes, antlers snaking out. A picture of Jesus bare-chested and bloodied. The picture moved when you moved. Jesus's eyes opened and closed as you traveled across the living room. His eyes followed you with anguish, begged you with hurting. When I was real little, Meghan pointed to the picture, asked, "Why is Jesus bleeding?"

"Because he loves me," I'd responded.

I shut off the vacuum and pretended to be dusting. It was best to be on guard with Father, to know what sort of mood he was in. I heard Mother whispering to him in the kitchen. Harsh undertones. Fearful murmurs. He came into the living room. I didn't look up from dusting the big box television. It was best to pretend he wasn't there.

"Pearl, get on outside." I could smell the shit and blood on him. I looked sideways. He had the rifle resting along his arm. I stared straight up the barrel. Every time he had that rifle on his arm, it seemed the barrel pointed right at my head. Since I could remember, I'd thought, *This man wants me dead.*

"I heard all about that nonsense in the garden. So, you better get yourself outside." I stood and followed him. Gangly legs in loose jeans, he always walked as if he was about to tip over. His red hair stood aflame, his boots and legs slathered in mud, mucking up the floors we'd already cleaned, that gun like an extension of himself, like a third arm.

There were a dozen small squirrels on a string on the ground. The sun threw a halo that turned the burnt grass to a circle of lime. He threw the line of beasts into the halo of light. A great sadness swelled up. My arms grew numb. The vision had done something to me, or re-done it, because all I felt was grief for the lost life of the tiny creatures.

Father knelt on one knee, untied the legs of the dead squirrels. "You're going skin all these." He thrust his browned hunting knife into my palm.

Of course I'd done a lot of butchering, a hundred, a thousand times. I was thirteen, for God's sake. I took the knife like I was swimming against some vicious current. The squirrels on the ground warbled and warped in crazy vision. I let the knife drop.

Father bent and shoved the knife back into my hand. He spoke as if he was underwater. I had to watch his lips to understand. "Do it."

I knelt, took the squirrel, bent its tail back, feeling drugged or drunk. Around me, a boiling wind blew branches in epic dance, as if the trees were trying to speak. I cut where tail met spine. I'd done it so many times. I pulled and the fur came off like a miniature coat. I stood slowly, like Joan of Arc on the way to the fire that would burn her to hell, and put the tail under my boot, took the hind legs and yanked until all the fur was around the head. I stared at the tip of the knife before niggling it into the fur around the neck, cutting off the pelt and throwing it on the grass. I didn't cut off the head because Father liked to eat the brains.

He took the squirrel out of my hands, kneeled in the grass, held the legs, and put the pink body belly up.

"I'll gut it." His eyes were bloodshot. He held his tongue between his teeth, bent his head, his hair like a slather of wet red paint. His face was rough and pockmarked, a dry landscape full of craters and cracked river beds. I turned my face away.

"Don't you turn your head. Don't you turn your face away from this. This here is survival. This here is what keeps you alive."

My mind warped. I watched as the bloodied pink squirrel became Father. Morphed into me. Became a miniature version of Mother. We were the shorn and exposed body of these skittering mammals. We were this naked beast. I wanted to scream, *Father, we're butchering ourselves!*

His head snapped up. Had I said the words out loud? A mighty energy worked his limbs. He stood, his long skinny fingers stained with blood. Father's anger was monstrous. If he wanted something and you misunderstood, he blew into a fury storm. If you asked him about his past, a question about his sister or father, the clouds engulfed him, blood boiled his pocked face. He'd rise from his chair at dinner time, stand above you with raised bony fist. I learned real quick not to ask. Not to speak.

He held the knife to my face, spoke dry and hard. "You take this here knife, and you skin every one of those. Then you gut every single one of them." He pointed the sharp tip of the knife at my nose. "This here is real life. Real life." His whole body was shaking. "No daughter of mine—" He didn't finish. He couldn't seem to finish. His pocked face was purple. He looked like he would explode. He dropped the knife, turned and tipped sideways as he walked back to the house.

When I finished skinning and gutting, I was washed in sweat. I felt almost loopy, like laughing hysterically. I put the intestines into a banged-up pot, walked them down the hill to where Lady Luck was chained. Lady Luck was a boy; Father named him. It was his sense of humor. You wouldn't know it most of the time, but Father had a strong sense of humor. He had a bumper sticker on his truck: "A fool and his money are soon partying."

Lady Luck was a bird dog, meant for running and fetching. He was kept chained all day. His life was a circle of worn dirt, his whole universe the length of his chain. I came up to where he lay on his belly whimpering. I turned over the squirrel innards and plopped them into the dirt.

God was in the details, or the devil. Did it matter? Was there a difference? I came into the kitchen. Mother had on a patterned polyester blouse, cream trousers with an elastic waistband. Mud-stained flat sneakers. The details. She smelled like dirt—not fresh earth but grime. She was always cleaning something. Back centuries, the women were always put to work cleaning up the messes.

I handed the pink bodies to her in the kitchen as she stood bent at the counter. "Good girl," she said and turned on the tap. "I forgot to fill the zink. Get the rest out of the icebox." She used *zink* instead of *sink*, *icebox* instead of *refrigerator*. She'd say, "I'm going to wash your mouth out with soap." "You made your bed, now sleep in it." Father would say, "I'll wring your scrawny neck," and "Get on out outside and cut your own switch."

I went to the round and rusted refrigerator, pulled the long crowbar handle. On the top shelf sat a bowl of bodies. They smelled cold, and the blood swished around the clear glass.

"That refrigerator," I said, disgusted. Everything seemed deprived and smelly to me right then.

"Pearl, you don't know what poor is." She said it real quiet, like a prayer. Her whole life, Mother planted the earth, harvested, shucked, chopped, canned. She butchered, gutted, dried, and froze. She pinned, cut, sewed. She knitted. She stewed. She boiled, baked, fried. She laundered. She vacuumed. She scrubbed. Her hands were raw. Her fingers long and bony, her knuckles swollen hard like marbles. Her back was curved. She'd grown up having to take care of eleven brothers and sisters, and even though there were three of us, she couldn't get out of the habit and worked like we were a dozen mouths to feed, baby birds begging, *feed me*.

I always thought Mother was just so very tired. I often thought that Mother was exhausted beyond all reason.

She palmed a squirrel. I guess I had tears on my face. I guess the color of my skin was a slime green. I felt so sick. Mother looked sideways. "I thought we put all this behind us, Pearl." She spoke soft and gentle. I loved when she spoke soft and gentle; it wasn't often. "You was doing real good there for a while." I didn't know what she was talking about. Had the vision happened before? I didn't know what she was saying.

Father walked by us to go outside. The screen door slamming sounded like someone screaming. Mother took the knife, leaned over the cutting board and cut the squirrel's legs off, chop, chop, chop, chop. She said, still softly, without looking up, "Your Aunt Nadine had the gift. You don't know what that woman did to your father." Aunt Nadine was Father's sister, the family shame, in and out of the nuthouse. Funny Farm Nadine, Nuthouse Nadine? Was I like Nadine? Mother said in a whisper, "What the world did to that woman."

"Pearl, you got to survive in this world. You got to be tough to survive. You can't live like this—you'll get crushed. Smashed right down. I seen it happen with Nadine."

She handed me a severed head. I put it on a flowered platter on the counter. She handed me the chopped-off legs. The torso. I put each on the platter.

The next day was Saturday. I woke up just at dawn and climbed out my bedroom window while Mother and Father slept. I climbed out a lot after Meghan left, onto the roof, across oak limbs, down the belly-burning trunk.

The woods behind the house, just on the other side of Lady Luck's dog house, leaned away like a great wind had sucked them from behind. It was the same woods that went all the way to the farm. A fist of brambles and underbrush, and nobody ever walked all the way through it to the farm. I'd always thought Mother liked it this way, the farm's stink and toil sitting behind a wall, giving her house an aura of being that much closer to town.

As I passed the doghouse, Lady Luck raised his head from the dirt and whined. We'd had him two years, and nobody ever touched him. It just wasn't done. Animals were animals. They had no relationship to us but as food, or as chasers of food.

As I rushed past, his pitched moan seemed to chase me. I flung myself deep into the thicket and stumbled over roots as I went deeper and deeper into the woods. Finally, I came to the sassafras. Behind it was a clearing, a secret place that as far as I knew nobody else had discovered. I flattened my palm on the nubby bark of the sassafras, flesh of an old friend.

I came to the clearing a lot right after Meghan left, to get away from the blown-up fear in the house, to ponder my sister. A patch of scrub grass like hair. A copse of speckled alders in strict formation. A pond and mulched log for sitting. Dragonflies buzzed low over the slimy, stagnant water. Branches of pawpaw and sweet gum moaned in the wind. A bush rustled, a twig broke from small mammals skittering. Around me bird chatter, sudden scramble of forest critter. And behind it all, Lady Luck with that low, vibrating whine that pulsed its way into flesh, lodged its way into throat, until his whine became mine.

I'd sit on the mulched log and feel like I was no different than every leaf floating down from every tree in that clearing. Over time, I found dozens of arrowheads sticking up from the soil. Carved from cliff rock, the color of limestone and granite, they were jagged-edged and burnished to a shine. They felt good in the pocket. I'd run through the woods, slapping my mouth, howling like an Osage. I wanted to be that wild. I wanted to have that connection, that legend to tell. I thought that with the power of those arrowheads, I could do anything. I could even bring my sister back.

The vision of the Native woman had made everything shift, and the clearing glowed up something fierce. White light streamed off bark and branch. I went over to where the creek dribbled through, stared at the phosphorescent water, kneeled beside it.

I put my hand in the creek water. As liquid hit flesh, something happened. The water flowed backward, forward, upward, down into the soil, all at the same time. Like my idea of direction was all wrong. I knew this way of seeing was something to do with the vision, knew it was a step up from when I was a kid and saw myself as every other living thing. Then the flesh of my hand started to become liquid, flesh, bone. Sinew flowed with the water, kept form only vaguely. I turned my hand in the creek, over and over in awe.

Later, spacey and light, I roamed out of the woods, back up to the house. I forgot to climb up through my bedroom and come down the stairs. Mother stood at the stove, frying up eggs. "Where have you been? We got a lot to do today," she said, but I ignored her and made my way upstairs.

I dug under my bed until I found the old Bible in its torn box. I lugged it into the upstairs bathroom and locked myself in. Nobody was going to tell me what was happening to me, and I needed to find some answers. I had nowhere to go for answers. The bathroom was no bigger than a closet, with low roof beams, an exposed bulb, a showerhead. I sat on the toilet lid, balanced on my toes, opened the book across my knees.

That *King James Bible* and an almanac were the only books we ever had in the house. Once, a hardbound *Reader's Digest* Father had found in the woods, some of the pages so speckled with mold you could make out only sixty percent of the words. All my life I was starving for books. Hungry for story.

I'd already read the Old Testament. After Meghan left, I'd locked myself in the bathroom and covered the begetting and begatting, brother killing brother, being forced off the land, tossed off the earth, ripped from the magic of the soil. Lobbing a rock, flailing a bit of a plow, cracking a sibling over the head. Blood flowing and soaking. Forced to roam. Some crazy, heart-wrenching, gut-wrenching universal plan.

In my house, nobody ever told tales. It wasn't just my parents. My relatives were all shut up too. The silence of my kinfolk wove core-deep. So few stories, you could fit them in the palm of your hand. Poor folk didn't talk about themselves, wary of what specters such stories might invoke. I was surrounded by clenched jaws, thinned and bitter lips. My story was a lack of story, a poverty of legend, a dearth of poetry. I wanted to tell Mother that our being poor wasn't just about food—we were starved for legend.

When I was in the third grade, the nuns at Holy Cross brought us to Mass early on a Tuesday. We went to Mass twice a week as part of school, and my family went on Sundays, too. Church had a few things going for it. Light threw rainbows from the stained glass, frankincense billowed fragrant fog, candles flickered in brass. The priests' fluid gowns, the harmony of hymns, the cavernous grunt of organ. We didn't have much ritual on the farm. The sensual luxury craved me to dance, to bark, to bellow.

That Tuesday, Father Michael came down from the altar, and the altar boys lugged boxes from the back room. The priest reached in, presented one *Bible* to each of us with both hands, as if it were a precious, kingly offering. The book was in a box lined with rice paper. Inside, the thick black cover embossed in gold. My first book! I printed my name in awkward lettering on the first page.

In the bathroom, I opened to the New Testament. I cradled the book like a newborn baby. I petted the page like it was the head of a calf. I would study Jesus, see if he could tell me what was going on. See if he had some answers to life.

Over the next few days, the earth went back to normal. It was good. I could not hide myself in that state, and I could not bear Mother's and Father's reactions. I still didn't have any answers as the world around me returned to its dull grey.

Three weeks later, it was nighttime and we were watching *Hee Haw* on the big TV. Mother and Father were lying together on the sofa. Most of the time, Father acted like he was the kid and she was the mom. He called her "Mother," and when I was telling her something, he'd interrupt, like we were two kids competing for her attention.

Other times, they had this love that kept you excluded, that kept you starving while they feasted. They'd lie in each other's arms all evening on the plaid, scratchy sofa, like they were one person.

They'd say maybe two sentences all night: *Sarah, your hair's gettin' in the way*, or *Terrence, my arm's gone all tingly again.*

I sat Indian style on the shag in front of the TV. *Gloom, despair, and agony on me. Ooooh. Deep, dark depression, excessive misery. Ooooh. If it weren't for bad luck, I'd have no luck at all. Ooooh. Gloom, despair, and agony on me.*

It happened so suddenly, I was up and on tiptoe before I knew what was going on. Energy took me from above, shook me from below, pulled me to the very tips of my toes. Again, the core of me became root stem, carved hard and furious through the living room floor, down into the basement, smacked fiercely through the concrete, until the tuber hit soil, the root plunged deep and root hairs spread like flames. My body became bark, my arms twisted branches that broke through ceiling plaster and roof shingle, begged up into night sky.

A white light sucked through the gaping maw of the ceiling. The Native woman. She whipped in like a tornado, a whirling ball of light. Her face rocked into mine. The wind of her blew like an air stream through the upper limbs of my old-growth arms.

The walls of the house fell, and the land outside, the hill leading to Lady Luck's doghouse and the forest beyond, tore up as before, a great force that broke trees and cracked soil. I heard wailing, a cry that came from all corners of the planet. The pain of it was excruciating. It tortured me, broke every one of my bones, sent fire through my veins. Again, the Native woman opened her mouth to speak, again she croaked out air, again no words came.

I saw Father grab my arms from some far-off place, heard Mother say, "Terrence, Terrence" in that pleading voice, but still he held tight, his fear leaving bruises. When I came to, he was dragging me up the stairs. His body shook with rage and fear.

Later, I lay on top of the quilt on my bed. What was happening to me? What was going on? What was this Osage woman trying to tell me? Was there something I was supposed to do?

"What is it you want from me?" I cried. I repeated it like a mantra: "What do you want? What do you want? What do you want?"

My belly filled with fists of anxiety. I fell into a nightmare sleep of medieval proportions.

chapter 3

"RUN!" I TURNED and screamed. "Run, I said run!"

Jason just stood and stared at me. I ran like mad up Powwow. He stood on the side of the dirt road skipping like a boxer, throwing punches. If he didn't take the racing seriously, he was never ever going to survive.

"Goddamnit, Jason, pick up your stupid feet!" I'd taken up cursing. At Holy Cross, the nuns taught us not to use God's name in vain and how it was a sin to curse with God's name, but since I'd taken up cursing, I'd lie in bed and the words *God shit, God shit, God shit* would fill my head to rattling. I couldn't stop it. *God shit, God shit, God shit.* I knew I was going to hell.

"Sonofabitch, Jason," I screamed. I was at the top of Powwow, about to run onto Tomahawk. He stared at something in the grass. He usually had his sketch book, but I guess he left it back at his bike. Father called him lazy. Mother said, *No wonder that family's so poor.* Bonnie was still at the bottom, heaving because of her weight. I knew he was waiting for Bonnie. Jason was always waiting for people.

I hadn't been at school for a couple of days because the vision had left me floppy, sick and bedridden. Bonnie and Jason rode their bikes over to see what was up. They were like angels, leaning their faces against the back screen door. Father was still so angry. The grimy smell of ham hock and beans.

"Can Pearl come out for a race?" they yelled through the screen. Bonnie and Jason always showed up when I needed them most. I bolted up, and without asking to be excused, I ran headlong out the screen door. I nearly knocked over a smiling Bonnie. I ran past Jason. I bolted into the middle of the dirt road and just kept running.

"Slow down!" Jason yelled. "You're acting like the world's going to end."

I was the fastest kid in the county, faster than anyone from town. A few nights a week, kids came to the door and asked for a race. I always complied. I always won.

"Jason, if you ain't gonna run, I'll just meet you back at the house," I screamed back at him.

"Just go, then." I heard Jason's voice float on the wind. I noticed the blood on my thumb and stuck it in my mouth intermittently as I ran. I had this bad habit of picking at my thumbs. In the dishwater, the flesh had craters. *Jason, if you're not willing to run, not willing to run as hard and fast as you are able, not willing to do whatever it takes to beat them all, to leave them all behind, I can't help you. There's not a thing I can do for you.*

After Tomahawk, the plunge down Mohawk let me blow it all out, a big gush as if I'd been holding my breath for years. My head bobbed, my shoulders tangoed backward. Around me, farm houses and barns fought savage branches, creeping roots, vicious brambles. We lived just this side of wild primal force. The earth snaked up, threatened to tear the buildings to pieces. I loved the power of the soil, how it didn't care about human-built things. As I ran, I could smell the musk of the past, the cold, dark pheromones of it—a primordial legacy slumbering just inches beneath the fertile soil.

We lived in the middle of the middle of the middle. Landlocked. Missouri was a place where the people may have been poor, but the land was stinking rich. In the woods, rattlesnake and deer, skittering mammals dragging fur-bellied along the debris of the earth. In the depths of hundreds of waterways, carp, trout, muddy-bellied catfish. Turtles the size of small children Mother plopped into a pot to boil. Skies teemed a rainbow of bluebirds, red robins, crimson cardinals, blackbirds. The body of the landscape rose up in limestone and dolomite cliffs. Most nights, a blackness so deep, a speckling of fireflies so glittering that a mythology grew in the stars of the sky.

No mountains or oceans existed anywhere near Missouri to impede the forces of air that barreled down, that blew upward, that slammed together in the heartland. Tornadoes whipped and pummeled, smacked the pulsing earth. Seasons thumped and walloped—livid heat, perishing cold. The landscape braced the soul, defined the flesh. Summer burned your soul, autumn sank your heart, winter froze the very core, and spring was the only season of hope.

On the steep final push back up Powwow, my mind slipped off its post. This was why I ran: to forget, to lose myself. All that was left was salty sweat falling like a promise across my lips and wind so strong it washed everything, absolutely everything, right out of my head.

I came to a stop in the scrubby front yard of the house. I paced the yard waiting for Jason. I paced the yard, thinking.

I had Nadine's address and phone on a slip of paper wrapped around the arrowhead in my pouch. I'd snuck into Mother's purse to find it. Nadine lived in Hermann. I had to figure out what she knew about visions. I had to understand what was going on. I picked my thumb. I went and stood in the middle of the dirt road in front of our house and sucked it, thinking, thinking.

It took a long time before Jason appeared at the bottom of Powwow, still shadow boxing as he ran. Bonnie was nowhere to be seen. I watched him run. He was thin and blonde, had a dancing way of moving his body. Other boys beat him up a lot. I was waiting for the bus once. He was yards away, walking toward me. I watched as two boys came up behind him, knocked him down, and took turns jumping on his stomach. I left my body and watched.

"Why didn't you wait?" Jason gasped. He was beside me. He bent over his knees to catch his breath.

"Time, tide and Pearl wait for no man," I said. I thought that line a lot in my head, but I'd never said it out loud. Since the visions, I kept letting things slip, kept finding it harder to hide myself.

earth

He burst out laughing. He stumbled onto the front lawn, held his guffawing stomach and fell sideways. Despite myself, I started giggling. I went up to his writhing body and pushed at his shoulder. He grabbed my arm and pulled me down and we rolled. Bonnie showed up a while later. Jason stood up and was helping me off the ground when Bonnie dive-bombed on top of me. I lay flattened beneath her, winded. She was so danged fat.

"What's so funny?" Bonnie asked, poker-faced, jiggling her fat body and making me gasp with giggles. The smell of her was like carrots with the dirt still clinging. Jason looked at my smashed skinny body and set off laughing again. The three of us rolled like happy puppies across our scrubby, balding yard.

One week later, Jason and I stood at the rock cut, panting, straddling our bikes. I'd talked Jason into going on the paper route with me. I could talk Jason into almost anything. We were about six miles from my house.

I needed Jason so I could find the entrance to the highway in town. I figured if I got him to the cut, we'd just take the new road straight in.

They'd just blasted the rock a couple of months earlier. Before, the end of my paper route was a dead end. The rock cut was all jagged outcropping and smooth stones in rough patterns, like a prickly, filthy quilt. People came from all around to watch the blasting. It was twenty-five feet high, sixty feet long. They'd put up signs: "Watch out for Falling Rock."

Hidden beneath burlap in the wire baskets on my bike was a map I bought from the gas station. I'd inked in the route to Hermann. I could've told Jason what I was doing, but I would have had to tell him everything, and I didn't trust anyone with the truth. I didn't trust anyone with anything, ever. I found people were not to be trusted.

Also in the basket, a fried chicken leg, a breast of duck, two slices of homemade bread, and three strands of deer jerky left over from last fall. In my pocket, $6.45 I'd earned from my paper route.

"Do you know who Falling Rock is?" I asked Jason, pointing at the sign.

Jason groaned. I was always telling stories. Mother said, *The worst thing you can do is not let Pearl tell her stories. She can take anything else, but don't interrupt her when she's telling one of her tales.*

"Actually, my father told me this."

"Oh, that's even better," Jason said. He got off his bike, leaned it and himself against the cut, folded his arms.

I didn't say, *Like you're the one to talk with that mother of yours.*

Jason had a glow about him, a yellow cloud of something like joy that followed him. He had no reason to be so happy, with that mother and the way the boys beat him up, but he carried happiness in his flesh. He couldn't have shaken it if he tried.

A bumble bee troubled my hair, and I swiped like a madwoman at the air.

"You know who Falling Rock is, don't you?" Father had asked, in that mumbling stumbling way. We were in the truck on Sunday on our way back from Mass, right after they'd opened the road. I wore this peach dress that Mother had sewn. In one month I'd outgrown it, and it pulled tight and awkward at my armpits. I was all gangly legs and arms, and my nose was too big for my face.

"You know who Falling Rock is?" Father repeated, because nobody responded.

"Not who, what. What," I said as if talking to a retarded child. It was getting harder and harder to hide my real thoughts. It was going to become a bona fide problem if I didn't watch it.

"Don't get smart with me." His long neck craned down. "Falling Rock was an Native He loved a woman name of …" He

27

paused, looked around. We were passing a small apple orchard. "Apple Tree."

I giggled. He turned and gave me that fisted look, and I swallowed it quick.

Jason had his arms crossed and stared at me, waiting for me to start.

"Oh sorry," I said and shook myself. I had this problem sometimes. I got lost in my mind. I had to be careful, because I thought others were following along with me as I told stories in my head, but really I hadn't spoken a word. This was the only story Father had ever told, as far as I could remember, and it was a fable, not real at all. Maybe he thought he told me more. Maybe he thought he'd given me the map of his childhood or related the goings-on of our ancestors. Maybe like me, tales spun like tornadoes inside his skull, and he thought the anecdotes were spilling from him, when really they were locked up tight like prisoners, forbidden to leave.

I repeated to Jason how Falling Rock had fallen in love with a woman named Apple Tree.

"Apple Tree," I continued, "had to go far to visit her mother in another village—far, far away. So far away it took her weeks to walk." I swiped the air and felt the small body of the bee brush my palm.

"Falling Rock missed her. But he had to stay behind because there was this big hunt, and he was some big Injun."

Jason groaned. He hated how the older folks in Missouri mocked the Indians, not that any of them knew any. More than a hundred years before, all the Osage and the other tribes had been forced off their land, and now their descendants all lived in a reservation somewhere in Oklahoma. Jason was as fascinated with the Osage as I was, had his own collection of arrowheads, and even a fish scaler, a curved rock that I would've thrown back not knowing what it was.

"I'm using my father's voice," I said.

"Well, that makes it OK then." Jason rolled his eyes. I hated anyone telling me what to do, so I put on an even thicker redneck accent.

"Fallin' Rock n' Apple Tree used ta sit out under them there stars and make themselves up some stories. Like they'd see themselves a few stars in a triangle and pretend it was a teepee and it was where Mother Bear lived, and they'd make up Mother Bear stories. They come up with their own legends. He loved her with all his heart." At this point, in the truck, Father had looked at Mother, and they'd merged, and despite the heat I'd felt bitterly cold. It was as if I didn't exist.

"Well Apple Tree somehow got lost. Nobody could find her. Nobody had word of her. They sent search parties, but they just couldn't find her. So Falling Rock left the village forever and promised himself he wouldn't come back until she was found. He wandered here and there, year after year, searching for Apple Tree, searching for his heart. He's still looking." I pointed to a road sign in front of us. "That's why they got signs, 'Watch out for Falling Rock.'"

I went up to Jason, pointed to the top of the cut. "If you look real close, you can see him standin' at the top of the cut, lookin' lost and lonely."

Jason smirked. "I wouldn't look for Falling Rock. They should have signs, "Watch out for Apple Tree." We should all be searching for her." I looked at him closely. Sometimes he said the oddest things, things that made you think.

I changed the subject. "Hey, let's bike to town." I said it as nonchalantly as I could.

"Yeah, right, let's take off on our bikes, and you won't get home until after dark, and your dad will come after me with one of his rifles. That'll be fun."

"Come on. If I'm with you, he won't worry. It's just me going by myself, 'cause I'm this precious little flower." I batted my eyes, leaned and nudged him with my shoulder. Sweaty from the biking, mud tracks in the folds of our necks and elbows. Jason stank like a boy. "I know this Native American burial ground. I heard about it at school. It's right in town."

"What burial ground? I've never heard of a burial ground in town, and I've lived there all my life."

"It's new. They just discovered it," I lied.

He looked at me doubtfully. He stood from where he was leaning, walked out of the shadow into the blistering sun and looked up at the top of the cut as if he was really looking for Apple Tree. He stood so long, I began to grow nervous. I had only so much time to get to town and find the highway to Hermann. I knew better than to say anything, though, when he was in such a state.

"Listen," he said, still staring up at the top of the cut, "I want to give you something. I was thinking I could give it to you some other time, but I think I should give it to you now."

He pulled a folded-up piece of paper out of his back pocket. His face was barn-red as he came up to me with it. "Sorry, it got squished."

My fingers were black with newspaper ink, and I smudged the white paper as I opened it. It was a drawing. I'd always been Jason's biggest fan when it came to his art. Even when we were little, I'd force him to keep drawing. He told me once that I had a way of seeing people that could save their lives. I'd thought of Mother, Father, Meghan, those butchered squirrels—I hadn't saved anybody's life. I'd had nothing but trouble with the way I saw things since I could remember.

No, Jason was the one who had a way of seeing. I looked at the drawing. Along the top, he'd written, *Time, Tide and Pearl*. He'd drawn a picture of me running up the middle of a country lane, swamped by massive old-growth forest. He drew it with colored pencils from above, as if he was hovering above me in the sky. He'd colored me red, and I was no bigger than a fingernail. I looked so small, so vulnerable, against the huge forest swamping on both sides. Along the edge in a field, he'd added a red barn. The red of me and the red of the barn were like two spots of blood in a dark-green landscape. The picture was so beautiful it terrified me. I folded it quickly and shoved it in my front pocket.

"So, what do you think?" He reached toward my pocket. I jerked back.

"Sure, yeah, it's great," I said, walking toward my bike.

"It's OK if you don't like it," he called after me.

"Jesus, I like it!" I got on my bike and headed down the hill toward town.

I heard Jason scramble to his bike, pedal fast to catch up with me, and yell, "Goddamnit, Pearl! Your father is going to kill me." All I really was thinking about was that sketch. It was the first time I realized art could tell so much truth it could scare the pants off a person. It was the first time I realized art was like my visions and could change the world.

Town was a strip of stores, a couple of supermarkets, a mall with a near-empty parking lot, a bank, a post office, a bridal shop and copy place. I couldn't fathom what the fuss was about. I couldn't understand why Mother was so fascinated with town. All her life she'd wanted off the farm. All her life she'd wanted…this. I couldn't understand the draw of it.

Jason came up next to me and said he'd go with me to the fictional burial ground but only if we went to his house first. It wasted much-needed sunlight where I could've been on the road to Hermann, but I didn't see any other way.

His house had clapboard siding and a falling-down wire fence around a small, scrappy yard. It was in a neighborhood of other poor-looking houses. We went in, and Jason called, "Ma, I'm home. Pearl's here." No one answered. He bent and picked up empty wine bottles by the sofa, putting fingers into the lips and carrying them all at once like he'd done it a hundred times. Everyone at school knew Jason lived alone with his alcoholic mother. Jason didn't hide it. I was amazed by this because my house was all about hiding. I couldn't imagine telling the truth about what happened there. My silence was inherited, bled deep into cousins, aunts, grandparents. So few stories. The silence wove deep into the soul.

I followed Jason to the kitchen. Worn-out Formica, a sink full of filthy dishes, fruit flies. He put the bottles by the overloaded trash.

earth

We lived on a farm, so I was used to dirt, but Mother was such an obsessive cleaner, our house never looked like this. No matter how many times I came to Jason's house, it shocked me profoundly. I had a feeling Jason wanted a witness. He liked the truth, even if it was brutal.

"Ma, where are you?" he called. We went into a side room. It was an art studio. Walking into the room was like leaving a cave and entering the light, like an epiphany. Half-finished canvases glowed with swatches of blood red, burnt orange, fiery yellow. I could hardly breathe. Black erratic slashes marred the brutal color. The glory and despair of it.

"Your mother did these?" I knelt in front of a stack of canvases. I touched a crimson leaf and the paint came off on my finger. It was as if the canvas bled onto me, or it was his mother's blood.

"When she's sober," he said dryly.

Mrs. Paulson had once been a blue-eyed, red-haired beauty, Mother had told me. *She had a gift with the visual arts. You'd see her standing in a long dress, wearing a hat, painting right next to a field down a gravel road. She was a looker, I can tell you that. Men on her all the time like flies. She was from out of town, because no woman in their right mind would fritter away the time like that, painting pictures. And sure enough, some man did come along, taught her a lesson or two the hard way.*

I'd seen her a couple of times, when she was sober. Apparently she had long phases, sometimes even years, of being sober. During those times, she was a beauty, not in the physical sense, but something glowed up from her cherry hair, some energy came through her eyes when she looked at you. I always felt like a swirling rainbow of color when she stared at me—soft inside, and light.

As I stared at the canvas, the crumbling earth of my vision veered up, hit me in the belly like nausea. "I gotta get going." I stood up wobbly on weak knees.

"What's wrong?" Jason came up beside me.

"Nothing. It's just I want to show you that burial ground before it gets late." Still his mother's paintings glowed up and surrounded me, threatened to take away my will. I pulled at his shirt. "Come on."

As we walked to the door, he called, "Bye, Ma."

I heard a soft voice from the other room, a murmuring. I wanted to run in and kneel at that woman's feet, to rest my head in her lap. To rest. Just to rest for one second in my exhausting life. I shook myself. She was a crazy drunk. I *was* losing my mind.

"You sure you're alright?" Jason asked as we stumbled down the crooked front steps and mounted our bikes.

I took off hard and fast. "Hey Miss Universe, what's the rush?" Jason yelled as he pedaled hard to keep up. Miss Universe was my bike. The name was written in stars on the bike's cobalt metal plate. I was way too old for it now, but I loved that bike like a best friend. She was the only freedom I'd ever known.

I'd seen Miss Universe in a shop window in town when I was in second grade. Through the plate glass, the bike shone like a lone star, glowed like some sort of horse with wings. A deep navy-colored banana seat covered in stars. Scarlet handle bars. Iridescent streamers like mystical hair. I put my palms against the cold glass. I gulped the bitter air. I was barely able to breathe.

A floating dream, a fantasy. I would never own it. We were too poor. When we weren't living off the land, Father did odd jobs, hammering, hacking, hauling. Mother spent the cash on electricity, household items, barbed wire and feed, cheap fabric and thread.

That Christmas, I came down the stairs and fairy lights glimmered off the bike's metal frame. Mother, who rarely got store-bought things, who sewed all our clothes and canned all our food and even made the curtains by hand, had gone and bought me the bike. Oh, the glory of the birth of Jesus Christ our Lord.

Mother's Christmases were magic. She saved up joy for that one season. A massive evergreen in the corner. Every year, we'd take the truck a few miles to some field and trudge through snow to an evergreen forest and use a handsaw. Beneath my tennis shoes, Mother put Wonder Bread bags over my socks and attached them with a rubber band around my ankles. The snow was so deep, it was higher than the Wonder bags. Father dragged the huge evergreen behind us in the snow, carving a brushy path, leaving frazzled angels in our wake, my ankles on fire with the ice that'd seeped in.

Wrapped gifts flamed up the living room beneath the tree. Mother would bake for weeks: peanut brittle, chocolate clusters, star-shaped cookies. The whole family would be happy for days in a row. Even Meghan had gotten into the spirit of it, sitting cross-legged on the shag and using whatever scraps she could find to make crazy ornaments—paper bags, bent nails, rocks, the lace from an old bra.

Even though town was nothing more than a few shops, everything was so spread out that you could drive for miles between the post office, for example, and the shopping mall. On my map, I couldn't exactly tell where Highway 94 connected up in town. I told Jason the burial ground was right around where Huckleberry and Gooseberry met Main, which looked like it was about a block from the entrance to 94.

I stopped and waited for Jason to catch up. My body felt good, strong. I would say this much for my ancestors: We were all muscle and vigor. Our bodies were like good, reliable horses. Gooseberry was mostly a neighborhood of poor houses with a body shop and a dry cleaners facing Main. A freight train lumbered by on nearby rail tracks.

Jason came up, panting. "I told you there was no burial ground here. Just a bunch of crappy buildings."

"I'm sure if we search around we'll find it. Go on down Gooseberry and see if you see anything." I got off my bike and walked it down Main.

"What am I supposed to be looking for, anyway? A mound of earth? Wouldn't there be some kind of plaque?"

I called back, "Yeah, they honor the Osage all over town with plaques. What world are you living in? Just look. Go between the houses."

I had to walk several blocks before I saw the highway entrance. Cars zoomed by at horrific speeds. I had to take Highway 63 first, then get on Rural Route 94, which from the map looked like it followed the Missouri River into Hermann. I knew I had to go right then, or I'd either run out of daylight or lose my nerve, or both. I biked as fast as I could back to Jason. He'd parked his bike against one of the houses and was looking intently at something that had nothing to do with burial grounds. As I biked up, he looked at me, eyes unfocused. I handed him a folded piece of paper. "Here. Take this."

He stared at the paper like he was scared of it. He wouldn't take it. I crunched it into his hand and turned Miss Universe around.

"I'm sorry," I said. "I'm real sorry."

He opened the note. I took off without looking back, standing up on the pedals, the bike whipping back and forth between my thighs.

The note told him what to say if my father asked where I was— that Jason left me at the rock cut at the end of my paper route, and I'd bicycled toward home. I wrote that I had important matters to take care of that I couldn't discuss with anyone, and anyway he'd probably think I was crazy. I told him that I'd needed his help to find the highway, and I was sorry for using him. I wrote I'd be back sometime soon, and he shouldn't worry.

I was on the dirt shoulder, biking hard, the wind pushing me from behind. "Pearl, goddamnit!" floated up on the breeze. I didn't turn around. He wouldn't catch up. He *couldn't* catch up. Jason had never ever been able to keep up with me.

chapter 4

A SEMI BARRELED past, blowing gravel in sharp tweaks along my calves and kicking up wind that knocked me sideways. There was no shoulder. Next to me was a sudden edge of jagged pavement that threatened to catch my front tire. Next to the edge, a rocky ditch.

Every truck that zoomed past was Father. Every growl of engine his frustration. Every horn his rage. I pedaled as hard and fast as I could.

I didn't know how long it would take to get to Hermann. I couldn't figure out the math on the map. I could hardly figure out the map. How could blue and red lines equal farm land and stretches of highway? The farthest I'd gone on my bike was the twelve miles round-trip of my paper route, and I used farmhouses, bends in the road, trees as landmarks. This map thing was a whole different way of thinking.

I got started so late. The summer sun didn't set until nearly nine thirty, and I hoped that was enough time for me to get there. I didn't have lights on the bike. As soon as night fell, I'd be screwed. I'd be a sitting duck. It was the first I'd thought of it. I stood up on the pedals and biked hard.

It was the stinking hottest, driest summer anyone could remember. I was sweating like a pig. The heat sent my hair into an afro frizz, burnt my lungs like fire. Even normal summers in Missouri were a sudden thrust. Blasting heat. Boiling tar. Sweating streets. But today was an impulsive hell. These heat waves seemed to be increasing, seemed to be occurring so regularly they were becoming the norm. I could barely breathe. The heat sweated fingertips, turned the handlebars to fire. A swarm of insects buzzed, sawed, titillated the air. I kept swallowing bugs. It was an exceptionally dry, dull, burnt season. Sweat running beneath pits and between thighs season. It was a suffocating season. That scorching summer took us all over, forced us, stirred us painfully, relentlessly forward.

I'd never been this far from home on my own. Miles of rolling burnt copper fields, sudden tufts of green like quick glimpses of beauty, of relief. Scalded leaves hung in limp submission from the trees. I had hoped to be right next to the river, hoped for the muddy coolness of the Missouri, but the river was off to the side through scrubby forest and shrubs. And next to me, a relentless stream of speeding cars and trucks, the hot-slip stream threatening to blow me sideways.

Besides the force of air generated by the traffic, the wind also blew a steady stream of dust and dirt off the rock cliffs and filled my straining lungs with dry powder. I biked past Wainwright, Tebbets, Mokane—small, square towns no bigger than your tight fist. On the main road an old brick fire house, a courthouse with pillars. On the outskirts, caved-in barns and broken clapboard houses. In Wainwright, I heard the far-off echo of a ball hitting a bat, some boys hollering, blunt voices carried on hollow wind. Outside Tebbetts, I had to brake suddenly for a Bluetick that bolted from a bank of trees with a bloody creature clenched in its jaws.

I got so hot and tired I had to slow down, even though I needed to hurry. I figured I was about three-quarters of the way there. The sun was low on the horizon, beginning to smolder, throwing a flush on the grey road as it receded into the distance.

I was biking hunched over and spent when a truck sidled up. A scarred and rusted red truck. I nearly jumped out of my skin. I sped up. The truck sped up, too, and kept pace. I was too nervous to look over. The driver leaned over and rolled his passenger window down and said something, but the wind took it.

I'd been with Father once crossing the Current Bridge, and a woman with ratty bleached hair and a matted fur coat was walking along the side. He'd said, "Pearl, that there's a prostitute." He kept pace with her as she walked. She'd been on my side of the road, and he kept staring at her through my window. He said, "Whore," slow and low under his breath. I'd pressed myself back into the torn seat of the truck so the word would go out the window and not land on me.

Finally, I looked over. Some bald man with whiskers. For some reason I laughed. He smiled and some teeth were missing. I remembered the whore, put my face straight, waved my hand in dismissal. He continued his slow shadowing. He was listening to some preacher on the AM radio. *This is Jesus Radio. All God, all day.*

"Can you give me some directions? I sure am lost," the man hollered from his hollow mouth. Still I wouldn't look. For a moment, I wished it *was* Father. I realized then for the first time that there might be some things worse than Father.

Up ahead I could see a long, gravel road that led to a house and barn. I stood up, rode the pedals hard. He sped up, too. I turned into the gravel road like it was my way home.

He honked behind me and yelled something, but I didn't turn. I biked all the way up to the house. A fat woman in an apron came outside. I wanted to ask her how far Hermann was, but I didn't want to leave any clues. I wanted to ask for water, because I'd forgotten to hide some in my metal side baskets.

"Is Eddie here?" I asked, smiling real bright to show I meant no harm. I swiped a clammy arm across my face and came back with smeared sweat and dust that looked like pale mud.

"Who?"

"Doesn't Eddie live here?"

"No, there's no Eddies here." She wiped her hands on a flowered towel. "What's the last name? I know everybody around here."

"He don't actually live around here," I said. "He's a cousin to somebody."

"Well, what's the last name?" I looked behind me the quarter mile back to the highway. The man in the blue truck appeared to be gone.

The woman looked at me suspiciously. "What'd you say your name was?"

"Oh," I said, turning my bike around. "I just remembered. He's not on this street at all. Thanks anyway! See you later." I biked down the spindly gravel, waving and kicking up dust. I was a good liar. Even Jason thought so. When you come from a family full of secrets, lying becomes your truth until it doesn't seem like you're lying at all.

Miles later, I struggled with the pedaling, too tired to go faster than a crawl. A storm was brewing. I could smell it. The weather seeped with mugginess, poured buckets of sweat down spine. The spread-out flash of heat lightning turned to long, sharp lines on the dark horizon behind me. The thunder rumbled, deep-bellied. In the flatlands of Missouri, you could watch the rain move across the land, watch it pour heavy and hard just across a field, while you stood there dry. I loved the storms. On any other day, I would've stopped my bike and watched in awe as the row of black clouds turned day into night in their wake.

The clouds were like Father, sudden and lethal. When Meghan ran away, he'd gone ballistic. He'd shaken me, pelted me with questions. *Where was she? What did she tell me?* I sobbed. I didn't know anything. Why didn't I know anything? I should've known something. I didn't show him the pearl, scared he'd take it away from me. I was just a kid, but I'd heard rumors about what happened. He drove all over in his truck, screamed at the Holy Cross principal, scared the hell out of Meghan's friends. He looked for her for months. He searched for her for years. But then one day, he gave up. We weren't allowed to mention her name anymore. Her being gone settled deep and scary inside him.

The deep thump, thump, thump of heart, the leaves hit by the storm wind, a shouting band of geese scattering in frightened flight, like some elemental chaos. I went into a sort of trance. I could sense another heartbeat below, in the subterranean roots and geological faults. I could feel the earth's erratic storm pulse. Thump, pow, thump.

I went into a vision. My body became again that hulking tree of engorged root and muscular limb. In the distance, in the yellowed hills, a mirage of Native Americans, shadowy men, women and children. They seemed so exhausted, so broken, so without will. The sky blew black and ferocious. The trees bowed in wind rage.

A wall of black forced the Osage onward. The ones who could sprinted madly forward. The earth howled and crumbled, tore up beneath their feet, sent them crumbling and stumbling. The sky cracked open and spit out sharp shards of hail. I heard from the earth a whine so high-pitched it caught me in the ribs.

If you love the earth, and they kill the earth, why wouldn't they kill you? If you felt yourself the same as oak flesh, and they chopped the oak down without any thought at all, why wouldn't they chop you down? Without any thought at all? If they killed the Osage, drove them to death on a Trail of Tears, why wouldn't they drive you to death? Why wouldn't they kill you?

A woman among the stumbling natives flew up out of the crowd, snaked on a wind stream toward me. It was the Osage woman. She flew with right arm outstretched, her straight black hair no longer in a braid but streaming straight out behind her, her face piercing the air, white light throwing daggers. All the colors of her were gone; all that ruby and emerald glow was just gone.

She stopped in front of me, her wan face inches from mine. She opened her mouth, her eyes pools of such depth, it was as if I fell into a world full of dimensions I could barely understand. I reached a hand as she reached forward. She opened her mouth to speak.

With sudden force, she was whipped and sucked back, yanked back to her tribe, her hand as she withdrew still reaching out.

I screamed, "What is it you want from me?" Just then, the rain reached me, hit the top of my head like a heavy foreboding. "What do you want?" That was the last thing I remembered.

It was dawn when I awoke, lying in a puddle, hidden behind the limbs of a weeping willow. How I had gotten there was anybody's guess. I'd slept the whole evening and the entire night through. I was learning the visions left me exhausted beyond all reason. I opened my palm to see that I was clutching the pearl. I'd clenched it so tight all night long, it left a mark like a stigmata in the center of my palm.

I spread the limp willow boughs like hair and came out to find the tree I'd slept under was in a field thirty yards from the highway. My bike lay on its side about ten yards away. How had I gotten there? It was the safest place I could've slept, hidden from bald men in trucks and the creatures of the forest.

The storm and the vision had spread me wide open again. I could see myself in every morsel of the world. Without Father to fear it out of me, or Mother there to protect me, I could just roam the field and experience the glowing morning field, the dew licking my calves. Everything glowed in dawn light. Light shot sparks in a cacophony of glimmerings. I couldn't get Mrs. Paulson's paintings out of my mind as I stared for whole minutes, transfixed by the liquid day. My own heart was the layers of rising sun streaming lines of light through the branches of the far-off tree line.

If the visions just did this to me then I'd be OK. But they opened my heart so wide that it ripped raw, opened not just to the glory but to the trauma of the whole blessed earth. I worried what I was feeling went even further than that, beyond the earth to the whole wretched universe.

I grew ravenous and leaned in the wet grass to my bike basket. The food was soaked. I flung the sopping bread to the grass. I dug for the wet chicken leg and devoured it. I inhaled the duck like some wild beast.

chapter 5

I ONLY MET Nadine once. I was small, five or six. We were at a barbecue after the double funeral of Grandpa and Grandma Swinton. We stood in podunk Vienna, Missouri, on top of fresh-mowed crabgrass on a rutted scrap of land next to their sunken silver trailer near a stagnant pond called Lake Margaret.

Grandpa always said, "If Pearl ever dies, I'm going into them woods and puttin' a bullet into my head." Pearl was my grandma's name. I was named after both grandmothers: Pearl for Father's mother, Elizabeth for Mother's. It was a name laden with expectation. It was a name that nearly bent a person in half. Grandpa mumbled like Father. He had whiskers that spat from a cratered mole, a jaw imploded by rotted teeth. He'd hunch like a broken scarecrow, his bony bottom peeking through a torn lawn chair. He smelled like melons left to rot on the vine.

Grandma Pearl came down with leukemia and died. Harold went into the woods and did what he always said he would.

I wandered in a sea of legs. Around me, the men and women wore dress clothes from the Montgomery Ward catalogue. The boys' hair was greased sideways with Vitalis. My relatives. They clung to paper plates of barbecued pork and angel food cake. I couldn't find Meghan. I was always looking for her for as long as I could remember—her long, thin, black hair, those outrageous clothes that made her look like some crazy Christmas ornament.

Because nobody told stories, I knew so little about the people around me. I knew only what I'd witnessed myself. All I could piece together was that my ancestors were all peasants. They could barely read. They worked the land. They followed the seasons. They didn't have the time or the desire to ponder themselves. There was no space or time to wonder, to wander, to brood, to ruminate on the stars, on the mythology of their lives. Such luxury was for rich folk. They toiled. They fell back onto spring mattresses in dilapidated trailers on scrubby patches of exhausted land. They procreated.

Mother stood by the food tables looking scared toward the line of forest at the other side of the lake. I'd seen Father disappear into the woods a few minutes earlier. Meghan was nowhere. The shut-down silence of my kin grew up my legs and thighs and torso. I seemed to become swollen with their quiet. It filled up my head with air. It brought my limbs to a place heavier than a plow. I couldn't move. A black hole. I felt myself falling.

"Hey, you girl." A woman's voice from far away, but heard as if in my ear. She glowed at the edge of the crowd. Black straight hair, black dress, black circles beneath black eyes. Most of the others were fattened up by a farm diet of fresh milk, fresh cream, corn-fed beef, but she was all bone: her long, angular face, hip bones visible through her dress, her black shoes heavy dumbbells on the end of skinny ankles.

I went to where Mother absently stirred a massive bowl of potato salad, still staring at the tree line. My back to the crowd, I whispered sideways. "Who's that lady over there in black?"

She said with annoyance, "You should be over here helping us with the food, Pearl." She was always trying to make me do women's work.

"On the edge over there, by the lake," I whispered. "The skinny one. Who is that?"

"Who?" Mother started on the coleslaw. She looked up. "Who?"

I pointed, shielding my finger with my body.

"Oh, come on, that's Nadine. Don't you even know your own aunt?" She and Father never took me to visit relatives, and then they'd say, *Don't you know anybody? You know you had an Uncle Roy who shot himself in the head. Don't you know nothing?* It was ridiculous.

Crazy Nadine. Funny Farm Nadine. I stole glances over my shoulder. Mother tried to hand me some cake to distribute, but I took one piece and wandered off.

I walked in wide arcs through the crowd, getting closer and closer. Finally, I was almost next to her. I could see the tremors in her body, twitches that moved her hand sideways, that worked her jaw as if she were perpetually playing Chinese Whispers. Her right shoulder was aimed toward the crowd, but the rest of her reached out toward the forest beyond. She ate bits of salad leaves like a bird.

"I like the forest, too," I said, but it came out like a whisper. I said louder, "I like the woods."

Her head came up. She swung around. A cherry tomato flew from her plate.

"I'm Pearl." I put my hand out. She took it reluctantly, her knuckles bony. Her eyes seemed to glaze over. "I'm Terry's girl," I said.

"Terry's girl?" Her eyes cleared. She smiled and was almost pretty. She knelt in the grass. Her knee landed on a sharp rock. "You're Terry's girl?" She smiled again, wide over too-big white, perfect teeth.

I nodded. She moved her hand to touch my hair, which in the humidity veered up like black smoke. I could feel the electricity as her hand grew near, and I knew the touch would do something to me, good or bad, it didn't matter. Before her hand reached me, I heard Mother's voice. "Nadine?" I looked up to see her walking toward us. "Nadine?"

Nadine's hand touched a strand of my frizzed-up hair, and I started to feel it, this sudden connection, like she was me and I was her.

Mother reached us and took Nadine's hand and held it. She pulled her up from kneeling position. The rock had left a deep imprint on her knee.

"Why don't you go on over there and get yourself a piece of angel food cake," Mother said to her.

Nadine looked at her vaguely. "Angel food cake?" she repeated, like she was being stupid on purpose. "Angel food cake?" Mother got her walking toward the food tables, then came back to me.

"Why are you always doin' the opposite of what you're supposed to?" She pointed to the trailer. "Go on inside the trailer and see if there's anything you want. Meghan's already been in."

Grandpa and Grandma lived their last twenty years in that trailer. I trudged through waist-high weeds to get to the rusted metal stairs. I swung open the door and it made a grunting sound. This was my legacy. Matted, rotting carpet. Wasps buzzing over sticky surfaces. Flies taking refuge up my nose. Torn plaid sofa. A bed with the weight of generations bowing down the middle. The smell of mold, grease, sweat, urine.

Folks had rifled through everything. The cupboard, the dresser, the narrow closet—doors flapped loose. The story of my grandparents handed out in meager possessions. Now that my grandparents' stars had burned out, their stories—like their paltry belongings—were dispersed, heartbeats fading to little more than echoes in the world's deepest chambers.

In the debris, I uncovered salt and pepper shakers shaped like chipmunks and put them in my pockets. As I was leaving, I saw a filthy picture hanging crooked on the paneling. I took it down. The glass was so dirty, you couldn't make out the image. I used the dish towel to smudge away the grease. It was a picture of a boy and a girl. I knew immediately the boy was Father, and the girl Nadine. He was real little, like three or four. He held a live chicken up against his plaid shirt. The two were turned sideways, and they laughed into each other's faces. Like somebody had told a joke right before the picture was taken. I put the picture in the waistband of my shorts.

I came out and heard crying. Nadine was in the scrub at the back of the trailer hugging her arms. I walked through the scratchy grass toward her. Mother shouted, "Pearl, get on over here. Now." I looked back and forth between the two. I was being tugged between Mother's fear and Nadine's pain. Mother called again, and I had to leave Nadine there, sobbing in the weeds.

Mother drove us home. Meghan sat squeezed up next to her. In her lap, she held a bag of pink plastic forks and knives covered in grime that she'd taken from the trailer. She held it in both hands like some sort of prize. I sat next to Father. He smelled of Schlitz and his head bobbed like a dashboard dog. His cavernous blood-red eyes. I'd been with Mother when he finally came out of the forest. She breathed such a sigh of relief seeing him. I wanted him to feel better so I reached in my shorts, pulled out the picture and handed it to him. He looked down with eyes full of death. Full of pain. Compassion tapped nerve endings that blew pain into my core.

There had to be more to his story. His rage was epic; there had to be more. What a gaping hole an untold story left. What confusion for generation after generation. What scattered echoes.

He snatched the picture from my hands. He rolled down the truck window. He threw the picture hard. It hit the side of an oak, smashed to smithereens.

Hermann, Missouri was built on a grid. It was a German town. Mother was German, and I knew how they liked to keep things organized. It made finding Nadine's house easy. Before I even knew what I was going to say, how I was going to handle things, I stood in front of her pale brick house, perched on Miss Universe.

I wasn't looking real pretty. Behind the willow, I'd taken off my T-shirt, wrung it, and used it to wipe my face and smash down my hair. Now the grey T-shirt I wore had long smudges. My hair had its own personality: big, frizzy, coal-black. The kids at Holy Cross gave me a nickname because of my hair: Wicked Witch of the West.

I'd taken off my pedal pushers and wrung them out, too. I did number one and number two, kicked some dirt on top. Still, as I stood outside Nadine's house, every part of me was covered with shit and stink. Even Miss Universe. I just hoped I didn't scare Nadine half to death when she answered the door.

earth

The house was built near the street, with a small front yard. Dozens of houses nearly the same dotted the square neighborhood. The street was wide and clean. Nadine's grass was brown, but that was true of a lot of houses in the horrible Missouri heat.

I walked my bike up the sidewalk, parked it near the hydrangeas. A wrought iron railing led up concrete steps to the small front porch. It was burning hot to the palm. I did my best to smash down my wild hair. I lifted my hand to knock, but before I could, the door was yanked open from inside.

Nadine blinked in the afternoon sun as if she'd come out of a cave. She was skinnier than I remembered, paler, taller. Her chin was as sharp as the tip of my arrowhead. I wiggled my fingers and said brightly, "Hi."

"What do you want?" She shifted her head and refocused slowly on the bike in the front yard. "I told you kids to leave me be." She started to swing the door closed, and I raised my hand.

"I'm Pearl." I put out my hand for her to shake. "Terry's girl."

"Terry's girl?" Her voice filled with hope. She fell forward a step and looked behind me. "Is Terrence here?" She thrust her neck to look down the road.

"No." She kept looking around as if Father would suddenly appear. "Do you mind if I come in?" I was so thirsty. She turned back and stared straight through me. There was something fixed and wrong about her eyes. She didn't seem to be in her body, just this shell of a woman. When she didn't answer, I said, "Thanks, I'll just come in then," and moved around her.

The house was shadowy. I passed a living room with the bulky drapes drawn, and in the dark I made out a beige sofa and floral chairs that looked like they'd never been sat on, with all the pieces too squared up. Farther inside, in the dim depths, I almost ran into the dining table before I saw it. It had four pushed-in chairs and a centerpiece with a candle that had never been lit.

I went into the kitchen to help myself to some water. I knew it wasn't polite, but I was dying. I opened a cupboard, and inside the cups and plates were organized like they were never used. I brought down a glass with strawberries on it. We had some at home. You bought the jam from the grocery store, and when you were finished, you had a glass to drink out of. I opened the refrigerator freezer and there was just an emptiness: two ice trays and nothing.

Nadine stood watching me. I sat at the polished kitchen table and started to put the sweating glass down but worried it'd leave a water mark, so I held the glass instead and let it drip in my lap. After a while, she picked her way over and lowered herself into a chair opposite me, clasped her bony hands hard until her knuckles turned pink, her liver spots twitching with unnatural energy. Her gaunt shoulders seemed heavy with gravity as she leaned over the table, her face near the surface. I was amazed to see she was beautiful up close: ivory skin, none of Father's scars, broad eyes, spider lashes, a stretched mouth. Like one of those old-time movie stars, ugly and beautiful all at the same time.

She said slow like it took a while for her mind to make sense of things, "You here all alone?"

"No." I hadn't thought up the lie, but it came spilling out of my mouth. "Mother's in town shopping for fabric." It was a good one because she was always looking for cheap fabric. She liked anything in a floral.

Nadine sat staring, eyes glassy. A wall clock ticked, dull like the heartbeat of a sick person. The lights were off, and the curtains on the window created a muted glow. It was sweltering. The windows stood open behind the drapes and the ceiling fan was on, but the air was an inferno. I picked the flesh around my thumb, then put it bleeding in my mouth.

She said, "But you got that bicycle outside. How could your mother be shopping, when you got that bike with you?"

"Yes," I said, slowly. "Yes. It was in the back of the truck, and Mother said, 'Go on and take your bike so you can have some fun with your aunt.' So, I took my bike out and she drove off." I'd heard somewhere that they cannot tell you're lying if you use a lot of details. I was good at dishonest specifics.

"She didn't want to stop in herself?" She looked so horribly sad, like nobody ever stopped in. I didn't want to lie and hurt her feelings more, so I just sat there silent.

"I don't know," she said. "I just don't know." Then she sat quiet again. I didn't know how I was going to approach talking to her about the visions when she was in such a state. I waited for some shift or opening. The heat was like we were sitting in some big slow cooker, heating up our insides to bursting. The repetitive whooshing of the fan above the table, Nadine's low-lying pulsations, my bloody thumb.

Nadine got up slowly, using her flat palm against the table surface for balance. She tottered to the black phone attached to the kitchen wall and took down the receiver. On the counter was an address book. She opened it, found the number and began to dial. "I'm calling your house," she said.

I ran up to her. She smelled of lemon cleaner, like Mother's just-washed linoleum. "Please, please, Nadine, just wait." She stared down at me. "Sorry, *Aunt* Nadine, I mean. Aunt Nadine."

I groped for what to say. "I'm having these visions." I let out a long breath. "I keep seeing the soil tear up, and I swear people are screaming …"

She started shaking, tried to hang the phone back up but missed. She slammed her fist on the countertop. "No!" she said. "No!" She hit the countertop again. "Shut your mouth." She raised her bony hand in a fist toward me, just like Father.

I reached my hand and touched the quivering flesh of her forearm. The moment my fingers made contact, she arched. She threw her head up. Her eyes rolled back. Something was happening that only she could see. Her body gave out from under her. As she went down, I reached out to stop her, but I was too late. She hit the counter with elbow and chin and landed on her stomach on the floor.

I stood above my aunt not knowing what to do. Finally, I flipped her on her back, grabbed her ankles, and pulled her down the hallway to her room. I propped her feet on the mattress, got my arms beneath her, and hauled her onto the bed. She was shockingly light.

"Nadine?" I said. "Aunt Nadine?" It looked like it took her a while to recognize me, then her eyes moved this way and that like she was trying to escape. She whined and rolled her face into the pillow.

"Where's your mother?" she groaned.

I wasn't good at comforting people and stood beside the bed looking down at her. Again that stringent smell of lemon cleaner. I thought she'd gone to sleep, and was about to turn and go out, when I heard her voice muffled by the pillow.

"Go, find your mother. Leave." She wailed, "Leave me be."

I needed time to think. Obviously this woman wasn't going to help me find a way to raise myself up. I went out the back door and paced the long, narrow backyard. It was dusk. The grass was mown, the hedges clipped, the yard as unused as the house. The setting sun didn't dull the heat, and my flesh was covered in a slime of sweat. I thought about the first time I knew I was going to have to raise myself up. Mother had stood at the stove frying up eggs and hash browns. Father sat at the kitchen table. I was five, and I did not exist to them. I was invisible. I looked up at my mother and knew I had to raise myself up. I knew that at best these people would ignore me, and at worst beat me to within an inch of my soul. They didn't know how to raise me up. I was five and I knew from that moment forward, it was all up to me.

A summer night in Missouri was the noisiest you ever heard— an orchestra of barks, croaks, chirps, peeps—low echoes that fell upon each other like water rolling over river stone. Here in this town, even though it was a small town, the noises were muted, as if a veil lay over the land.

I noticed there were no fireflies. You could see other folks' backyards and no sudden pinpoints of light. I figured it had something to do with how manicured everything was. The closer you got to town, the farther you moved from the magic of the earth.

An old red bike leaned against the house. Weeds had grown up through the spokes, and it was rusted. I stared at it uncomprehending for whole minutes. I touched the torn black seat. It was Meghan's. I recognized it from when we were kids; I'd even ridden it myself a few times. How did Meghan's bike get here?

My brain seemed to move in slow motion. There was no other answer. Meghan had taken her bike when she ran away. My sister had come here after she ran away. She'd been here. Meghan had always been Nadine's favorite. When we visited Nadine, which was rare, Meghan and Nadine always stuck together like shipwreck victims, like they were clinging to a life raft. They'd stand at the edge of the kitchen and talk low. At the end, when we were leaving, they'd hug, making everybody uncomfortable. Nobody hugged.

I ran my hand on the metal over the back tire. It was banged out with a hammer. I'd watched Meghan bang it out myself after our bike accident.

How memories could be locked up inside you, and something would trigger one that you didn't even know was still there, how you had all these stories inside you just waiting to be remembered.

The bike wreck was one of those tales that became part of our family story. One of those metaphors that said way more about us than the actual facts. How the smallest story can say so much, can carry the weight of past, present and future.

When I was six, I'd begged Meghan to let me ride her down Powwow. She was plopped cross legged on the dried grass in the front yard, her shoulders heavy.

"No way. Kid, you gotta be joking," she'd said.

"Please," I begged. I did a cartwheel, a backflip. I finished with a backbend and looked at her upside down. "Please. Pleeeeeaaaase, Meghan?"

She grabbed a strand of my hair. "How can I say no to this hair?" She liked to make fun of my hair, spoke to it sometimes like it was a separate person.

Powwow was a monster, one of the steepest roads around, with a curve at the bottom that was lethal. I had the shakes as we walked the bike up the hill. Meghan and I wore matching cotton blouses with embroidered patches. Mine was a smiley face and hers was a cat. I'd begged Mother to make us matching shirts. I smiled up at my sister.

We were like twins. We were like strangers. We were soul mates. We were not alike at all.

We reached the top of the hill. Bonnie and Jason were already at the top of the road with their bikes. Everyone seemed to have a bike but me. Meghan mounted hers, helped me onto the seat, and kept her feet on the ground while I tested the pedals. In front of us, the nearly vertical pitted gravel road.

"You all go first," she said over her shoulder to Bonnie and Jason.

"Yeah right," Jason responded. "You'll wreck and take us down with you. I'll follow behind, thank you very much." Even then, Jason was too smart for his britches. Bonnie smiled. Bonnie was always smiling, smiling. Bonnie was always smiling.

Meghan pushed hard with her foot. "Wait," I said, but it was too late. We were plummeting.

We picked up speed fast, sweat and wild wind whipping hair, insects stinging death on cheeks. We jiggled down the wide gravel road, barreled down, down, down. Just before the steep curve near the bottom, we started to wobble. The front tire did a jig. A quick to and fro. Meghan had her hands on my shoulders.

I could sense she would throw us over. Meghan had a lot of fear. She was never good at waiting for disaster, would throw herself over so that the terrible future would be acted out as soon as possible. Her fear had always scared me. Somebody else's story could become yours if you weren't watching real close.

How clear my mind was when the tire did its jig again. I begged Meghan silently, *Hold steady. Hold your nerve.* We were whipping so fast. *Do not throw us over, hold on, even if we're wobbly now, there's a chance we will come out of it.* The day was hot, muddy lines of sweat and dirt behind knees and down spines. My thick black hair stuck in a congealed pool at the base of my neck. The hot wind came at me like a perpetual slap in the face.

We were just at the curve where the road plunged into steepness. The tire wobbled again. *Oh Jesus, please. Meghan, please.*

earth

She threw her body sideways. How a second can be a lifetime in the universe of the mind. Bare-legged and bare-armed I hit the gravel at twenty miles an hour. She landed on top of me, her weight as familiar as the morning, as normal as the sound of a truck engine just before dawn. Gravel whirring beneath flesh, eyes wide open, witnessing speed and perspective, the momentum of road and bike and bodies at strange and twisted angles. I could smell the blood. I could feel the flesh ripping. Oh, this is what an arm on fire feels like. Oh, this is what the dark fumes of baked human flesh smell like. We didn't stop our tumblings until the very bottom.

Meghan got off me, burst into a high-pitched wail. I put my hand to my head. It was covered in blood. The skin was burnt off my right forearm; gravel had embedded deep into bloody flesh.

Jason and Bonnie braked and stared at us. Bonnie was smiling, smiling. I stood on bloody and scratched legs. Meghan limped up the road, crying. I picked up the bicycle, gripped it with my good arm, dragged it. The back wheel was awfully bent. Bonnie and Jason were there and then they weren't.

Mother stood alone in the kitchen, a curve to her shoulders. Steam rose from pots on the stovetop. The limp scent of green beans. The spongy blandness of ham hock and beans.

When Meghan walked in crying with me behind her, she said, "I told you kids not to ride down that road," without turning around. "Go lie down." She moved her hands quickly over carrots, chopping them. "Don't expect any help from me," she said as we picked our way up the stairs. She never took care of anyone hurt by the consequences of their own actions. "You made your bed." *You made your bed. You sleep in it.*

She'd made hers. She was sleeping in hers.

Before Meghan shut herself in her room, she turned and yelled at me, "Get your own bike."

I went into the bathroom, looked at the small vague mirror over the sink. Half my face was swollen up, eye puffed up and closed. I picked gravel out of the open wound on my right arm.

I heard somebody knocking on the kitchen's screen door downstairs. I heard Mother answer it. I heard Mrs. Willard, the widow who owned the small farm next door, talking. I limped downstairs. Mrs. Willard looked up and saw me, then she barked with fright. Mother kept her eyes averted. Mrs. Willard looked from her to me.

"I saw them go flying down the hill. I saw them wreck. You think Meghan being so much older woulda known better. I watched them coming up the hill crying after the accident. I saw them both limpin' up the road and cryin'," Mrs. Willard said.

But I wasn't. It wasn't proper to talk back so I didn't say it out loud. I stood there all swollen and bloody and didn't speak. She didn't know the half of it.

I didn't cry. Not once.

I wasn't crying.

I smelled cigarette smoke. I was gripping the black seat of the bike. Nadine stood on the back stoop smoking a Salem. Night was falling. How long had I been outside? I looked up at her standing there, a long, thin strip of a looming woman, the setting sun glowing like a far-off crown, vague around the top of her head. Despite the heat, she held her arms across her body. She'd changed into a cotton housedress. A blue bruise grew from her elbow where she hit the counter. I moved away from the bike.

Thoughts were still whirring around my head about Meghan, about Meghan's bike being here, about Nadine knowing where my sister was. I didn't want Nadine to know these thoughts. I had to keep my intentions secret. From everyone.

"I called your house," she said, stomping out the cigarette with her fuzzy slippers.

I jumped and looked around like I was trapped.

"Nobody was home."

I breathed an elongated sigh. She looked down at me.

earth

"I wouldn't let nobody hear you say the kind of nonsense you were talking about in that kitchen."

I looked up at her with my mouth open. I was so tired of the centuries of denial that coursed through my family's blood. I was so fed up with the silence. The words came out hard, angry, hoarse.

"Listen, I came all the way up here by myself on my bike. I deserve answers. You just had a vision right before my eyes. Are we going to pretend that didn't happen?"

She raised her fist at me, her face shaking.

"You adults," I screamed. "You don't do nothing for us kids. You expect us kids to be the one to figure out the mess, and you won't help at all!"

I turned my back on her. I had to think. If she wasn't going to help me, who would? I had to find Meghan. Nadine surely had an address. I went and lay on my back in the grass and stared up at the stars. For a long time, I didn't saying anything. It felt like everyone was always trying to shut up the truth. Like there was a conspiracy against truth that was too heavy to bear.

Nadine came and sat cross-legged on the grass next to me. I didn't look at her. She said, "OK," then went into a coughing fit.

"OK, what?" I asked, when she finished.

"Ask me."

I wanted to ask about the visions but thought I'd start with something easier. "Meghan was here?"

She blinked, shifted on the grass and didn't speak.

"That's her bike right there leaning up against your house."

"She was. That was years ago now."

"Father went crazy looking for her."

"I swear she was gone by the time he got up here. Left in the middle of the night before I could talk her out of it."

"You didn't even call him?"

She gave me a look. I shut up. She'd just *tried* to call him about me, and he was probably going crazy looking for me. The thought humbled me. I said softly, "Can you tell me about the visions?"

The muscles of her face twitched every which way. Her jaw clenched. Her shoulders fell like there was a heavy weight on her back. The words came out of her like they were forced. Her jaw was so tight, I thought she might break. "They started when I was ten."

"Floods." She spoke in monotone. "Everything, everybody underwater. The screaming." She put her right hand up, cocked her wrist, palm to sky, like she was invoking the heavens. A cigarette smoked between her fingers. She listed other calamities: earthquakes, sickness, drought, like she was reciting the book of Revelations. The heaviness of her weighed on me like she was obese and not skinny at all.

When she finished, she looked over at me with such needy eyes, as if I were the adult and she were the child, as if I had some answers to give her and not the other way around. This happened to me a lot. Even nuns at Holy Cross would lean into me sometimes with pained eyes, like they were seeking some explanation for why things were so wrong. It exhausted me. It bent me nearly in half.

She forced the smoke out between clenched lips. "My mother sent me to Fulton." Fulton State Mental Hospital, everybody knew it. The nut house, the funny farm.

In the silence that followed, I heard whispers of untold stories, things that had happened that she probably never told anyone, and I wasn't sure I wanted to know. I could tell they'd done something to her head. She was full of some energy that wasn't animal, vegetable, or mineral.

"I don't know why she sent Terry with me. He was so little." Her voice was foggy, muffled.

"She sent Father to Fulton?" I asked, aghast.

Nadine was crying. The cigarette had burned down to her fingers and she flicked her hand from the sudden heat. "To our Great Aunt Hilda's. After I got out, we were sent to her farm in the middle of nowhere, hours and hours away. Thirteen kids and just the two of us got sent away."

earth

I thought of Vienna, Missouri, where her parents had lived. That was already the middle of nowhere. The aunt's house must've been some serious backwater.

"Terry was so little. He had no Mama, nobody but me. I was no good for anyone after that hospital, so I guess you could say he was all alone. Terry blamed me for everything. He stopped talking to me."

I knew she'd gone back a few times to Fulton as a grown-up, but I didn't want to ask, didn't want to know. I'd come here to see if she had visions, and now that I knew, I didn't want to know any more, didn't want to be anything like her, didn't want to be in the grass next to her. I wanted some hope, some explanation for how to manage them, someone to say how they were a gift, and I was a gift and it would be all okay.

She reached into a pocket, took out an orange pill bottle. "These are supposed to keep my head straight. I get bad if I forget. I must've forgot to take them today."

She shook the bottle and it clanked like a lethargic child's rattle. "Now I just get nightmares." She turned her narrow chin up. "Nightmares are acceptable. Nightmares don't get you sent to the farm."

We stayed there quiet for a long time, both staring up at the stars. I tried to digest what she told me. I fell into a dark brooding. If Nadine was like this after a life of having visions, what hope did I have? What was the whole point of the visions, just to drive a person crazy?

As if she read my mind, Nadine said, "You got something I never had. Some strength. I saw it the first time I met you. Terry had it, too."

I looked at her surprised. Father had strength?

She took a pack of Salems from her front pocket, extracted one with her long, skinny fingers, and lit it. "Some of us just don't have the will for it." She went quiet then. I felt her fall down into herself, so far down that no matter how deep you reached you could not put your hand inside her and yank her back up again.

I turned back to the stars, tried to figure out how to make her feel better. With my family, there was so little joy. It was as if pain, hard work, and depression was all that was allowed, as if joy was a precious commodity that nobody could afford.

"I can remember being born," I said louder than I meant to.

Nadine went into a coughing fit, and I waited for her to stop.

"Mother was in the hospital bed, and I was wrapped tight, held by this nurse." I could feel my mother lying in that hospital bed, the wrench of her, the raw animal force of her. She was so profoundly happy. I was this ball of pure energy.

"The nurse picked up a black pen at the end of this chain attached to a clipboard, and I remember it like it was yesterday, the chain shot these silver balls of light. It was like a string of stars, a constellation, and I kept trying to reach for it with my chubby fingers. I was so excited I sprayed a line of yellow urine like sunshine along the length of the swaddle.

"The nurse carried me down this long hall and it was like a tunnel of light. I could read everyone's mind. I mean it. As a baby, I could read absolutely everyone's mind. I could feel and hear the souls of the other babies in their cribs, and all this joy was like an orchestra of thoughts, like some beautiful song.

"I could understand everything I was about to become, the family I was born into, the patch of earth I'd call home. It felt real heavy, that much knowing.

"This ball of light, I thought it was an angel, fluttered out of the top of my head, edged toward a window, flew into the night sky. I followed it in my imagination and watched the light separate into three stars. A star for heart. A star for womb. A star for shoulder. The three starting points of my mythology. Then, alone in the crib, I forgot everything I knew when I was born. Everything. Darkness fell."

Smoke went up my nostril, and I coughed. Nadine hugged her knees, smoked, stared upward and rocked her body back and forth.

"After that, I don't remember anything again until I was about four or five." I didn't tell Nadine that as I grew up, I kept seeing fragments of myself, just like in that crib at the hospital, balls of light spin from the top of my head, fly up and out, and swirl into the sky. With each loss, I became more of a shell. At some point, I'd have to figure out how to retrieve the parts. I'd have to go find the lost parts of me, put them all out in front, connect the dots, create a constellation. Reform myself from the dust and light of the universe.

The quiet between us drew out long and low into the night. I thought Nadine had gone to sleep. "Terry and I used to do this," she whispered finally. I jerked a look at her. Her face was so wide open. She looked real young, like someone my own age. I thought, *You had the strength, too, Nadine, when you were little. I can see it in your face. They beat that strength out of you, but you've got it. Don't shortchange yourself.*

"Before he hated me, we'd sneak out late and lay on our backs in the grass. It was so tall, that grass, and we'd sink down and disappear." She exhaled and the smoke wafted like miniature smoke signals. "Compared to out there, the stars here are nothing. Terry started it. He pointed out a group of stars and named it. He'd name them after dogs, cows, people we knew. Then he'd make up these stories. Just like that off the top of his head. He was always so magical about his stories, just like you."

I barked a snort. Father, magical? He was just an angry, pacing, tied-up dog. She gave me a look, and I stopped guffawing.

"Where is it?" She swiveled in a circle on her bony bottom. "There." She pointed the burning Salem toward the sky at the end of the long backyard. "See that triangle?"

I lifted my head. "Sure." I didn't say that you could see a triangle of stars almost anywhere you looked. "Sure," I repeated.

"That one he called Nadine. Terry said I was nothing but sharp points."

I laughed. It seemed like a lifetime since I laughed in a good happy way. I looked into Nadine's face. Her dentures glowed bright beneath wide stretched lips as she broke into a smile. She lay back down. We stared up at the night sky and didn't talk for a long while.

I thought of Father as a boy. I'd never thought of him as a boy before, and since I'd come to Nadine's, I kept seeing him as a boy in my mind's eye. This was the poverty I wanted to tell Mother about. Not telling stories about your relatives was like starving yourself to death.

Around three o'clock the next morning, I got off the couch. I hadn't slept. I pondered what to do. I had come this far, and I needed some answers. All I could think about was finding Meghan.

I snuck into the kitchen. I took the address book that I'd seen Nadine using before, flipped to the S's. Meghan's address wasn't there. I checked the M's. No luck. I carefully opened kitchen drawers and cupboards. I found a box on a shelf filled with letters. I flipped through them, but still nothing. I saw some mail collecting dust in a wooden letter holder next to the phone. I found a birthday card to Nadine from Meghan with a return address.

My hand shook as I wrote the address on a scrap of paper. East St. Louis. Meghan lived in East St. Louis. The place was infamous. Even at Holy Cross we'd heard the rumors—cars breaking down and the occupants going missing; muggings, rapes, knifings, shootings.

I'd convinced Nadine to wait and call my parents in the morning. It wasn't difficult. I reminded her how enraged Father would be when he stormed up in his truck, and besides I thought she was so lonely that even a thirteen-year-old was better than nobody. Anyway, after her vision and our talk, she was so exhausted; she was barely able to walk from the backyard to her bedroom. She passed out with her slippers still on.

I felt horrible raiding her refrigerator and stealing food. All I could find anyway was a bowl of green Jell-O and a pack of bologna. I plopped some of the Jell-O into one of the strawberry glasses, found a lid in the drawer. I put two pieces of the bologna and the jar of Jell-O in a brown paper bag I found under the sink.

I rooted around in the drawers for cash, found a five and pocketed it. I knew I was getting her into real trouble by taking off in the middle of the night. She'd surely call my parents as soon as she woke up. If Father hated her before …

I debated whether I should leave her a note. I found paper and pencil, and as I went toward the window to see by the moonlight, something flashed in the backyard. It flashed again, and I stood and looked out. At first I thought it was a lightning bug.

Nadine was on her back in the grass, smoking, staring up at the stars. The only movement was her arm bringing the cigarette up to her lips. She exhaled smoke signals that floated heavenward. I watched her. She just stared up at those stars and smoked.

I felt a wide-open love blow up my heart. I'd only felt this before with Mother. How do you love your relatives when they are so messed up? When all you wanted to do was run away from them? But still, my heart seemed to balloon, float out and surround Nadine in the grass. She looked back as if she could sense me. I ducked just in time.

chapter 6

MEGHAN PUT THE pan of boiling water in front of me. I always had to dunk. She hated the stench of it. We were next to the chicken coop sitting on tree stumps, surrounded by scrubby weeds. It was dawn. Autumn dropped a fine mist on the fields, in the forest.

Father had just butchered twenty hens. After he cut their heads off, their bloody bodies flew across the field, like white hot shots of crimson lightning. I had to run after them and collect them in a pile. Meghan stood back watching it all with her arms crossed and her face disgusted.

I held the first body upside down by the ankles and dunked it into the boiling water. The stench of matted feathers, boiled skin, and blood steamed up into my hair. The rancid smell of it entered the nostrils, lined the back of the throat.

I handed Meghan the chicken and she pulled the feathers out distastefully, with fingernails covered in chipped burgundy paint. I grabbed great handfuls and pulled; the plastic tips were filled with a murky fluid. The remaining hairs were thin and fine, and it was a lot of work to gather them up and pull them out. Meghan never finished hers, always handed them to me to do the fine-tuning.

Later, she would have to stand at the kitchen sink back at the house and gut them. It was her job. I thought that with her wild way of seeing, gutting probably wasn't a good thing for her. She'd cut bodies, take entrails into palm. Watch blood and guts drip between fingers.

The pile grew. Meghan picked up one of the now-bald chickens by the feet and smacked it hard with an open palm. The chicken squawked. We both looked up, surprised. She did it again, slapping randomly up the bald flesh of the chicken until she caught the voice box again. The squawk came when she hit the vocal cords just where the bleeding neck met the torso.

She did it again. The dead chicken squawked loud and clear. Thwack-squawk. Thwack-squawk. She stood up and danced in a circle thwacking the headless chicken.

I grabbed a plucked chicken and hit it too. Squawk. I giggled and wiggled my foot. Squawk. Skip. Thwack-squawk.

Meghan and I walked in a circle, beat a rhythm, two quick squawks, pause, and a sharp one. We trailed a line of blood from their necks in the dirt. Squawk, squawk, pause, squawk. We danced. We filled that farm with shadow song.

I was in a ditch beside Route 66. Miss Universe was on her side. A smart-ass in a Mustang had driven my bike off the road, and I'd landed in a Slurpee; my hair was crusted with the purple drink. I had a bloody palm with gravel in it.

I heard Mother's voice: *If you don't live in this world, you ain't never going to survive.* I looked at the cars speeding by on the highway, at the fumes. Maybe Mother was right. I picked up my bike. I did agree with her on one thing. How does a person survive in this world? How?

At dawn, when I'd first hit Route 66, it wasn't so bad. But as I looked up now at the six-lane highway leading into St. Louis, the cars were chockablock, trucks with tires bigger than my bike, fumes so heavy they looked like storm clouds. The chaos set my head to spinning. *Mother,* I thought, *if this is what town is with a capital T, you can have it. It's all yours. I don't want any of it.*

Meghan's address was not on the map. East St. Louis was in Illinois. I'd have to buy another map and, by the feel of my palm, some antiseptic and Band-Aids. I was desperate to get to her place before nightfall.

I realized it was too dangerous on Miss Universe. I'd be spotted right away. Father would find me. By now Nadine had called him, but she didn't know where I was heading, so maybe he would drive back toward home, looking. I thought of him looking for Meghan this way and felt bad, but there was nothing I could do but keep going. I realized Miss Universe's glittering brilliance made cars honk and catcall. I needed to hide her.

I labored the two painful miles to the next exit, found a gas station with a convenience store, leaned Miss Universe against the glass. I'd never needed to lock her before, so I had nothing to secure her with. I walked around the store, twisting this way and that to keep my eye on it in case someone tried to steal it. I grabbed an Illinois map, Band-Aids, hydrogen peroxide, a baseball cap, a can of black spray paint, and the only T-shirt left. It had the Mobile logo on the back and *I've Got Gas* on the front. The teller was a pimply teenager who didn't look up as he took nine of my remaining eleven dollars.

I rushed the bike to the side of the gas station, squatted, mumbled a quick apology, shook the can, and started spraying Miss Universe. I began by blacking out her name on the metal plate. It felt horrible, like something was changing forever, seeing her name blackened out like that. But I forced myself to keep spraying. I proceeded to the striped metal. I couldn't bear turning the starry seat black, so I left it. I tore the gold streamers from the handle bars. When I was finished, she looked like death.

The can said "quick-drying." I had thirty minutes. I walked Miss Universe with me into the big station restroom. I hydrogen-peroxided my palm and covered it with Band-Aids. The wound dried out fast and hurt like hell when I moved my fingers. I threw away my shirt and put on the new one, which went down to my knees. I shoved my hair up into the baseball cap and it stuck on top of my head like a clown's hat. I looked at myself in the mirror, hoping that I looked enough like a boy to pass, but I just looked more like a clown, like a circus act, like an easy target.

When I was finally crossing the bridge over the Mississippi to East St. Louis, my hands shook from the highway, the noise, the throat-closing exhaust fumes. I was also starving. I'd eaten the bologna and Jell-O and now my hands shook from hunger. I had to be careful. I could feel a vision threatening.

The sun was getting low over the muddy river. I tried to keep the bike straight, with a railing on one side that plunged to the Mississippi, and honking, screaming cars on the other. The hat seemed to help. Fewer cars were slowing to stare. I couldn't believe being a boy was that much easier. Being a girl seemed to be one lesson after another in terror and hiding.

The river below me had a sheen I did not recognize. It reflected the setting sun almost like a mirror. I stopped to look. It took me a while to remember that I was staring at an oil spill. I'd heard about it on the radio station Mother and Father listened to in the mornings. Some refinery had leaked barrels. I watched the goo slush down the river in slow motion, felt it enter me, run thick and dark in my veins.

The base of my brain buzzed. I clenched my jaw and bore down hard. *Not a vision here. Not here, please, God in heaven, please.* Below, a group of young Native American men appeared on the shore. Bare-chested and shaved, the young Osage lifted a pelt and hauled it into a tree canoe. The base of my skull buzzed ferociously. *Damn it,* I shouted to the universe, *make it stop.*

The Osage guys hauled the canoe into the Mississippi. They got in and looked around, confused. They were stuck in the oil. Past and present merged as the natives fought what should have been water.

I felt the presence of the Native woman and screamed, "No!" I wrestled my shoulders back and away as if someone were grabbing at me. Finally, the vision stopped.

I stood there panting and looking around. It really stopped. Could I really have some control? The thought gave me something like hope, something like deep-down relief, something like the possibility of a life.

I looked down at the river. The Osage boys were not there. I looked up and down the broken shore. A duck flew low and landed on the oil slick and flapped its useless wings. I turned and noticed more cars were slowing down to stare at me. I shook myself. Even an almost-vision would get me in deep trouble here. I noticed the sun was getting dangerously low. I started pedaling. The oil seemed to follow me, seemed to balloon up from the water and enter the top of my head and fill my body with a darkness, a blackness. How could I live in such a toxic world? How could anyone survive this world?

I pedaled off the bridge and entered what looked like a bombed-out city in another part of the world. Potholes threatened to send the bike flying; shells of buildings were choked by ivy and grass. The sun threw long and low beams across the streets as it set—red because of the smog. The sudden twinkling of neon announced liquor stores or naked dancing girls, and everywhere empty lots were piled with trash. So many shells of buildings, boarded up. So much emptiness.

I kept having to veer to avoid nature. Tree roots tore up concrete. Thick, tall grass sprouted from street craters. The earth found its own way. No matter how much concrete we poured, how much oil we spilled, the earth figured out a way. We thought we could smash the land down, but it still grew. It took whatever light filtered, matured with whatever nurturance it could get. Like people, it grew, sideways if it had to, branched leftward, adapted vertically. I saw myself as a crooked tree with twisted, eccentric roots.

I thought I was seeing some kind of mirage when I spied a field of crops, all this green in rows behind a chain-link fence, between a liquor store and a trash lot. I biked up to the fence. A homeless man clasping a bottle to his chest scrambled away, like I was some thief after his booze. It was a field of corn. Someone had put in corn. The gate was locked tight with a padlock, or I swear I would've gone in, laid down amidst the stalks, and gone long and hard to sleep.

It was dark now and the air seemed to howl. Cursing, sirens, howling, thumping. I kept my face forward. A low-riding T-Bird slowed. I put my hand up and noticed a long strand of thick hair had come loose from under the hat. I tried to sneak it back, but it was too late.

The thumping car kept pace. The driver slurred something out the window, and I popped the front tire of my bike onto the sidewalk. I had to veer around bands of drunks who gathered beneath infrequent neon. Still the T-Bird lingered.

I came to Meghan's street. I turned and the car turned with me. I glanced over fast and saw the burning tips of two, maybe three cigarettes. The guy wasn't alone. On the stereo, Black Sabbath. *Children of tomorrow live in the tears that fall today.*

On Meghan's street, the houses looked like broken castles: columns out front, neck-high weeds in the yard, some windows with the glass blown out. I found the house number. A brick building with a massive cracked sidewalk that led to a once-grand porch. The door was boarded up with an orange X painted on it. I jumped off my bike and ran it up the fractured sidewalk. The T-Bird idled. A terror grew in my belly. I pounded on the door. The driver yelled something out the car window. I knocked hard. Harder and harder.

"Yeah, just knock on a nailed-up door, *someone* will answer." I turned, held blackened Miss Universe between me and the speaker. It was a large woman, in her hand a brown paper bag of groceries, two cartons of Lucky Strikes sticking out like long loaves of french bread. She laughed like a crazy woman, jiggled so much she almost lost a carton.

"My sister lives here."

A guy in the backseat of the car catcalled something about me having a sister.

The old woman looked from me to the car. She shrugged. "It's your funeral." She laughed to herself and continued her hobbled walk down the sidewalk. She yelled without turning to look at me. "Try around back, genius."

I went to the side of the building. I had to leave Miss Universe, something I fiercely didn't want to do. The alleyway was narrow, littered with fast-food wrappers, empty cartons and broken glass. The whole time I was sure that I'd hear the creak of the T-Bird door and footsteps following.

At the end of the alley, I thought I saw a pile of clothes as I squeezed past a dumpster. It moved, and I froze. A homeless man. He opened his left eye and looked right into me. I stopped. I never felt I was any different from anybody, no better or no worse. I was no different from the kid who kept having epileptic fits at Holy Cross during gym class, and I was no different from this homeless man. That way of seeing always got me into trouble. As I looked at that homeless man, I looked into myself, and I was paralyzed for a moment.

I heard a car door slam. I gasped and ran to the back of the building. The back door was steel and had rivets and was lit up by a bare outside bulb. I knocked. Nobody answered. I heard footsteps coming down the side of the building. I hauled a pipe off the ground, smashed it against the door. Clang. Echo. Clang. Someone yelled, "Shut the fuck up," out the window.

I ran to a light shining through a murky ground-floor window. I found a crate, scooted it, stood, looked in. The window was barred, and I could barely see. A living room. A young woman with dark hair walked by holding a cigarette. There was a man there but he was in the shadows. I raised my bandaged hand and knocked on the glass. The girl exhaled a stream of cigarette smoke and turned toward the window. I heard shuffling, and she was at the back door, opening it, holding a baseball bat, just as someone turned the corner of the building and came running at me.

"Who's out here?" the woman yelled. She put her hand up to her eyes to block the glare of the bare bulb.

The man ran past her and grabbed my arm. I screamed and tried to pull away. "Pearl, goddamnit," the man yelled. It was Father.

"Who is that?" the young woman yelled.

Father looked like a deer caught in the headlights as he stared at the young woman.

"Oh my God! Dad?" the young woman said. She took a few tentative steps forward, then turned to me. "Oh my God. No way. Pearl? No way!"

"Meghan?" I said in low croak. I tried to loosen Father's grip, but he held hard.

"Go get in the truck," he said. I didn't move. I couldn't move. His face blew plum and the pockmarks stood out like measles. I stared at my sister. She was wearing all black, and as she moved away from the light, all I could see was the white of her face and the pale wood of the bat. She was like some ghost.

She put the bat by her side. "So, you finally found me," she said to Father.

He worked his cheeks, like each phrase was a marble he was spewing out. "Ain't nobody been lookin' for you." He squeezed my arm. "I said get in the truck." He turned back to Meghan. "Don't lure her up here again, you hear me? She's going to have a good life. She's got family."

Meghan flinched like he'd sucker-punched her. She raised the bat. "What did you do to make her run?"

"What did I do? Maybe you should be asking yourself what you did."

She ran up and pushed at him with her free arm, still holding the bat. He shoved her back. "What did *you* do, Meghan?" he snarled.

The two stared at each other. I did not exist. Just the two of them locked in their own universe of hurt.

He pulled me toward the alley. His hand was shaking. He pulled me past the dumpster and the homeless man, who watched us behind black-smeared eyes.

"Let her go!" Meghan yelled.

"This is none of your business. This is *family* business." He said the words low, muddy.

Meghan swung the bat. Father palmed the wood and struggled to yank it from her hands. As they yanked and pulled, I was a puppet attached to Father's fist, a shadow dancer to their fight. He shoved her. The bat rolled. Meghan fell.

She hacked a cough. Father dragged me forward. She said in a little girl voice, "Pearl." She broke into a coughing fit. "Pearl."

I looked straight and clear into the homeless guy's face. I saw myself there. I looked deep into him, and I saw Meghan and Father there, too. I saw all of us inside that one man. We were all that destitute. We were all that homeless.

As we plunged down the alley, Meghan's cries were like echoes of some trapped bird. It took all my air, the sounds of her grief. Father deposited me into the cab of the truck. I saw Miss Universe on its side in the truck bed. The T-Bird was nowhere to be seen.

The drive home was silent, with the furies screeching below the surface. He drove the route that I'd just biked, and it was as if we were rewinding the last couple of days—washed-out highways, whirring farms, bleeding trees. I was being sucked back, pulled hard back toward the farm, toward the people who wanted me dead, toward my tribe.

chapter 7

BONNIE AND I sat in our one-pieces in the mud and rocks on the shore of the Current. I'd been back a week. My swimsuit was pink-and-purple striped, synthetic. Bonnie's was black, frayed around the bottom. You couldn't swim in the Current. Bonnie's mom and dad, Val and Wilbur, brought us. I guess it was their sense of humor. They sat just behind the tree line in their powder-blue Cadillac, him drinking from a flask and her drinking Tab.

Bonnie was my best friend since kindergarten. We'd spent half our lives playing Hangman in her living room. They were the only family for miles with air-conditioning. W-h-i-s-k-e-y. Val would walk in and tell us about sex with Wilbur. She would tell us about *not* having sex with Wilbur. On scrap paper with colored pencils, I would hang Bonnie's man by the neck 'til he was dead. I-n-t-e-r-c-o-u-r-s-e. *Wilbur wouldn't touch me last night. It's been years since I've gotten any.* Val was skinny and tanned. She'd lean over Bonnie and pinch her belly. *You're gettin' a little roly poly there.* Bonnie would push her off. *You're gettin' some jelly welly alright.* P-a-r-e-n-t-i-n-g.

Bonnie had certain phrases for me. She'd say, *You smart. Me dumb.* She'd hold her hand up like a Native American saying *How,* and say it in a monotone. Ten times a day. *You smart. Me dumb.* It all started with some report card of mine she saw at Holy Cross. She also said, *I sure need a dictionary when I'm hangin' around you.*

Wilbur's basement office was filled with toys—plastic men in outhouses who peed at the push of a button, women whose clothes flew off when you turned the pen upside down, a stack of *Hustlers* not so hidden in a filing cabinet. At eye level on desks were half-filled tumblers of scotch, cubes of melting ice in awkward decomposition. The dark, brutal smell of it. *Wilbur wouldn't make love to me last night.*

We sat on the sand and gravel of the muddy Current shore. I kept singing beneath my breath. *Gloom, despair, and agony on me. Ooooh. Deep, dark depression, excessive misery. Ooooh. If it weren't for bad luck I'd have no luck at all. Ooooh. Gloom, despair, and agony on me.*

"Are you going to tell me where you went off to?" Bonnie asked, chubby arms wrapped around fat legs. "Jason is so mad at you." Her belly got in the way, and she strained to hold the position. "Your dad comes over, acting like I was some murderer. Screaming at me, hollering at my dad. Your dad is scary."

What could I say? Bonnie, I'm having these visitations from the spirit world, and either the world's going to end or my sister is going to die. So I went to see my aunt, you know the one in and out of the nuthouse, to see if she could help, and then I went to East St. Louis to find my missing sister. And I found her, and so did my dad, and we had one little happy reunion.

"Just needed to get away." Gravel dug into my bottom, and I shifted from one cheek to the other. I'd only been back a week, and already I'd had two more visions. I couldn't stop them, and I couldn't stop Father's fury at them.

Bonnie ran flat hands over and over a patch of muddy sand, flattening it down. She didn't say anything more. This was conversation in Missouri. Everybody felt real deep, but it just wasn't done to talk too much.

I watched the Current whip by in muddy fury. It was deceptively small, ordinary, but so ornery. It was just a few feet wide and tempted you with its normality. But everyone knew the Current was nothing to be messed with. Every year, a couple of kids died in the Current. We all knew the stories.

In Missouri, there were two rivers that got all the attention: the lugubrious Mississippi, now slimy with oil, and the stout and muddy Missouri. But dozens of other rivers snaked the countryside, sent mucky water like blood up and down the animal veins of the landscape.

Bonnie drew a scaffolding in her flattened area of sand. She drew some lines for letters. I knew what she was doing, but I didn't even have the letters for what I was feeling. So I stood, kicked off my flip-flops, hobbled my way to the water. The brown river jerked in fast, furious shifts. The river was talking, a babble of boulder and brack.

"Yeah, go swimming. Bright idea," Bonnie hollered after me. I put my feet in. You couldn't even paddle in the Current; the pull of it was relentless, vicious. "Seriously, Pearl." I picked my way into the water, rocks piercing the soft underbelly of my feet. I swam out to the middle and doggy paddled. "Goddamnit! I'm not going to save you if that's what you think."

I barely could keep myself aligned with where she sat; the current yanked and pulled like an angry dog. I paddled harder, trying to get back to the shore, but I was barely able to stay in place. Bonnie looked at me with wild eyes. "Goddamnit, Pearl!"

"Bonnie, I can't—" I sputtered water. "I can't—"

Bonnie stood up. She was slow-moving. She muttered something under her breath, and all I could make out was "…always getting me into trouble."

She waded out into the water, paddled to where I was, the current ripping and yanking her. I was swallowing and spitting out water and losing strength.

She took my hand. "Let go!"

We rushed downstream. Our heads reeled along the top of the mucky river—on both sides, heavy brambly forest. Bonnie floated easily, her chubbiness keeping her head well above the water line. Her breasts floated in front of her. I hadn't noticed her breasts had grown. We were growing up. This was me reaching maturity. I laughed and choked and spat. Bonnie tugged hard at my arm to keep me above the surface. We rushed with the current for what seemed like miles.

Tree branches grew long and snarling over the river water. Bonnie reached up and grabbed at a branch and missed. We kept rushing backward down the muddy water. More branches, more grabbing. She caught one, her arm scratched up and bleeding. The branch bent with us as the current pulled us all downstream. She held the branch until it pulled taut, and we stopped.

"You gotta reach over me, grab the branch and pull yourself out." She held me in one arm and the branch in the other. I coughed. She squeezed my arm 'til it hurt. "Jesus, just do it."

I reached over and grabbed the limb above where she held it. I flipped myself over her, submerging her, but she was ready for it, scrunched up her face and held her breath. I climbed hand over fist to the bank. My arms bled from the twig-poking and scratching. Bonnie followed. I flopped on my back. She knelt beside me and turned my body sideways. I coughed up river.

"What the hell," she said. "Jesus H. Christ." She gave me a dark and hard look, of anger, but some knowing, too. This was as far as talking went with Bonnie and me.

When I could stand, we looked around. We were at least three miles from the car, surrounded by thick underbrush. We stood barefoot in swimming suits, looking into a forest with no path.

Bonnie pulled bushes apart, placed her feet where she could.

"You smart. Me dumb," I said from behind, holding up my palm. But she didn't turn around, didn't respond, kept trudging forward while I followed.

Forty-five minutes later, we were back at the car. Bonnie opened the back door.

"Put a towel down or you're going to get the seat wet," Val said from the front. Bonnie took a folded towel off the back seat and laid it flat. We both got in. Val reached into the cooler at her feet and handed us each an ice-cold Tab. "You girls have fun?" she asked. Wilbur started the car.

Jason and I walked low and long into the forest behind the house. Lady Luck whined. Lady Luck moaned. His sobs flew on the wind and cried up the threatening air. Already that day, I'd shucked, peeled, boiled, brewed. I'd boned, bailed, blanched. I'd mucked, mowed, mopped.

We trudged through brambles and vines, fighting thorns and jagged branches. Twigs caught at my hair. My hair grew ratty and thick. Whole families of birds could have nested there. We picked our way through cockspur, thorns like sharpened fingernails digging ruby tracks along forearm and cheek. Jason worked his way through the thicket like a delicate creature, like a fawn. He moved like a dancer, a fairy.

At the clearing he sat beside me on the log. "Would you just tell me what's going on?"

I leaned away from him. I'd already told him about going to Nadine's and finding Meghan. I had not told him about the visions. I didn't think he'd understand. And I had not told him about what'd happened since I came back from Nadine's and Meghan's.

Did I tell him about Mother in the kitchen, standing in front of Father like some football player, blocking him as he swung and snapped his black leather belt? Me on the floor having just had a vision? Father pushing her sideways into the sink, her falling to the floor, him coming at me like some crazed bull? Did I tell him how Mother came and sat on the side of my bed, how she begged me to stop having the visions, pleaded with me not to run away, beseeched me to give up whatever nonsense was going on inside my head? Did I tell Jason how I'd said, *He's a jerk! He's a mean jerk.* Did I tell him she'd responded, *Don't you dare go talking about my husband like that. I'll wash your mouth out with soap!* Did I tell him how she forced my mouth open and inserted the big green bar of Zest?

So many untold stories. I felt so heavy looking at his freckled hands covered in flecks of paint. Those delicate fingers.

earth

I wanted to tell him about the visions—the rest I would never tell. I'd push those stories down deep in my belly until they never got out.

"If you mock me, I swear I'll never ever talk to you again." I meant it. I'd cut him off. It was hard enough dealing with parents and nuns. Jason put his palms up like he was surrendering.

I told him about the visions, starting with the very first one in the garden. I told him about the earth crumbling.

"What do you mean, a vision? A premonition?"

"If a premonition is like being zapped by an electric fence and makes you feel like crap, then yeah, sure, a premonition."

He sat quiet for a moment. "You really saw an Osage?" He was fascinated with everything Osage. Even though the Osage had lived right on the land where Jason and I were sitting, even though they probably had their village right where we sat, we never learned about them at school. It was what I meant by poverty of story. "What is she trying to tell you?"

I shrugged. "The world is going to end? I just don't know. Every time she's about to say something, the vision stops."

"I think there's some other meaning. I think it's like dreaming. There's a kind of code or something. Maybe we just need to figure out the symbols or something."

I felt a buzzing at the back of my head and clenched my fists, held my body rigid like a petrified tree.

Jason said softly, "I wish I had your way of seeing."

"I don't wish my way of seeing on my worst enemy." I bent over my knees. The base of my skull was throbbing.

He put his palm flat on my back. In our family, nobody touched, and the feel of his hand sent me soft, then more rigid than before. "I know you feel alone, Pearl. But I'm here."

I wanted to say, *I don't feel alone in the forest*, but he was right—in that other world, I felt so alone it nearly killed me.

He pulled my face up with his thumb. "Listen, you aren't the only one with troubles." I shook my head. "Truly. I got some of my own." I thought about his drunk mom. I thought how much feeling your own pain made it hard to look in the face of someone else's.

"And you know the Osage sure didn't have it easy." I shook my body, stood up and turned my back on him. Like it helped that the whole world was so messed up? Like that was supposed to help?

"Anyway, you got to stay alive," he said.

"What do you mean? That thing that happened at the Current with Bonnie? What did she say? I was just goofing," I said.

He rolled his eyes. "Pearl, you've got to stay alive at least to find out what this Osage woman business is all about. That's worth living for, right?"

I rolled my eyes and picked hard at my thumb.

The energy grabbed me by the front of the T-shirt, like a fist in the solar plexus, lifted me up and up, nearly off my feet. Roots lunged into soil, branches soared upward.

I heard Jason yell, "Pearl!"

The Native woman, not as a spirit but as a human being, stood next to me with two children, a boy and a girl. She wasn't a white light this time, but a flesh-and-blood human. She huddled with the boy and girl around something in the blackberry bushes. They carried spears and bows and arrows. Squirrels and wild rabbit hung from a strip of leather on the side of the Osage woman's dress.

A bird scrambled around the base of the blackberry bush. The girl cried. The teenage boy was clear-skinned, clear-eyed, elegant, bare-chested with a shaved head. Bracelets on one forearm. His skin was dark, his face open. He was simple in his strength. He looked so healthy. The fledgling robin hopped about the base of the bush as if it were lost or confused or hurt.

"It's hurt, do something," the girl said. They spoke their own language, but I could understand.

"We don't always need to do something," the mother said. "Sometimes leaving it alone is the best you can do."

"Do something," the girl cried.

Her mother reached down to the bird, picked it up. It was hurt after all, a featherless gash to its side. She cupped the bird in both hands. The boy and girl watched like they'd seen this a dozen times. A light grew from her hands, spread around the bird. The light was so attractive, like you'd give anything for that woman to touch you like that. The bird fluttered in her hands, but she held on a while longer, then opened her fingers, and the bird flew like a red-hot ball of fire skyward.

Without warning, their future flashed like a bolt behind my eyes. It was their Trail of Tears, like I'd seen on my bike on the side of the highway. The mother and daughter were dying of some sickness by the side of the road. Snow covered the earth, hundreds of bedraggled Native Americans walked past them, the boy knelt beside them in terrible despair. He didn't look so healthy in this future place.

The Osage woman in the clearing jerked her head toward me. Her body arched as if she too were going into a vision. I saw her children each take one arm, like they'd seen this happen a dozen times, too. The white light version of the Native woman streamed from the top of her head, flew up to me. The white light face came close to mine.

This light woman glanced around the clearing, a look of knowing, a look of despair. She seemed to fall then, back and down. She was back in her own body, her children holding her up on each side. She turned to them, said in an exhausted, harsh whisper, "Let's go now. A storm is coming."

She ran in awkward exhaustion with the children, labored them through the alders. She looked behind her, straight at me. The boy followed her gaze, but his eyes scanned the forest and seemed to see nothing. I watched as they galloped away, the children like deer, muscular in forest light.

Jason was shaking me. I was in the dirt and he was holding me. His face was sheet-white, his eyes reeling orbs. "What the hell just happened?"

In the distance, Lady Luck's voice stretched long, low and wide in aching hum.

chapter 8

M s. Castle, the seventh-grade English teacher, kept staring at me during sixth period. Holy Cross was a compound of a brick church, two schoolhouses, rectory and convent, surrounded by a strict wire fence. It was a mini-universe of God, nuns and priests. Green-and-blue-plaid uniforms, skirt hems six inches above the knee. They had us kneel while one of the nuns measured.

Ms. Castle was a lay teacher. Every once in a while, Holy Cross could hold onto a lay teacher for more than a year. As the bell rang, she said, "Pearl, I need to talk to you."

I hauled my books to the front. She waited for the other kids to stream out, then bent her knees and put her face low to look into mine. "Is there anything you need to talk about?"

She had permed dark hair; blue-framed glasses that covered most of her face; soft, pale skin; light-blue eyes. What was I supposed to say? What could I possibly say? She used some kind of lavender scent, stood in front of me smelling of flowers.

"How are things at home?"

I shrugged. The distant echo of kids' chatter. The scratchy taste of chalk dust floating in the air. Luckily, I'd never had a vision at school. I couldn't figure out why, other than not much of school engaged me. I made good grades. It was just memorization. A monkey could memorize. The teachers mostly left me alone.

earth

Ms. Castle stood, stretched her back, sighed. She walked to the corner and put her hand on the knob of the teacher's closet, a white door with horizontal slats. She spoke in her teacher's voice. "I expect you to be responsible. I expect you to be careful. I expect you to be respectful."

I followed her. I had no idea what she was talking about. What had I done wrong? What was I in trouble for now? I kept my head bent low.

"One at a time," she said, opening the door. "You must put one back before you take another." She swept her hand toward the back of the closet. In front of us was a wall of tattered paperbacks. I was drawn forward, magnetically. I kept looking back at Ms. Castle, terrified this was some kind of trick, and she'd slam the door before I had a chance to reach the books. I stared at her permed hair, her blue eyes. She was the only "Ms." I'd ever met. Was this what being a Ms. meant, row after row of glorious books?

At home, we still only owned a *King James Bible* and a *Farmer's Almanac*. I'd never seen so many books owned by one person.

I ran my sweaty palm over the rough spines of the paperbacks like a blind person reading in quick succession. Whole universes to explore. Whole universes that were there the whole time. I couldn't see the titles; everything was a blur. I grabbed one on top of the second row, didn't look at it, held it against my chest.

"Only one at a time," she repeated. "Put that one back before you take another."

I nodded. She looked at me hard, looked about to say something, but then didn't.

When I got home, I locked myself in the bathroom. I took the paperback out of my book bag. On the front cover stood a lone tree on a hill. The back said it was about a Jewish girl, Rachel, in one of the concentration camps during World War II. An orphan in a group of orphans.

I finished it the next day at recess, sitting on the cold metal of the fire escape outside the second-graders' classroom. Screams echoed on the playground. I was so deep inside the book. Rachel and the group of orphans were released from the camp. They were moved to a big house in the countryside. Someone gave them apples, a salty soup. A few of the children got sick. Rachel walked out of the house, around the fields. She found a lone tree on a hill. She climbed slowly, because she was so tired, up that hill.

As she stood on that hill with that tree, a statement came up from her belly and out of her lips: *I am Rachel.* She started running down the hill, yelling her name. *I am Rachel! My name is Rachel.* Screaming and running, hair flying, like her very life depended on it. I clung to the metal railing of the fire escape. I wanted to stand up and scream, but I scrunched myself up. I held it in.

When I wasn't laboring, I was running. I ran when a vision threatened, ran when Father was in a rage, ran at recess when the nuns got on my nerves, ran whenever, wherever and however I was allowed. I ran the mile track to the farm and back, the roads around our farmhouse, up Powwow, onto Tomahawk, down Mohawk and back up Powwow. I ran laps around the playground at recess. When a vision threatened to overwhelm, I ran like my very life depended on it.

The visions found another way. They pounded my dreams. Nights were full of thunderbolts and thrashings. Mornings were knotted up in sweaty sheets. My eyes became painted with charcoal shadows. The problem with visions was they gave you enough to scare the hell out of you, but not enough to let you know what you were supposed to do about it.

I couldn't keep my visions solely in the dream world. It could never be that easy. They still erupted, still forced me onto tip-toe, still landed me more often than I could count on the wrong side of a belt.

earth

Mother got Father a job in town, construction. Maybe she was helping me out. Maybe she was getting him out of the house so he wouldn't witness so many visions. But really, deep down I believed she wanted store-bought things. Mother wanted so desperately away from the earth.

A family portrait at breakfast one morning: a still life, a snapshot of that moment when life turns from one thing to something else. Father with Vitalis like an oil slick in red hair, a starched work shirt, a crease in his work trousers, old brutal boots. The Pall Mall pack in his front pocket. Mother handing him a black arched lunch box. The little boy look on his face, like summer vacation was over and he had to go back to school. The truck door slamming, the engine coughing with reticence. Afterward, Mother going to her stash of JC Penney catalogues hidden behind the pressure cooker in the kitchen cupboard.

The job in town seemed to make things even worse. Before, he'd spent most days out in the woods hunting or on one of the rivers fishing. Now, Mother had put him in starched clothes and sent him to town. She'd put him into a cage. At night, after work, his bony fingers went more often to the cans of Schlitz malt liquor in the fridge, to the pack of Pall Malls in his shirt pocket. It sent his bony fingers to his belt to appease his growing rage. I studied this rage. Like I tried to discern the visions, I tried to discern his anger, to make a note of its peculiarities, to fathom how past and present created his rageful future, and mine.

I was at the clearing. The patch of tall grass flamed sparks. The grass spoke to me. A burning bush. A talking bush. If you cared to listen. I was trying to listen. I didn't know how long I was there, when I heard the screech. It pained up the air, shimmied the branches, set my nerves rattling. Wary, I scrambled up the long hill that led to our house. The ground was pale and dry as rock. I came out of the forest, walked up over a small rise.

Father's gangly form, his shock of auburn hair like an inferno. He stood over Lady Luck. The dog stood looking up at him, mangy, long and potbellied, wobbly on bony legs. On his snout, silver whiskers.

Father pulled his leg back and swung his foot into the dog's soft underbelly. "Quit your whining!" The dog was chained and could not get away.

Father lost balance, stumbled back a couple of steps. He looked around. His legs like too-long toothpicks. His face was always full of ravines and crevasses, a cracked face, a tortured face.

"Quit." Kick-screech.

"Your." Kick-moan.

"Whining!"

Beneath my feet, the ground was so parched. Straggling weeds grew in uneven clumps. Cracks like lightning snaked out from the bottom of my shoes. The screaming bird dog cracking the earth wide open. The screeching father. I stood for an eternity. I stood for seconds or centuries, white light pouring from the top of the head, veering up to God knows where, more parts of me disappearing into the universe. I picked my thumb until it bled. From my belly a desperate whimper, from my gut a raw caw. A devastation from dog to man to soil. A tearing asunder.

Father was the chained dog. Father was kicking himself.

When the noise stopped, I looked up. Lady Luck was on his side in the dirt, whimpering, pleading. Father ran his sleeve across his face. He turned toward the house, hitched up his trousers and stumbled up the concrete steps to the side door.

I walked on unsteady legs past Lady Luck and up the steps to the back door. In the kitchen, Mother was bent forward at the stove. She looked sideways. She held a wooden spoon up like a conductor over an orchestra of eggs. Father sat behind her at the kitchen table, one arm resting on the tabletop, looking down at nothing, looking exhausted.

"Your shoes are dirty," she said.

"What?" I thought she was talking to Father, but she was looking at me. I owned only two pairs: patent leather flats for church and school, and boots for farm. Both were too small, and my toes hurt. Usually I went barefoot. I looked down at my boots. They were covered in caked dirt.

"Go clean yourself up." She took the cast-iron skillet off the stove. "Breakfast is ready."

Again, I thought about how I was going to have to raise myself up. Nobody here was capable of it. I knew I had to raise myself up, and I had no idea how.

Dinnertime. A white pile of Wonder Bread. Thick, bloody steaks. Mashed potatoes, gravy. Green beans. Cole slaw. On the counter, the Wonder Bread wrapper, the red, blue and yellow-colored circle a sign to Mother of better things. Still, despite more store-bought items, we mostly ingested the land. It was the earth that lodged beneath our fingernails and dissolved in our gullets. It was the earth that we purged in our shit.

It was autumn. Billowing curtains, empty echoes. Outside the window, a skinned deer hung from the old oak. It was deer season. Father had got a twelve-point buck. The head would join the others in the living room.

Father said without looking up, "You got your head too much in books." I'd tried to hide my reading in the locked bathroom. I'd tried to reserve my immersion to the toilet seat, but there was no way to conceal it all. I was voracious for story. Starved for legend. I read book after book after book.

Mother looked at me. Strangely. Something was brewing. Something had to pop. The strain in the house now that Father had to work was like a weather pressure system on the verge of bursting. I watched Mother watch me. She never looked at you directly unless you were in trouble. I brought a fork heavy with steak to my lips. She said, "That's Baby you're eating."

I pulled the cold tongs from between my lips, metal scraping teeth. I stared at her, helpless. Baby was a brother to me. Baby was my favorite calf ever. I'd bottle-fed him and loved him like a pet. She knew that. *Toughen up,* her glowing green irises said. *Toughen up, Pearl. Get your head out of books. You got to survive the real world.*

I swallowed the bite nearly whole, and the meat made a hard lump in my throat. Do not love the earth. Do not become attached to it. Do not bond. Do not think you are that hoof, that forehead, those deep pools. If you do, there is no room for you. You will be beaten as if you were a beast. Gutted. You will be kicked in the gut again and again. You will be thrown off the land. You will find less and less of the earth to call your own.

I had no stomach for the rest of the meal. I pushed my chair back, and the leg grunted like a fart against the linoleum. Father mumbled something toward his plate. It was hard to translate him normally, but the grunting chair made it hopeless. I stopped mid-air, hand next to the cutlery. If you didn't get him what he wanted, when he wanted it, there was always hell to pay.

"Go on outside and wait for me," he growled, gesturing a fork toward the door.

I went out across the scrubby front yard and sat on the grass. I picked the skin around my thumbs until they bled. I watched the leaves twirl in tiny whirlwinds on the gravel road.

The screen door slammed. I stood up and wiped the blood from my picked-over thumb onto my palm. He smashed a path across the front yard, retrieved a sliver of something from between his teeth with a toothpick. His left trouser leg flapped from the top of his work boot like a fish in the bottom of a boat. He walked past me without looking up, went into the middle of the road and stood with his legs apart.

"Come on. Get on over here," he said. He looked straight up the hill.

It dawned on me what he wanted. It dawned on me what he wanted to do. I went to the middle of the road. He smelled dark and hard like yellowed work socks after a long day of construction. There was no way, no way at all, he was going to win this one.

I put my right foot forward and my right hand on my knee. I looked over and saw Mother looking at us through the curtains of the front window.

"One…Two…Three!" I shouted. I took off like a shot, punching the air with my fists. If he wanted a race, he'd get a race. No problem. No problem at all.

I ran hard uphill on Powwow. I was about to turn onto Tomahawk and whipped a glance back. He seemed to move in slow motion, skinny legs pulling up in front of him, boots flapping against the road. His mouth hung open in heavy breathing. That head of hair like a sudden forest fire.

Tomahawk was potholed from farmers' trucks running it winter after winter. A normal road, a road like any other street in some rural byway. It helped me to think I was normal and the running was normal, racing a father was normal, an everyday, straightforward thing. Val drove by in the baby blue Caddy. I waved. She lifted her sunglasses to stare at Father behind me. I turned and saw Father hacking and holding his side. She parked in the middle of the road and got out to make sure he was OK, but he threw her arm off and stumbled forward. I turned my focus back, whipped hard down Mohawk.

I was back at the house in record time, my mind so beautifully clear before the despair crept slowly like rainwater back into a leaky rooftop. Minutes went by before Father turned the corner at the bottom of Powwow. His boots flapped this way and that, clown shoes on stick legs winging sideways even as they barely left the street. He was rasping, coughing, hacking up phlegm, spitting. His face blew Pall Mall red. I could see his knobby knees through the faded cloth of his work pants. His blue shirt was soaked in sweat.

On the straight uphill, he clenched his hands by his shoulders and pumped his elbows. The hill got even steeper, and he leaned his upper body forward and spat. I walked into the middle of the street. He stumbled and leaned toward me, looking like a baby reaching out as he took his first steps. A line of slobber ran through the crevasses and potholes along his long, thin chin. I nearly put my arms out, nearly urged him toward me. I kept thinking of what Nadine told me about him as a boy. I should help him. I should try. But as I stood there, I could feel a heaviness from him that would surely drown me. He was too much weight. A load of untold stories—not just his, but generations of untold truths. I would never be able to bear it and survive. I turned my back on him. I dug my fists deep into my pockets. I went to pace the front yard.

He sputtered to a stop next to me, coughed for breath, bent over his knees, laughed. The problem was that running always led you back to this house, no matter how fast you were, how good. Father had that problem, too. We were all leashed up like Lady Luck.

He bent over, gasping. I took a sideways glance at the sweat on the back of his thin neck. I stretched my hand out. I just wanted to touch him while my mind was clear, just some sort of contact. Blood of my blood. Flesh of my flesh. Was there a way to make contact where I didn't have to bear the entire weight of him? I didn't know. I wasn't sure. My fingers came close to his neck, but before I reached him, he stood abruptly and turned toward the house. Mother was in the window.

"Mother," he called, limping across the grass. "Mother!" He coughed. I heard the screen door open and slam. "I did it!" I heard him yell. "Goddamn, I did it."

Not all my visions were bad. Some were full of so much light and love that it filled my body up to bursting. I had a lime-green desk in the dormer window in my bedroom. Mother and I picked it up at a yard sale and used an old bucket of paint in the basement to cover up its scars. I painted the wooden knobs yellow. I sat at that desk to do my homework, the view out the window of forest and hills. One blissful vision happened at that desk. The Native woman came and flew me out the window on blistery winds over Lady Luck's broken doghouse, over the forest with the clearing, to the barn and the massive vegetable garden, farther beyond our property over fields parceled out like a rag quilt. We soared along black skies, over barren fields and rocky and wild mountains, across oceans, to foreign lands. Everything I saw, animal, vegetable, mineral, was full of texture and tint, and was just perfect, so perfect just as it was.

Another time at that desk, I had a vision where I entered a single drop of dew; inside that drop, I fell from a swollen leaf, slapping another leaf as I splashed down and down until I entered the relief of moist soil. I was in the vegetable garden. I was a single drop of living water. I awoke from this one feeling like I wanted to go out and lick the ground.

Nighttime. We all sat out back. Just as the visions weren't all bad, life at our house wasn't all bad either. We had our moments. It was just that all the trauma seemed to fire our synapses so hard and fast it trumped the tenderness. The hard stories buried the delicate moments beneath mounds of pain. You had to look hard to find a seedling of hope amidst all the devastation.

This night, all around, the orchestra of the forest, low rhythm of cricket, croak of tree frog, zip of flying insect. I was catching fireflies in a canning jar. They flashed like stars in the palms of my hands. My body absorbed the sounds and vibrations of the wild night, became a quilt of rustling and cooing. Father and Mother sat swinging on the porch.

Father had his fiddle. He knew about ten tunes, played maybe twice a year. He held the swing still with one foot while he worked the strings. Mother kept her hands tight in her lap and nodded. He stared at Mother as he played "Mississippi Sawyer." I watched them through the glass of my mason jar; in the dry grass, flashes of light mixed with those edgy strings. The music glided along, breathed up the late summer air. From his strings, I felt the rivers he fished, the currents long and slow, and beneath, muddy sounds, cavernous. The pull of the current, the random meandering of muddy, scaly, ugly fish. The music was the story of the river.

I looked through the prism of fireflies at the blaze of Father's red hair, the black-violet night of Mother's. I saw him trying to bring the river to her, trying to love her with the sway and heft of the ponderous waters of that landlocked place.

As he played, I found myself in the water, the moon between my fingers on the river's surface, the water like molten silver. In front of me sat my father's silver fishing boat, the sun pink and streaked and slow. It wasn't a vision; it was more like the way I used to experience the world when I was young. To the heavy music, I sunk deep until I was in the muddy bottom waters, swimming with fish as ancient as the land.

He'd stopped. I was standing in front of them at the swing. I didn't know how I got there. They were holding hands. I was staring at him. I was touching the fiddle on the swing next to him. Father's body was arched on the swing. His eyes were thrown back. He was trying to control it, but I could tell. He was playing music and he'd had a vision. His visions weren't as strong as mine or he wouldn't have been able to control them, but he was definitely having a vision. I stood dumbfounded. Father had visions. That's why his mother sent him off with Nadine.

"You have them too," I croaked.

"What did you say?" He nearly screamed it, grasping tight to my mother's hand. His other hand became a fist.

"Pearl, go on in the house," Mother said.

"I just…It's just …" I put my hand on the fiddle again. "I didn't mean to …" All of the air went out of me. I wanted to say, *Your music is beautiful. It's amazing. Your visions sing the song of the earth. Your music chants the language of the river.*

"Git. Go on. Git," he said, fist up and ready.

I clenched my jaw tight. I went into the house.

chapter 9

M S. CASTLE GAVE me a notebook. It was in a narrow brown paper bag, and it was black. *For your own stories*, she'd said.

At first, bent over the lined pages, tongue between teeth, I tried too hard; the pushing and wedging destroyed the stories. I had to stop trying so damned hard. I had to place the stories out in front of me and back up. I had to draw lines from tale to tale, fashion a constellation, give each a name, turn them into myth.

The difficult stories had to come out first. Hard times shot electrical storms that transformed the geography of my brain. Because of the pain, the awful stories burned brightest. Trauma trumped tenderness. The difficult stories came first.

After that stubborn earth was turned over, tenacious root and clinging weed dug under and up and laid bare; only then could the more gentle moments sprout; only then did the delicate stories even have a chance. To open. To speak.

Day after day, I purged upon the page.

If I didn't tell the stories of my ancestors, who would? If not me, who? I imagined these untold legends as voices speaking over and under each other, running in deep caverns in the belly of the earth. I couldn't hear what they were saying—the voices drowned each other out, affected everyone with their noise. These were not just the untold tales of my own ancestors, but those of everyone in the world. What a racket they made. What a desperate fuss to be heard.

earth

If I wrote the stories, the little I knew, could I purge myself of the weight? Could I change my own plot? I wrote Father's story, what I remembered about Meghan. I knew only four stories from Mother's childhood. A smattering of brutalities.

I wrote about the one time Mother took me to see her bedridden mother. I was five. She drove the truck out of town, deep into farm country. She turned down a single-lane dirt track; we bumped and jostled until we pulled up to a falling-down house.

We were in woods I'd never seen before, and an excitement charged through my veins, a primal force. I wanted to go into those trees, to get to know them, but I was wearing a dress and Mother wouldn't allow it.

A dishwater blonde woman with brown teeth in her thirties answered the door. We entered a low-ceiling house. The interior had dark-maple paneling and thick beams. The smell was of illness. The smell was deep, pungent, rotten. I felt the odor in my shoulders. I felt the pong creep down my spine.

The woman took us into the sitting room. An old woman was in a bed in the middle of the room, a skeleton beneath piles of rag quilts.

"This is your Grandmother Elizabeth," Mother said to me.

I went up to the bed. I stared. She was sunken and emaciated. Agony was etched into the deep wrinkles on her bony, petrified face. Thin strands of black hair fell across her cheek. She had no teeth, and the center of her face had caved inward; wrinkles sprayed out from her lips like a cat's whiskers. She writhed in the bed, gumming nonsensical syllables. Beneath the quilt, where her legs should be, an emptiness. I knew Mother paid this woman to be a caregiver. I didn't know why I was only brought to meet my grandmother once. Maybe I was brought as a baby, but I didn't remember it.

When my own mother was little, she'd had to take care of her mother. Grandmother Elizabeth had had bad arthritis and ended up losing her legs. Mother went to school until she was ten. They couldn't afford shoes for everyone, so they took her out of school. Besides, they needed her as a caregiver. There was nothing to protect the soft padding of Mother's feet. Anyway, she was needed around the house.

This was one of the stories I knew about Mother. How that first day they took her out of school, she stood and watched the dust of the school bus on that long dirt road as it took her brothers away. She went barefoot behind the barn and squatted in the sharp, scratchy grass. She wailed. She tore at the weeds with thin fingers. She pummeled the earth with young fists. She wanted books more than anything, and they took it all away.

She was put in charge of caring for her mom and feeding eleven kids. She argued with the dry earth for meager roots. She fought with the cracked land for torn greens. She begged the scrawny chickens. She snuck about to steal the money from her father's pockets before he could get to the bar and waste it on whiskey. She tried to feed them all. Two brothers died from malnutrition. Their death weighed heavily on her.

Most of her other brothers grew up so sensitive, so undernourished, they drank like their daddy. I imagined that they were farmer-artists. Fragile shoots exposed too soon. One after the other, these boys shot themselves in the head. It was a legacy, these suicides, an acceptable form of not living. We didn't talk about any of it. Their deaths were never mentioned. Their stories were never told.

When Mother was seventeen, she met her savior, her knight in shining armor, her ticket out of hell. My widowed father showed up in town with a little Meghan in tow. Mother was small, dark, shy. He was tall, rugged, tortured. He swept in like a tsunami; they clung to each other like shipwreck victims. They married after seven months of courtship.

As I stood over Grandmother's bed, a boy of about five or six ran from a back room and out the front door, his shoes echoing a solemn drum beat against the hardwood. Thump-thump-thump. That sound, and the squawk of my nearly dead grandmother. The dank smell. I thought, *What would it be like to be that boy, an old woman dying in the sitting room.*

"She's flushin' the pills again," the blonde woman said. She paced the sitting room, shoulders slumped.

"None of them getting down?" Mother asked.

"No, she says she don't like how they make her all fuzzy-headed. I take her into the bathroom, lift her on the toilet. She's got the pills in her hands ready to take 'em. I turn my back, and she's gone and flushed 'em."

"No, no, no," Grandmother said, twisting her head on the pillow.

Mother came up. She did not touch her mother. I stood by Mother. We did not touch. It wasn't done.

The caregiver said, "Sarah, your Pearl sure does look like her granny."

My head snapped back like I'd been slapped.

Writing about my ancestors caused me much pain, their lives such dreadful drudgery, their despair as recurring as the seasons. But I couldn't seem to avoid their story. My story seemed to be accessed down that icy path, across that arduous, slippery slope.

I just knew when my grandparents' stars burned out, their stories, like their meager belongings, would be dispersed. Mother and Father were unwilling to fill in the blanks, terrified of what specters such remembering might invoke. I wanted to tell the little I did know. As a record, a flimsy summary, the shadow of a myth.

I wrote about the Osage, about the people before us. It seemed right. I wrote what I knew from my visions. Their lack of story was a deep hole, a missing piece to the earth's story. The way to kill a whole group of people? Kill their story.

Different people had different ways of looking at the world, different pairs of glasses that highlighted different things. I loved all the different perspectives like I loved that clearing. What would it be without the eccentricities of that sassafras, without the goofiness of the sudden patch of grass? How boring life would become if we all told the same story. The way even the land had a story to tell, told in the bones, whispered in the blood, fables without words, fairy tales of the flesh. The way the land had so much to say. That way.

Stories were as important as food. *Toughen up or you'll never survive,* Mother and Father said. I thought, *Listen up, too, or you won't ever survive. Listen. Up.*

Stories weren't just about the telling, but about who told them. Not just about who, but how. Not just how, but why.

I wrote about third grade at Holy Cross, about the infamous Sister Theodora. She had no room for anybody else's stories, had no space in her soul for other ways of seeing.

I wrote about how I stood at the big globe in the corner of the classroom. I had a ruler. I said, "Excuse me, Sister." We called her "Sir Ted." She was bent and severe in cat eyeglasses, twisted and drawn in full habit. Someone must've done a number on the nuns, because they took all the joy of living and smashed it, beat it senselessly over our heads, tore it from our bellies and threw the guts of it to the dogs.

Sir Ted kept writing on the board, and I yelled louder, "Sister, I said excuse me." She turned and caught me in her glare.

I pointed the ruler to the Soviet Union. I asked, "If the Russians tell their stories and we tell ours, which story is really the truth?" It was the Cold War. We had atomic bomb drills once a month. We floated daily in the terror of Communism. "If they're just saying how they see life, and we're just saying how we see it, why is our way of seeing things right and their way wrong?"

"Sit down, Pearl," she said, arm and yardstick raised. "I won't have none of that nonsense from you today. We got a lot of material to cover."

"But why would they possibly think we're right?" I said. Sir Ted came up to Bonnie's desk, holding the ruler like a sword, as if challenging me to a duel. Bonnie shot her hand in the air. Sir Ted slapped the ruler down hard on the surface of Bonnie's desk, the thwack ringing like a shot. "Don't you dare let Pearl drag you into her nonsense, Bonnie May Johnson. You hear me? There is nothing but trouble down that path."

Sir Ted came toward me. "I said sit down!"

I went to my desk. *Sit down, Pearl. Sit down, Pearl. Sit down. Squelch it. Lock it up. Lock it down. Bury it. Bury yourself.*

Sit. Down.

Sit.

Down.

Soon afterward, Sir Ted started a no-clapping rule school-wide. We were only allowed to tap our index fingers together. There was too much voice in clapping, too much vigor. At school assemblies, hundreds of students tapped their index fingers, pa-pa-pa, the sound like shallow intakes of breath.

One day I was looking out the window, down on the heads of some second-graders running across the parking lot. Our classroom was on the second floor, and the building sat on a hill. A lay teacher was with them; she hadn't been at the school long. The kids hollered, sprinted to a small square of grass. She clapped some rhythm and they all started clapping.

Surely the lay teacher knew the no-clapping rule. There were signs everywhere, like no smoking, but with two clapping hands in a circle, and a red line striking through.

A group of nuns emerged from the front door of the convent just on the edge of the schoolyard. Five of them. One started running across the parking lot to the small field, and the others followed. They held their arms out in front of them and ran, tapping their index fingers. Pa-pa-pa. Their habits, skirts and black cloaks flew out behind them and they looked like a flock of birds. The kids and teacher in the field slowly stopped clapping. They looked over, mouths open, hands falling to their sides. Pa-pa-pa-pa-pa.

I carved, composed, created. I scribbled, scrawled, inscribed. My hand moved on its own as if some spirit were guiding it. The second notebook filled. I wrote smaller. I fit whole worlds in tiny script into books of fifty pages.

I wrote about the past so hard, so full of heart, that sometimes I'd look up from my notebook and not know if I was in third grade or seventh. I'd have to force my head clear—the stories took over my life like the visions. I had to remember that I was thirteen now, a big girl, with access to a closet full of books and a head full of stories. It was a responsibility. In that rural place, it was important to keep my wits about me.

One day, I found a book in Ms. Castle's closet. It was set on top of the rest. I swore it hadn't been there before. The pages were too fresh, the cover too unscratched. On the front, a Native American standing, holding up a stick with feathers like he was praying. My arm trembled as I stared at it.

Black Elk Speaks, Being the Life Story of a Holy Man of the Oglala Sioux. On the back, they called it a "religious classic by an American Indian." He was a warrior, medicine man and visionary. A person didn't come across such books in a Catholic school in the 1970s. I carried it conspicuously past Ms. Castle's desk so she'd look up, so I could wink at her for putting it there for me. But when she did glance up from grading papers and I winked, she sort of frowned, looked perplexed and went back to her paperwork.

I couldn't figure how the book got there if she didn't put it there for me. I didn't want to open it during recess and have the reading spoiled by a fly ball or snotty-nosed kid, so I waited 'til I got home, waited for the safety of a locked door, the comfort of the toilet lid.

Instead of locked in the bathroom, I found myself in the clearing reading the book. A rattled bird flew some fall leaves off a tree branch and I came to, noticed where I was. I didn't remember coming to the clearing. I went back to the book.

Black Elk had visions. He was nine when he had the first one, and when he came out of it he wouldn't tell anyone because he was scared they'd think he was crazy. He went hunting with his bow and arrow and killed an animal like boys in his tribe always did, but this time he felt horrible about it.

Black Elk said what I felt. *The thunder beings were like relatives to me.* He looked at his people and thought, *They seemed heavy, heavy and dark; and they could not know they were heavy and dark.* Like Nadine and me, he had terrible fears that the world was in a horrible state. He told his story to a poet in 1931 who wrote it all down. All I could think was if Black Elk thought it was bad then, he should see the world in 1979.

It was getting dark and I hadn't noticed. I carried the book like a Bible through the woods and up past Lady Luck whining in the dirt. I went up the back stairs and got a couple slices of bologna and went back and threw them in the dirt for him. Father wasn't home from work yet. I went to the living room, sat cross-legged and foggy-headed on the orange shag carpet. I turned on the big-box TV for some reason and Tony Orlando and Dawn were singing "Tie a Yellow Ribbon Round the Ole Oak Tree."

I wasn't watching the TV. My face was close to Black Elk's words. I heard Father enter the living room. I knew better than this. I knew better than to be reading when he got home from work. Usually I listened for the crunch of his truck tires on gravel and ran and locked myself in my bedroom. Or I started setting the kitchen table so he'd think I was a good, hard-working little woman, the kind some hard-working man would want to marry someday.

I hunched my shoulders. He stood behind me. I could feel the rage of him like insects crawling beneath the skin.

"What trash are you reading now?" he asked.

Filled with the spirit of Black Elk, I thought, *Why can't I tell my father about the visions? Why can't I explain that what we all have is a gift?* Father with his fiddle, with his love of the woods, had the gift, too. Black Elk had brought me hope and turned me stupid.

I held up the front cover to him, said, "He had visions just like mine, just like Nadine's." I didn't add, *just like yours.*

He grabbed the book from my hand, turned it over and read the back. He was nearly illiterate, so it was a long wait while he mouthed the words. He finished and turned the book and looked at the cover, stared at it and looked about to sob—not the kind of crying because he'd had a hard day at work, but the kind akin to a lifelong crevasse of wailing.

I stood, went up and put my hand on the book to take it back. I said real gentle, "You can read it if you want."

"All you two got is a one-way ticket to Fulton," he said so quiet, so marble-mouthed, I nearly didn't hear. "Ever since you turned thirteen, you're …" He didn't finish. I tried to pull the book from his fingers. He yanked it from me and held it like a sack of rotten tomatoes at his side.

"Give it," I said with a low growl.

"Git on in the kitchen and help your mother with dinner."

"I said give it." I wasn't whining. I said it straight and hard. He wasn't used to me not whining.

He raised a fist. I ran at him, went for the book, caught the edge. He held on, and his whole body shook as he struggled against me. We played tug-of-war with the book until it popped out of our hands, flew across the living room and hit the plate-glass window. I was staring at the book on the shag and didn't notice him come at me. He slapped me hard on the side of the head.

"Git in that kitchen."

I turned to face him. I looked back at the book. I was breathing hard. I lunged for the book.

He grabbed the back of my shirt, hauled me up. He spun me around and hit me. An open-handed, meaty slap. My head snapped back. My cheeks burned. He'd only ever 'spanked' before, if you could call his beatings spanking. The slap to the face was personal, shocked me with its intimacy.

I yanked out of his grasp and went for the book again. He slapped me back: one, two, three, four, ear, cheek, head. I was forced back and back, toward the staircase. I put my hands out toward the book, the crumpled thing helpless on its side on the shag. Ms. Castle would never lend me a book again if I didn't save that book. My life would be over if I couldn't get to that book.

earth

I swung my arms wildly, flung myself forward. I couldn't get around him. He kept slapping. He backed me up, all lanky angry muscle, his bony elbows flying out sideways.

I raised my arms to protect my face. I was losing touch with reality. My body changed. I became his mother who sent him away, Nadine who caused him to lose his family. I shifted into Meghan. I was every woman to betray him.

I dropped my arms. Where there should've been fight in me, there was this whirring vortex, this hole. Between slaps, snapshots of his mother, whose name was mine; his first wife, who'd up and died on him; of Nadine lying in the grass; snapshots of Meghan's face through murky glass. Snap. Snap. Snap.

He stopped finally, stood in front of me breathing hard. I stumbled away, ran up the stairs. "You think I want to end up like you?" The book was still on that cursed living room floor. "I'll kill myself before I end up like you," I screamed.

chapter 10

IT WAS MY fourteenth birthday. I decided it was my turn to kill. I begged. Mother said no and no again, that hunting was men's work. Maybe, she suggested, I would want a sewing box for my birthday. I beseeched and whined. I stomped and slammed. Finally Father snapped, screamed that my head was too much in books, and maybe this would teach me a thing or two about the real world.

When I was real little, I was no different from the earth, but by the time I had my first vision in the garden at thirteen, most of that connection had been beaten out of me. Now with the visions, I could feel that connection again, and I wanted it dead. I wanted to sever all my feeling for the land, to stab it and gut it and get it out of me.

Wet twigs muffled underfoot. Scuttering animals, a prattling creek, a low echo to the sky. The smell was dank earth and far-off wood fire. Father and I left the farm and walked deeper and deeper. We had acres to roam. I cradled a 12-gauge.

I knew it meant spending a day alone with him, but there was no other way. If I wanted to go hunting, if I wanted to kill, it had to be with him. It was a sacrifice I was willing to endure.

I never saw the Black Elk book again. I was too horrified to tell Ms. Castle what had happened. I stopped borrowing books. Stopped writing. She watched me darkly, looked like she wanted to have another after-class talk, but she didn't say a word.

Father came to a stop and, with the tip of his boot, rolled russet heart-shaped droppings. Deer droppings. He said nothing, went and sat beneath a nearby oak. I followed, climbed up the backside of the tree, dragged the shotgun with me, the bark rough through thin jacket and jeans. Atop a thick branch, I looked down on the top of Father's head, thick red hair aiming in all directions. He took sips from a thermos he kept in the large side pocket of his coat. I could smell it on him, the dark musky whiskey. Since he'd started working in town, he'd traded in Schlitz for something stronger. His hand crept more often to his Pall Mall pocket. With every rustle in the forest, he brought up his rifle and peered through the site.

I put up my shotgun and pointed it around the forest, then aimed it downward at Father's head. He had some grey showing. *Pow*, I thought. *Blam.* I turned the shotgun again on the forest and glimpsed deer from my vantage point, but didn't say anything and didn't shoot. I cradled the gun in a nearby crook of a branch, leaned forward and put my belly against the thick limb, turned my face so the bark chafed my cheek. I was so tired. I stared at the few leaves left on the branches. They danced in crazy circles—light on one side and dark on the other, light and dark, light and dark, light and dark. So very tired.

I had almost hypnotized myself when a shot slapped through the forest, a guttural ricochet. I flinched, fell forward and clung to the branch to keep from falling. I saw Father vanishing fast below, running in his nose-first way, his orange reflector coat appearing and disappearing like mini-explosions.

I sat up, saw a deer running in the opposite direction from where Father was running. I grabbed my 12-gauge and, without much aim, shot. I'd fired a 12-gauge a thousand times at cans and bottles, and I wasn't a bad shot. The deer stumbled. The dancing deer fumbled. It slipped to its knees.

I felt horror and something like electricity. I held the rifle, scrambled down the branches, slid the trunk, my belly taking heat against the bark. I ran headlong toward it.

When I was a few yards away, I stopped. The doe limped sideways, stumbled up a small incline toward a clearing, its black hooves slipping like high heels on the wet leaves and embedded rocks, the high white tail bobbing unpredictably. It made it to the clearing and fell on its side. I walked up the small hill and stood over it. Blood matted the fur of one of its flanks. The animal lifted its head and looked around, whining in high-pitched moan. White drool dribbled from her mouth to the dirt.

I was breathing so heavy, the air in my body dizzied up my head. I pulled a shell from my jacket and went to open the chamber to insert it. The chamber wouldn't budge. I slapped its side, tried again, but it was jammed. I put the butt of the shotgun in the dirt and used my boot to kick at the metal handle that opened the chamber, but it wouldn't shift. The doe whined and swiveled its head wildly. Despite the chill, I sweated a thick smell. I cursed and paced a circle of dirt.

The doe tried to stand, but her left leg slipped out, and she fell. She cried and whimpered something fierce. Father was nowhere around. I couldn't have found him if I tried—the forest went just too far in all directions.

I stood over her, my jaw tense, face damp with sweat. Had I wanted this? I felt like I was going to vomit.

I took the gun vertically in both hands and raised it above my head. I brought the butt of the gun down on the doe's head. There was a weak thud, the doe yelped, and its unwounded leg twitched. I felt the pain as if I hit myself in my own head. The still-living doe sent a whine up inside me, and I couldn't take its pain or my pain, and I brought the butt down again and again and again. Blood streamed from the nose of the doe into the dirt, but it was still breathing, belly rising and falling in erratic flutters. I knelt, held the butt with both hands and landed it squarely. There was a crack and the doe went limp. The deer was dead and maybe the girl was dead, too. I sat exhausted next to her, leaned my forehead against the barrel of the shotgun and closed my eyes.

"Well, look who bagged herself a doe." Father was dragging a twelve-point buck by its hind legs. He stood below and couldn't see the caved-in skull. I looked at him about to cry. "Don't you go bellyachin'. This was what you wanted. This was what you come for."

When I didn't move, he said, "Grab them legs and let's get movin'. I don't have no time for your nonsense."

I followed Father through the woods, dragging the doe behind me, streaks of blood marking a path in the dirt. The sky had grown dark with autumn overcast, the echoes slower and scarier than I could ever remember. I looked up and around but could no longer recognize the forest. For the first time, I felt frightened of the woods, terrified of bramble and branch. I'd never in my life before been scared of bark and roots.

At the truck, Father and I took the doe by the legs and swung it up into the flat bed. "What the hell happened to the head?" he asked.

"Gun jam," I said.

He snorted. "Ever hear of a knife?" He snapped the mottled leather pouch at his belt and took out his hunting knife, waved it like a wand in my face.

I couldn't speak. Nobody told me about carrying a knife. They all said toughen up or you won't make it in the world, but they never told you what you needed to survive, never gave you a clue what you needed.

We swung the buck on top of the doe. You had to slam the tailgate because it was dented, and he slammed it four times with no luck. Finally, he swung it up and kicked it hard with his boot. He left a dent there.

When we got home, he pulled the buck out of the bed and left it by the truck. He yanked the doe out and dragged it to the side yard, under the oak. I'd spent a lot of time climbing down that oak, sneaking out my bedroom window when I heard one of Father's rage fits, scrambling along limbs and branches, running headlong in the middle of the night to the clearing. That oak had seen a lot of deer hanging skinless from its branches.

I ran around the house, went inside and turned on the spotlight installed on the side of the house for butchering. I came back out and stood and stared until there was nothing else in the world but the circle of light, the gold and white glow of the doe's coat, the way the legs splayed out like an elegant dance against the grass. I backed up until my back was against the brick of the house.

He'd gotten his tools out of the truck and was sawing at the neck with a handsaw. "Wouldn't a mounted the head anyway," he mumbled. He held up the severed head when he finished, then put the shattered thing behind him in the grass. He looked around for me. He was blinded by the spotlight and had to squint.

"What are you doin' back there? This was the reason you went huntin'. This ain't stayin' inside doing women's work. This ain't books. This is real life. If you got the stomach to eat it, you got the stomach to gut it." Hunters and farmers all around mid-Missouri never could abide squeamish types, folks who wanted all their food to be cleaned up behind suction plastic. I couldn't stop staring at the doe's head. It looked like my head. I stared at myself, sideways and shattered in the grass.

"Git down there and grab the ankles," he hollered. When I didn't move, he yelled, "Pearl, goddamnit. Mother said you wouldn't be able to do this. I stood up for you. Now, git on over here!"

I walked weak-kneed, knelt in the grass, held the ankles of the hind legs in both hands. Father looked at me hard, his blue eyes wide open. "You always think we're again't you," he said, looking at me deep. "We ain't again't you, Pearl. We're for you. We're *for* you."

I didn't know what to say. If they were *for* me, why did I feel like dying? He put his tongue between his teeth, held the hunting knife, nicked the pelt, ran it from crotch to rib cage.

For the next forty minutes, he cut, ripped, disemboweled. He maneuvered, yanked, tore. He turned the doe's open belly sideways so the innards poured out, and with arms covered in blood, cut the diaphragm away. Out came the esophagus, heart and lungs, and the rest of the intestines. He swiped his palms flat on his trouser thighs.

A pulley system was permanently installed on the oak. He went up to the side of the house and readjusted the spotlight so it was trained on the tree, came back and dragged the deer to it. He showed me how to tie the rope around the front legs so it wouldn't come loose. He went behind the tree and pulled the rope hand over fist until the deer's back legs were a few inches off the ground. He came back around the tree, and the headless doe stood between us like a third person.

I thought it was finished, and turned. Just as I did, he reached around to adjust the rope and blocked me. I fell back into the open carcass of the doe, the warm, bloody body encircling me. I was an Osage wearing a pelt, a raw and bloody pelt. The smell was bitter, carnal.

Father stared down at me. In his eyes, such blood lust that my knees went weak. His whole body shook. I thought of the Osage. Is this what the settlers had felt? When they met the Osage, did they have a desire to devour them? Did they see something in the Osage that was so lush, that echoed an ancient full-bellied memory, that they just wanted to consume it?

I crouched, ran right between Father's long legs. I ran inside, upstairs, locked myself in the bathroom. Later, I peeked out the window. Father was pulling the fur off the deer, methodically. Finally he finished and the doe hung naked. He went behind the oak and hoisted the rope, pulled the deer up higher, the furless, headless beast moving up, up, up until it spun in the spotlight.

I had an image of Bonnie and me playing Hangman. The colored pencils. A headless body. Some letter, if I could just guess it, would end the game.

Father went to the back door. I heard it open. I heard him yell, "Pearl, get that there pot beneath the zink for these here intestines."

Sometimes places in legends become confused, bogged down by time folding in on itself. I was never able to separate the fight over Black Elk in the living room and that shattered doe with what happened next. It got mixed up in my head, confused. All the events merged into one eternal moment.

Father was going hunting with his men friends. It was Saturday. Mother bought new floral furniture. She'd dog-eared the page in the

JC Penney catalogue and stared at it daily since Father started working in town. The furniture was being delivered. A floral sofa, two floral overstuffed chairs, a heavy wooden coffee table, two side tables.

Father said, "Pearl, why don't you come hunting with us?" Ever since I'd gone hunting the first time, something deep had been shifting in him. Like he saw my going with him as an act of friendship. Maybe I was the boy he and Mother never could have.

"I need to help set up the furniture," I whined.

"Let Mother do her women's work," he said and came over and put his hand on my shoulder. The only touch I'd ever had from him was a whipping. I tensed. The hand there was heavy like lead, so many generations of weight. The heavy hand blew compassion in me. I could feel the bulk of the load he carried, a weight no single person should have to bear. I had an idea to take his hand, like the Osage woman had taken the bird, and wrap it in white light to give him just some relief, to give us all some little bit of relief.

"I can't kill another animal." It came out before I had a chance to stop it.

He dropped his hand. "You can eat it, but you can't kill it." He looked disgusted. "Go on, stay here and do women's work." He slammed out the door.

The delivery men brought in the furniture. Mother and I spent hours moving it around the living room. Her hands shook with excitement. We tried combination after combination. Nothing seemed to be just right.

Toward evening, the doorbell rang. We didn't have many people out there in the middle of nowhere ringing the doorbell. Neighbors knew to knock at the back door. Mother grabbed her purse; her eyes turned backward on the furniture. She muttered that she must've forgotten to pay the delivery driver.

Mother kept the chaos of her soul in her pocketbook. It was jam-packed with tissues, broken pencils, rubber bands. It was the one place she allowed herself to go crazy. She opened the door. She opened the purse. A wad of one-dollar bills fell to the floor, and I ran up, bent to retrieve them. How intense the smallest detail at the moment of greatest trauma. Mother had a red stain on her white sneakers. I noticed the man's boots. They were so black, so shiny.

Mother and I both looked at his face at the same time. It was a police officer. His belly hung yards over his belt. His jowly face was surprisingly young; pale-blue eyes; small, round, ruby lips. He looked at me while he spoke.

"Family to Terrence Swinton?"

"Yes," I said. Mother clutched the wad of bills to her breast.

"It is with great sympathy that I am here to inform you that Terrence Swinton was shot while hunting this afternoon. He was pronounced dead on the scene at one forty-five p.m. My deepest condolences to the family." He spoke a memorized sorrow.

Father had been hunting in the forest. Not the forest abutting the farm, a different one. He'd gone hunting with his buddies. He always went hunting with his buddies.

The cop handed me a card, said something about coming down to identify and claim the body, something about personal effects.

Mother shut the door while he was still talking. I looked helplessly at the small square of glass at the top of the closed door. She dribbled debris from her open purse as she walked toward the living room. I followed her. A floral chair sat facing a wall, not yet having found its proper home. She sat in it and put her purse in her lap. She sat and sat.

All day and all night she sat, staring at the wall.

I called the police. I finally got Mother to drive us down in the orange truck. I let her deal with everything with the police while I searched around the station for someone to give me the story. I had to know the story. Nobody would tell it, and they kept forwarding me around. Finally, some guy who looked too young to be a cop gave me the details. A college boy shot Father in the head. The boy was with another hunting party. It was his first time hunting. He saw something rustling in the bushes and shot at it. *Of course,* I thought. *That college kid had his head full of books. Nobody can survive in the world with their head full of books.*

My mind grew confused; I began to think I was the one who shot Father. If I would've been there, like Father had asked, I would've had my head too full of books and I would've been the one who shot him, right? Because I felt life too sorely, because I couldn't toughen up, it was this other kid who killed him instead. But it was like I killed him. Because I wanted him dead, I was sure I was the one who made him die.

Afterward, everything changed. Father had been our connection to the earth, our obstinate bond, our brutal glue. With Father, life was a series of explosions, earthquakes that tore at the soul, craters connected by jagged fissures. Father, even with his brokenness, his rage, the gaping wound of his heart, had kept us as close to the earth as we would ever get.

Afterward was a different story, an entirely different fairy tale. One book was closed. Another, a totally different story, opened. Mother wanted away from the land, so desperately away. After his death, it was as if the universe shouted, "Get out!" It pried our fingers loose, yanked us from the crooked soil, sent us like Cain toward civilization, toward town. A punishment for all the earth-hate, the self-hate—for all the inherited detestation.

part ii

chapter 11

I CRUMBLED MYSELF around Father's coffin. Great sky circles of mind-numbing heat. Indian summer. Early November and the humidity set a trap for you. At the graveyard, life shifted in and out of focus.

Voices sweated up from soil. Liquid vocabulary emerged from the loam. Not just the souls of those buried, but the earth itself spoke—the tree, the root, the branch. Behind the human babble, the land had an accent, a whisper, a yowl.

Even bruised, the earth had stories to tell. Delicate despite all odds. There for the telling, the looking, the touching, the smelling. I stood beside Father's grave and couldn't bear the listening. I wanted to tear myself from it. I wanted to bash myself over the head repeatedly until it all just stopped.

Centuries and miles of knowing. Enfolding. We beat it back, manicured it, built houses to hide it. But still it gathered, bushed, snaked. Ready to take us. Back.

All day, I sought Meghan in the crowd. At the gravesite, I swore I saw her, that ghostly face floating in and out of the crowd of my worn-out relatives, my tight-lipped kinfolk, my storyless tribe. She wore the black coat and black boots she had on in the alley, flitted like a black angel, appeared and disappeared like some dark ghost. Jason stood like a sapling, white light glowing from black suit, eyes closed; swaying, praying like a branch moved by a breeze. Nadine's skinny head stood above the others. She held herself bottle-stiff behind and away from the crowd. She was used to being banished, so she exiled herself.

earth

The Native woman hovered. She floated. She threatened like an unsettled sky. I tried to ignore her, thought of her as some grim reaper, come to take my life, come to use me. Up.

The priest's drone, the low sky, the cacophonous earth, the lingering Osage woman, the dark essence of my sister. I was told to claw a handful of dirt and dribble it onto the coffin. I leaned into the pit, over the box, and watched myself disintegrate, shoulder and chest, up and up to the side of my face, my flesh flaking to clods of dirt, my whole body raining thumpity thump upon the black box. I myself was burying Father. I was witnessing my whole self bury him. Join him. Join earth. I knew the soil better than I knew this world; this world I could not figure out. I began to fall, to tumble, headfirst into the grave. This world I was learning to hate. This world I wanted nothing to …

Mother.

She had me by the back of the dress. She pulled me, yanked me. Back. She took me by the shoulders, spun me. "Pearl. Wake up." She shook. I collapsed in her hands. "On the pain of Christ."

"I …" with each word, she shook.

"Cannot." Shake.

"Take."

"This."

I fell against her belly. She moved back. We didn't touch. It wasn't done. I looked down at my fingers, wrist, arm. I was flesh again. I did not want to be flesh. At the edge of the pit, I wailed.

For two years after the funeral, Mother and I floated, victims of the same casualty isolated in our separate universes, deep in our own black holes.

I had this foggy hypothesis. It was harder to lose a difficult father than a good one. Thorny fathers confused the heart, shredded the soul. A rotten man was like cantankerous roots: No matter how deep you dug, you couldn't claw the tendrils from the pits of your soil.

Like me, Father had never been able to discern himself from the earth. He grew up and couldn't discern himself from his children. Now I was growing up unable to discern myself from him. The unholy absorption.

We had Father's life insurance. For the first time in her life, Mother had all the store-bought ingredients she could ever want. Refined sugar and margarine. Chocolate chips. Canned cherries. She took to baking. From morning 'til night, she measured and mixed. She sifted and scraped. She folded and frosted. She stood crooked at the stove—standing straight might suck her into the earth. She was trying so hard to be free. From the rotting.

Cherry Delight. Oatmeal Cream Pies. Triple-Decker Peanut Butter and Jelly Pie. Apple Crisp. German Chocolate Cake. Mother's processed dreams.

She baked; I refused to eat. Hunger strike. I would desire nothing. *You cannot take from me that which I do not desire.* I would not desire the earth. I would not crave the soil. I would not want its food. I would not want *anything.*

A wasting. A wafting. A rootlessness. If I desire nothing, if I refuse to eat, you cannot then take sustenance from me, because I have already denied it.

Ten green beans, one teaspoon mashed potatoes, two bites store-bought chicken, and a mouthful of Wonder Bread. A half-piece bologna, three potato chips, a sip of Lipton Sun tea. Ten Cheerios floating in a bowl of milk, two sips orange juice, one bite toast.

I grew thinner, lighter. Two pounds, four pounds, six pounds; a sloughing, a wasting. A disappearing. Wisps of body, floating. Translucent, angelic, unrooted. It was the only way I knew to yank myself far from the sucking world.

earth

It was Christmas. The world skated a thin edge. Mother went by herself to the woods and cut down a tree, dragged it back. Through my translucent eyes, the house was aglow with tinsel and lights. The smell of flour, eggs and butter, of baking batter. The house was fat with intended joy.

There was a knock at the door. When someone knocks at the door to tell you someone you know has died, every future knock at the door fills you with doom. Mother sat on the sofa and steeled herself. I answered the door.

Aunt Nadine stood there. She stood crooked, and under her arm she bore a wrapped gift.

"I know I didn't call first, and maybe you don't want any company."

Folks in Missouri had so few social graces.

"Come on in, Nadine," I said. She looked skinnier than before, and I could tell by the way she looked me up and down, she noticed I was skinnier, too.

"Nadine," Mother said with hard-pressed lips from the sofa. In that one word, the distrust of this "crazy" woman, this woman who scared Father nearly to death, this woman who echoed her daughter. "Can I get you a drink?"

Nadine shook her head. "I don't mean to be bothering you. I just dropped in to give Pearl something."

Maybe in other Missouri families kinfolk dropping in to give you a gift at Christmas was normal, but not in our house. Nadine handed me the package and sat on the sofa next to my mother. They sat crooked and leaning toward each other but not touching. Mother never spent time with Nadine when Father was alive. We never visited her, and she never came to see us. We only saw her at reunions and funerals. Mother only knew Nadine from rumors and hearsay, from Father's fear, from mean stories about her madness. But as they sat there, I could see Mother liked her. Deep down, Mother wasn't a bad person. She had a good heart. It was just that it'd been broken into so many pieces over the years, it'd twisted her up.

I stared at the crooked bodies of my mother and Nadine. I couldn't see myself in them. In Missouri, I wasn't able to find a woman I wanted to be. I didn't know what Father's death did to Nadine, but I did know that Mother defined herself by her husband, and without him she didn't know who she was. I saw that a lot in Missouri—women whose only understanding of themselves was through their men. Outside of maybe Ms. Castle, there was no woman around me I wanted to be. I had to raise myself up, but I had no examples to go by.

I stood in front of them and opened the gift. Above them was the picture of Jesus nailed to a cross. I opened the gift with Jesus's eyes closed. The wrapping paper was damp, like Nadine had dropped it in the snow. It didn't tear with a whistle but disintegrated with a mush. I let the paper drop in a torn heap. I went ice cold when I saw what it was. If you didn't know me, you would've thought I was unhappy. But I wasn't. I went cold when something was too big to react to. When any reaction couldn't possibly cover the situation. In that family, I went cold a lot.

It was a book. *Little Women*, by Louisa May Alcott. I left my body. Because I received so few gifts as a child, I didn't know the art of receiving. I was frigid in that living room with my Aunt Nadine and my mother, a wad of red fragile wrapping paper on the floor, Jesus not watching, in some peripheral distance, the magic of the Christmas tree, colored lights flashing hope from the far-off evergreen.

I moved. Jesus's eyes opened. I looked at Aunt Nadine—those laser eyes. I met her gaze. We flew into each other's souls. We left our bodies and flew off the planet together. We became two stars dancing in the black universe, just the two of us in some wild place where anything was possible. I had to tear my eyes away, stare at the picture of Jesus, to bring myself back.

I'm sure I said thank you. The book was a blue, glossy hardback. I put the binding up to my nose and breathed it into my flesh. It smelled like glue. I worried the texture of a single page between my fingertips. I turned it over in my hands and put my palm

flat on the glossy cover. I rubbed my palm over and over that book—
for minutes, for days, for years. It was as if I were reading it through
my palm.

"Nadine, you want some Folgers? I can make a fresh pot."

"Sure, Sarah," Nadine said.

I stood there holding the book. I thought about Nadine's eyes. I
looked at Jesus. His eyes were open. I rocked back and forth hugging
the book.

I see you. I don't see you.

I see you.

I see you.

I see you.

Later, I happened upon Mother, after Nadine left, after we'd all
gone to bed. I'd come down to the kitchen for some water, but I
stopped at the doorway when I saw Mother in the glow of the light
from above the stove. She had *Little Women* in her hand and was
petting the cover and staring at it. I stayed there watching her stare at
that book.

Springtime. Jason stood at the back screen door, pale, out of focus, an
outline from a different life. I'd seen him at school, of course, but I'd
been ignoring him for so long. "Can Pearl come out for a race?"

In his knuckled fist, a messy bouquet of purple crocuses, like
some wild long-ago song. I stared at the flowers. It was the first I
noticed it was spring. He always saw too much.

"What do you want, Jason?" Not eating made me tired, and I
leaned against the wall. Behind me, Mother's gummy peach cobbler
carried toward us the deceptive aromas of normality.

"Race me." I looked at him through the screen. He was tall, and
his long arms had some muscle. I hadn't noticed at school. How'd he
grown up so fast? It made me nervous.

"Just leave me be." My voice cracked. I started to close the
wood door.

He said quickly to the closing door, "There's a time for everything. A time to weep, a time to laugh. A time to mourn, a time to dance."

I opened the door again. "Don't quote the Bible at me." He could be so annoying. "Like you even know the Bible."

A fierce smell rose up beside me. I bent down to the mess of shoes on the mat by the door. Father's boots were still there, the yellowed sweat of them. But there was something else. I dug around. Between two steel-toed boots, a brown starling.

"Is it dead?" Jason had opened the screen and was staring at the bird.

It flopped and turned itself belly up. "Wounded," I said. When you lived in the country, you were always finding dead or dying animals in the house. I couldn't think of a week that went by that there wasn't some small critter perishing on the carpeted floors of our house.

I thought of the Osage woman, leaned down and cupped the bird in both hands.

"Poor thing," Jason said. I pushed past him and went out to the backyard. I knelt in the grass where we used to skin squirrels. I could feel its heartbeat hammering fast and hard against its breast.

At first nothing happened, but even Jason was silent. Then the space between my cupped palms and the dark feathers grew with light. I felt a heat fly down my arms, a buzzing in my palms. The bird jittered and flipped. It reacted so hard it flopped right out of my hands into the grass. I reached to pick it up again, but it hopped once, twice, then took flight, flew up and up to the branches of a nearby maple.

I looked at Jason, then up into the maple branches, where the starling sat and tittered. Maybe it wasn't really that wounded. I kept looking until the starling took flight again and flew away. Something had just happened. My hands were afire, pulsing with heat. I held them out in front of me.

"Are you ok?" Jason asked from behind me.

"Did you see …" I turned and he was staring at my body. He was looking my body up and down. I put my palm out flat as if it would block his view. I wore baggy clothes to school, but since I was at home, I had on something tight and you could see my bones. Mother didn't seem to notice.

He grabbed my arm. His face fell. "What's going on?"

"Leave me alone." I yanked away. He'd completely ruined the moment with the bird.

"Look. I know life hasn't been a bowl of pumpkin seeds for you, but you've gotta pull it together!" He still clutched the flowers. I noticed a bruise beneath his left eye. There was a story in it, but I didn't want to know. *You're not the only one with problems, Pearl.*

I stumbled toward the house. *Jason would make me weak. Jason could make me feeble. I'd never be able to carry the load.* I opened the screen door. He caught the edge of it and wouldn't let me close it.

He thrust his face in the opening. He had whiskers now. When in the hell did he get whiskers? "You got a gift some of us would die for."

I snorted. Yeah, my life was a real birthday party.

"You got a gift and you're going to throw it all away."

"Leave me alone!" I screamed. We played tug-of-war with that screen door. "Go home."

He let go and put up his hands like it was a stick-up. The screen slammed with a wicked bang. Mother yelled, "What's going on?" I shut the main door, too, closed it right on his face. He yelled through the wood, "Maybe you need a friend, and maybe I need one, too. Did you ever think that?" He paused, and when I didn't open the door again, he said hard and quiet, but loud enough that it went through the wood, "I once knew a Pearl who would've never given up, who wouldn't ever let the bastards get her down."

I crossed my arms over my chest and sank back against the door. For a while after Nadine's visit, I'd felt better. I'd even started eating like a normal person again. But it only lasted a few months, and I felt the familiar suck backward.

I could see Jason through the window at the other end of the kitchen bicycling off in a fury. Later I went out to feed Lady Luck. I found the purple crocuses tumbling with the wind across the slushy backyard.

A starling trapped in the basement. One flew out of the fireplace. Another, then another. Some wounded, most not. One died inside. Day after day, I held them in hot palms or chased them. No matter what, I got most of them to the backyard, got most of them to fly.

I checked the screens on the windows, the doors, opened and closed the fireplace chute. I couldn't figure how they were getting in. Still they fluttered, frittered, foundered. I chased them with a desperate broom. I scrambled after them frantically because I wanted them to live. I shooed them madly. I cupped them with an intensity of will and light. They flapped crazy all over the house, fluttered distraught through living room and kitchen. I'd run skinny and flailing a broom wild and fanatical through that house, front and back door open, desperate to get them out to the open air, desperate for them to fly.

chapter 12

OTHER'S FEET WERE small. Tiny. If they hadn't been put to hard labor, they would've been fine-looking; white and petite, the toes like pearls. She came home one day in a new pair of shoes. Fancy, glowing, open-toed ruby heels. It was an omen. The shoes pulsed like backlit gems, Dorothy's ruby slippers, Cinderella's glass slippers. Magic shoes to transport her somewhere far, far away. I'd only ever seen her wear sneakers and rotted rubber boots. On Sundays for Mass, scuffed black flats.

She went missing behind the eyes. She'd put food in the oven and forget it and leave. I'd come into a kitchen fogged with smoke. Beaded boots, fabric flats, satin slip-ons—every week a new pair. I started listening for the slam of the screen door when she left the house, kept my nose open for the burning.

One morning for breakfast, she wore silver silken slippers. I came in all ratty-haired and skinny and couldn't stop staring at her feet. The morning light glittered off them like stars. She put her leg up and jiggled her foot, throwing sparks across the kitchen. "I can't wait for you to meet him, Pearl." She blushed like a little girl. On her feet, the power of one told story. We hadn't finished the first legend, and she was entering the plot of another. She defined herself by the men in her life, and without a man she was a blank page. She'd met someone. She was filling herself up with his story.

earth

I found Miss Universe covered in cobwebs down in the basement next to Father's boat. Since I'd painted her black, she'd lost a lot of her magic. I cleaned her off and oiled her and pedaled up Powwow. I was all gangly arms and legs, but I had more strength in me than I thought. By the time I made it to the rock cut, six miles away, I could feel the power in the muscles, sweat like promise on lips. I'd given up the paper route a long time ago, and I missed my solo jaunts into the mid-Missouri countryside. When I made it to the other side of the cut, I let it all out, whipped arms and legs into glorious cycling harmony. I flew on that bike.

When I got to Jason's house, I realized I felt good for the first time in years. He stood on his crooked porch, watching me get off Miss Universe. I stood staring back at him, in his white T-shirt, holding a paint brush, spattered painter's pants. How'd he gotten so tall, so filled out? It took my breath away. I tried to push the feelings down, but I was flushed to my hairline as he opened the door for me.

"What're you doing here?" His voice was cold. All the ignoring had hurt him. I knew and I was sorry, but I wasn't used to saying those words.

"I came over for a race," I answered in all truthfulness.

Besides the usual empty wine bottles, there were tall-neck brown beer bottles. Jason's mom had a new boyfriend again. These women with their new boyfriends. They kept plunging and plunging into another without even knowing who the hell they were. Fear whipped through that house, made me gasp a little, but I covered it with a cough.

I followed Jason to the corner of the living room where he had an easel set up on top of an old canvas drop cloth. All over the floor, mingled with the empty booze bottles were half-full paint tubes. The heady smell of beer, oil paint, red wine and turpentine.

On the canvas, a long, lonely road winding into the distance. It was the kind of road you saw in rural Missouri all the time, the kind that both gave you enough room to breathe and made you feel the loneliness of the whole planet in your rib cage.

I did a turn around the living room. Hanging all around were his paintings and his mother's—so much beauty shining out of so much misery. They'd captured Missouri, the landscape, the heart of it. Awe-inspiring splendor matched up with mud and misery. I didn't know if other places were different, if other places had milder ways, but I did know that glory and that wretchedness combined in each person's heart and made up the temperament of all the Missouri people I knew.

I came back to Jason's lonely road. He looked at me. I guess I had tears in my eyes. I wanted to say something about his mystical hands, something about his forlorn byway being more full than all the oceans of the world, but I had no words.

"Last one around the block is a rotten egg."

"What?" Before I knew what was going on, he dropped his paint brush and ran straight out the front door. I laughed hard and took out after him.

A rain started to fall. He only had the lead for about a block. It was hard to run and laugh at the same time. We kept barking out guffaws as we ran. Still, I passed him. Jason would never be able to keep up with me. He grabbed for me as I passed, and I did a jig, a quick to and fro, and he missed. Cars honked and cat-called. We laughed and ran. We didn't stop after one block. We ran. We ran and ran.

On weekends, Bonnie and I cruised in her mother's blue Caddy. McDonald's, Hardees, McDonald's, sometimes Montgomery Ward. It was what teenagers did in that rural place. I had become ravenous, insatiable, out of my mind with need. I wanted to devour, inhale, consume. I had a reputation for it. At school and at other schools, my hunger became well-known. Tall, lean guys in Wranglers. Boys in Levis with hay bailer arms. Thick-lipped hunters in plaid.

A time to laugh, a time to dance. We hollered redneck mating calls at jacked-up trucks, orange Camaros, smoky Trans Ams. *Yahoo.*

earth

Woohoo. Yeehaaaaaaaaaaaaaaw! Between our thighs, bottles of Tickle Pink in brown paper bags.

On the seat, drive-through meals. Metallic ketchup, burger wrappers smeared with gluey fat. I'd get a McDonald's hamburger and tear off the bottom bun, throw it back in the bag. I'd just eat the small burger and part of the top bun. I was still counting every bite.

Bonnie, though, ordered several times a night from the drive-through: double cheeseburgers, fish sandwiches, fries, onion rings. She was growing as big as a house. She had jelly welly alright. I drank my bottle and half of hers, my wine-stained smile a bruised purple.

We spread a black notebook wide on the white leather seat. Games of dirty Hangman. Pubes. Vagina. Genitalia. Any filthy word would do. Bosom. Scrotum. Man meat. Fuckwit. Shithead. Dickwad.

We were at St. Francis now, the Catholic high school. It sat on the edge of town, on the verge of rural, the cusp of city. Stocky brick buildings on a rigid slab of concrete surrounded by mesh fencing. An entrance of massive windows rose two stories, and behind them a twenty-foot statue of Jesus. The cross, the arms thrust out, the man impaled like a broken bird. A crown of thorns, a wailing face, blood spurting from forehead and chest.

I'd joined cross country. The track coach had been on me since I got to the school. My reputation as a fast runner followed me from Holy Cross. He was disappointed when I went for cross country, but I needed the distance. I needed to build the stamina. I needed to stop running around blocks, to stop ending up right back where I started. I needed to run miles, across town, out of town.

Nearly every day, I worked legs and lungs. Through heat waves, rain, fog, I jogged from pavement to street, to rural dirt roads, through forest, across field. My body grew strong. My lungs filled and refilled with air. My feet beat a tempo with breath, beat a tempo with heart, beat a tempo with the pulse of the very earth.

All the exercise seemed to manage my visions. I still had them, but they didn't appear as often, didn't seem to scare me as much, didn't leave a black hole where my heart should've been. Some were even simple and joyful.

A truck driver with naked girls on mud flaps motioned us over.

"My guy's the driver," I said to Bonnie. She smirked. The driver had a striking profile. The passenger's face throbbed with acne. "Dibs," I repeated, poking her chubby arm. She was no winner of arguments. You could get anything you wanted from Bonnie.

We pulled into The Hair Parlour. A strip mall of olde worlde (Mother pronounced it "oldy worldy") knickknacks, a fabric store, a dry cleaner. The parking lot was built on an incline and angled toward the street.

"What are you ladies up to?" the driver asked, leaning his head out and down to be heard by us below. The tires of his truck were as tall as the roof of the Caddy. He chewed tobacco, turned to spit into something on the seat. He had a head of auburn hair that lay heavy across his forehead. His face was long and his wide mouth stretched like Jason's painting of that lonely road. An empty gun rack hung behind his head. His stereo blared Def Leppard.

"Want some hair on your chest?" He handed down a bottle. Bonnie took a swig, grimaced, handed it to me. I took a mouthful, coughed. Mad Dog 20/20.

Bonnie reached up to him with her Tickle Pink. He took it in his long palm, peered down into the paper bag and laughed. He handed the bottle to his friend in the passenger seat, but the kid shook his head. He shrugged, eyed us sideways, tipped the bottle, thick-lipped, swiping at his mouth when he was finished with the back of his hand. "Not sure that dog'll hunt," he said.

"I hunt," I said, getting out of the Caddy with the Mad Dog. It was early November cold. I'd thrown my plaid wool coat in the backseat and shivered in a white patent leather miniskirt. I went to the driver's window, tipped the Mad Dog, took a deep swig.

"Well, let's see if we can't bag ourselves something." He leaned over and opened the passenger door and said to his friend, "Go on, git."

The skinny kid passed me with a dirty look. He was no looker, with that acne and those teeth.

I climbed up in the truck and took a look at the guy. His arms bulged from his shirt. These were hay bailer's arms. He smelled good too, like a big open hay field. I could smell the grit of his arm pits; musky smells wafted off him like a morning on the farm.

I grabbed his big face and kissed him hard. He kissed back. Whisker burn on cheeks and chin. The dark and gritty aftertaste of chew.

I straddled him. His face was so big. He shoved me up and back. Dry humping. *Burn it up. Let's go for broke. Watch the night go up in smoke.* Up and back. Through eye slits, I saw the scrawny guy making out with Bonnie through the side window. My guy's cock pressed hard and long beneath the fly of his Wranglers. He fumbled crazy at my belt. I wrestled with his hands. He tried to undo my Zenas. I smacked his hands. I didn't have sex. I couldn't believe the girls who were stupid enough to get pregnant, or even go steady. These boys grew up to be just like the rest of the sorry-ass Missouri men. Who wanted that? Who wanted any of that? Even Bonnie had said since she was a little girl all she ever wanted was to grow up and get married. I didn't understand it. I had a story I wanted to live out. I couldn't understand ditching that story for some guy. I couldn't fathom it. That's why I stayed clear of Jason. I didn't want love. Love got you stuck deep and hard in the mud.

I was so jacked up that I didn't feel the buzzing. I'd gotten good at predicting a vision, but this one was blocked by my boiling horniness. I arched. My eyes rolled back. I guess the guy thought I was coming, because he let out a holler and went harder and faster.

It was a Meghan vision. Worse than ever. She reached out needy arms to me. She was made of dirt and gritty roots, and as she reached out, her whole body started to crumble like the earth. She needed me. She desperately needed me.

I slumped out of it, just as the guy came with a hard grunt. Exhausted, I rolled off him. He pulled a white hankie out of his glove compartment. I reached for the door handle as if in slow motion.

"The name's Anthony," he said. He spoke to his belly button as he used the hankie to clean himself up. He finished, put the hankie back, took Red Man off the dash and pinched some into his cheek.

"Pearl," I answered weakly. I had to do something about Meghan. I opened the truck door, shivering in mini-convulsions, and walked in a daze to the Caddy.

"Pleased to make your acquaintance," Anthony called after me out the window.

I shooed the acne kid away, got in the car. Bonnie was buttoning her blouse. Without thinking, I said, "He wants to meet us in St. Louis to party." I didn't look at Bonnie. The lie fell from beneath my teeth, easy as that.

Bonnie giggled. "My guy'll be there, too, right?"

"Mmmm hmmm," I said.

"We'd better hurry up," she said as Anthony backed up the truck. "They're leaving."

"Don't follow them. They have to go somewhere else first. My guy gave me directions." I knew this would get us in a shitload of trouble with Bonnie's mother—the blue Caddy was her baby. I always thought that maybe she cared about it more than Bonnie, but I felt a scary need to get to my sister, to find Meghan. Right then.

Bonnie yelled out the window, "See you there, Blake!" The kid looked down as they passed with a confused stare, shrugged and picked something from between his braces.

Lord, it's the same old tune, fiddle and guitar. Where do we take it from here? I turned up the stereo. We'd been driving more than two hours. Bonnie did her old lady imitation, twenty under the speed limit, hands clenched. We inched along the busy highway into St. Louis. I looked around and thought of how young I'd been when I rode Miss Universe this way.

"You sure you know the way?" Bonnie asked. Her body was rigid behind the wheel. She wasn't used to driving in city traffic, in six lanes of honking, spewing cars.

"Of course," I said annoyed, forgetting that she thought we were going to hook up with the guys. She looked at me sideways. I said, "I got it memorized. Keep going. I'll tell you where to turn. Trust me."

"Yeah that's always worked out well for me in the past." She gave me a wary look.

I rolled the window down, and icy air competed in spurts with the grinding heat from the dashboard. When we hit the bridge to East St. Louis, I was glad it was so dark that Bonnie couldn't see how rough it was. From what I could tell, it'd gotten worse. More street lights broken, the cars dirtier, the river filthier, mournful.

"You sure he said this way? They didn't look like they was from the city. They looked local." A beat-up Impala slowed to stare, the guys wild-haired in the throbbing interior.

She swiveled her head and glared out her window, then out the windshield like she was trapped. I put my hand on her arm. "That guy really liked you." She wasn't used to boys liking her. "He thought you were foxy. What was his name?"

"Blake," she said. "He goes to St. Francis."

"Yeah, my guy, Anthony, said he was from St. Louis. He musta come down to visit Blake or something," I said.

Bonnie had this way of biting the side of her mouth when she was scared, her two front teeth smashing her lower lip. I quickly drew a scaffolding on the notebook between us, drew the lines for three words, sixteen letters. She guessed Bs and Ls and Es, and finally yelled the letters out above the sound of REO. B-o-n-n-i-e-l-o-v-e-s-B-l-a-k-e.

We entered East St. Louis. Pulsing neon, screaming sirens, thumping stereos—it all seemed scarier than I remembered. I kept her going with Hangman to distract us both and told her to turn here and there. We got a lot of interest from the other cars. They pulled up next to us to get a look.

Blood dripped on the white Caddy leather. I'd picked my thumb really deep without noticing. I smudged it up with my finger, stuck my thumb in my mouth, was sucking my thumb as we pulled up to Meghan's building.

"You've got to be kidding." Bonnie's teeth stuck out to her chin. "I'm not going in there!"

"I bet Blake's just sitting on the edge of his seat waiting for you."

She looked at me sideways. I grabbed her chubby upper arm, leaned my face in. "Oh, come on. Live a little."

I finally got her out of the car, helped her pick her way over the garbage in the dark by the side of the building. She was better at fording rivers than handling trash. She said under her breath, "You're going to get me killed." Above us, a couple broke out into a vicious fight. Their slurred, broken cursings rained on our heads like shattered glass.

I was relieved to see the light glowing from the back window. I pulled Bonnie along as I ran. She was a waddler. I grabbed a crate and put it beneath the barred window, stood on it. There was Meghan with some man in the living room. I put my hand through the bars and knocked on the glass. "Meghan!"

Bonnie hissed, "Meghan? Your sister? The guys are meeting us here?" Sometimes Bonnie was so slow.

"Meghan!" I called. "It's Pearl. I'm here. I'm here!"

chapter 13

HE ONE WHO tells the stories rules the world. We learned that Hopi proverb in social studies. We lived on Osage land and never studied them, were only taught about the Hopi and the Apaches. Such a poverty of legend.

I wrote down my stories in my black notebooks because I wanted to rule the world. I didn't want anyone else defining me. They defined you all wrong if they couldn't control you, defined you as sick or bad or stupid or worthless or killable. Or crazy. If I couldn't rule the whole world, maybe my stories would simply help me manage my own world. Maybe.

The stories in my black notebook were the truth, as close to the truth as I could get. My version was different than what others experienced. I always thought, *You tell your version. Let me tell mine.*

Some stories were the versions of me that Father and Mother told, ideas I was expected to swallow whole. Notions that got wedged in the throat. Sometimes, the world tried to force a story on you, tales that turned you into a monster or a hero, stories that made you a carnival cutout, with a hole to stick your face in. Stories that defined you as a mad woman.

Some tales emerged from behind a veil, played out in another dimension, an alternate reality, and when they ripped through normal, they shattered everything you knew about the world you lived in.

But some stories were the ones I told myself, shored-up half-truths, fantasies I blindly based a whole life on. These were the worst.

Meghan let us in. A tall man was with her in a rabbit fur coat. The coat was short like some of the girls at school wore, and his wrists dangled from the ends of the sleeves. He wore mirror sunglasses and had scrubby whiskers. He looked at Bonnie and me and barked to Meghan, "You ain't missin' another night."

I thought he was older, but when I passed close, I saw he was maybe in his twenties. He was so skinny that his legs beneath his corduroy trousers looked bowed like an old-fashioned cowboy's.

"Pardon me for ha'ing company," Meghan slurred. She swayed on her feet, her neck and jaw rigid, her head making crazy circles. She was skinnier than I remembered. Her jaw and cheekbones were sharper. She was still good-looking in an edgy way, but it was as if her chest had caved in.

I huddled with Bonnie by one wall, and she held my forearm so tight she was bruising me. The guy looked us over from head to foot. He grabbed Meghan's wrist hard, pulled her to the door. He spoke low and urgent. She slurred her responses. I couldn't hear it all, only that Meghan called him Russell and said, "You don't fahking own me." He laughed high-pitched like a girl. When she tried to pull her wrist back, he raised his fist.

Bonnie whispered, "The guys aren't coming at all, are they?" I put up my hand to shut her up. It took all I had not to run up and punch the guy in his mirrored sunglasses.

The guy lowered his fist, put his face in Meghan's. "I'll be waiting." She snorted. He put his fist back up. "Show up." He loped out and slammed the door.

Meghan turned toward us. Her eyes swam. "To what do I owe this honor?" She said it surprisingly clear and sober. She went to a stained chair spewing stuffing, flung herself sideways into it, leaned to the coffee table and grabbed a pack of Salem menthols. On the table were tall-neck Miller beers and tubes and baggies. She arched her body to extract a lighter from her tight jeans, lit the smoke and took a drag that sucked her cheeks inward. The place smelled like salty boiled water, something I couldn't put my finger on.

I came around and sat on the sofa. It was damp. There were chunks of plaster on the cushions. I looked up at a hole in the ceiling, swept the chunks onto the scarred hardwood. "You didn't come to the funeral." It wasn't what I meant to say. What did you say to someone you hadn't seen in so many years? I noticed it was freezing in her apartment and hunched forward to sit on my hands.

"I guess I couldn't find my dancing shoes." She coughed. She wobbled her head up, looked at me and smirked. "By the way, I'm fine, thank you. Thanks for asking."

I blushed, opened my mouth to speak, but she put up a jerky hand.

"Oh no, no. Let's talk about *him*. It's always about *him*. If not him *him*, then some *him* somewhere." She leaned over the edge of the chair and coughed. "Always about the fucking men." She had a cold sore on her lip covered in makeup, and the coughing set it to bleeding.

"Are you sick?" My voice cracked with the anxiety of the vision and her desperate arms beseeching me. The sentence came out high, like a whine. I felt a hand on my shoulder and looked up at Bonnie standing behind the sofa. She stared down at me, her eyes large and scared and intensely blue.

"What?" Meghan's voice was watery. "Sick?" She laughed and coughed again. "No." She paused and laughed again. "No." She stood, nearly fell over. Her tight black jeans were tucked into combat boots that laced up her calves, and she wore a torn Rolling Stones T-shirt with a rip across the pulsing red tongue that showed a lacy black bra. She wove down a long hallway toward the back of the apartment.

"Come on. We're leaving." Bonnie said, grabbing the top of my arm. I had a flashback of the Current River and sat frozen for a second.

"I'm going to leave you here. I swear I am." She looked at the door. "I'm not going to save you every time you get yourself into a mess." She kept staring at the door. I could see she was scared witless with the idea of walking back to the car alone, finding her way back to the bridge and back home.

earth

Meghan wove back in. She held a beer. She looked at us, held up the beer, said, "Shit, did you guys want one?"

"I gotta go," Bonnie blurted.

"Meghan, this is Bonnie."

"Hello," Meghan said, held her beer up, tried to bow but lost her footing.

"I've got to go," Bonnie said to her. "Pearl, you coming?"

"No," I said.

Meghan turned slowly as if it was hard for her to keep up with the conversation. She steadied herself with the back of the sofa, sloshed some beer onto the fabric. "Oh no, no, you can't stay." She went to the coffee table and lit a new cigarette with the embers of the one she was already smoking. "You've got to go with your friend Barbie."

"I'm staying," I said, holding the edges of the sofa cushion. "I'm staying."

"I didn't say you could," Meghan said.

Bonnie reached and grabbed my arm again. I pushed her away. "I'm staying."

"Well, I'm not," Bonnie spat. "Walk me to my car."

Meghan looked at both of us, confused. She turned to me, I was sure, to demand I leave, and I stopped her talking by saying, "We'll all go. Come on, Meghan. Let's walk Bonnie to her car."

"Well, la de da," Meghan said. "Let's all walk little Miss Barbie to her car then." She looked hard at Bonnie but followed us outside. She said to my back, "You can only stay one night. I mean it." Behind the building, something got into her, and she looked up at the sky, put her arms out, did a spin. "My sister's come to visit." She laughed and coughed. "My sister's here." She spun around until she had a full-blown coughing fit and had to bend over to catch her breath.

We picked our way by the side of the building. My heart sank when we got close to the car. The hubcaps were missing. Bonnie turned to me with a furious look.

"You're lucky the windows aren't smashed," Meghan slurred. She drunkenly cupped her face and looked in the window. "You still got your stereo!"

Bonnie opened the door, got in, started the engine. I opened the passenger door, turned to Meghan.

"Meghan, why don't you come home with Bonnie and me?"

"Home?" Meghan said, looking at me for a second like a little girl. Then her eyes hardened. "Home!" she spat. She turned to go back down the alley. I caught her arm.

"Come on. Just get in the car."

Bonnie had the heat on high and some of it reached out and warmed us.

"You fucking go home. Home?" she screamed. "Since when is that place my home?" She spat out the last word, pushed me and stumbled down the alley. I leaned in and got my notebook off the seat. I opened the back door and grabbed my plaid coat. I looked at Bonnie's eyes in the rearview mirror. I wanted to say sorry, but I just never used that word. Never. No one had *ever* said they were sorry to me, and I was damned if I was going to be the sorry one.

I put my palm flat. "You smart, me dumb."

"There's going to come a time," she said, looking at the steering wheel while she spoke, "when no one is going to be around to save you. Nobody is going to be there."

It felt like a curse. I closed the door. She drove off.

There was one memory of Meghan that stood out above the rest. It was so close to the surface, this memory, that it was there all the time, but because it was so close, it was sometimes hard to see.

I dreamt about it on her damp sofa that night, and thought about it as I woke to murky dawn smearing through the barred windows. She'd bought a full set of flowered dishes at a rummage sale at a nearby farm. I couldn't remember who drove us, but she brought me with her and we drove to this state park that had a cliff over a river. Sometimes kids jumped off the cliff. One from my school broke his neck.

Whoever drove us was waiting in the car nearby. Meghan hauled the dishes to the cliff. I followed her. We stood on the craggy outcropping; below us, the rushing river. She leaned down and took one of the plates and threw it over the cliff. Below us, it smashed into dozens of white flowered shards on the river bank. She leaned down again and handed one to me. I looked up at her and smiled.

Meghan used to call us "kitchen bitches." Father used to make us work so hard alongside Mother in the kitchen. Canning, stewing, baking, cooking, cleaning. Once a neighbor bought a dishwasher, and Father laughed and said to us, "I don't need no dishwasher. I got myself three." We were slaves to that man. Meghan hated it and yelled often about it, and got beaten for the fight in her. I hated it too, but kept my mouth shut and watched my sister get the belt.

I threw the plate hard over the edge of the cliff and screamed when it shattered. Meghan grabbed a bowl and threw it. I threw three coffee mugs in a row. Soon, it was raining dishes off the edge of that cliff, and Meghan and I were whooping and hollering something fierce. We didn't hear the park ranger until he was almost on top of us. Meghan grabbed my hand and we ran, the two of us laughing from deep in our bellies. We threw ourselves into the waiting car and sped off.

I lay on that damp sofa and realized Meghan was the only woman I'd met I could look up to. You could cut the air with a knife when she walked into the room, it was so thick with her energy. With her crazy clothes and wild design ideas, she was the only one I could see myself in. My only mirror. My cracked and knife-sharp shattered mirror.

That night after Bonnie left, I tried to talk to Meghan, but she grew more and more confused as the evening progressed, her slurred words giving way to babbling. Then she abruptly put on her coat and went out. I fell asleep on the sofa, fell into profound exhaustion, fell into a tiredness so deep, my head felt paralyzed, my limbs heavy like all my life I'd been carrying too much weight.

I got up and went to the bedroom to see if she'd come home while I was asleep. The room was empty; the mattress on the floor didn't appear to have been slept in. I walked around and checked out the room. One wall was dotted with full-figured Cross Your Heart bras, browned by cigarette smoke. The cups were stuffed with potpourri. I went up and sniffed one of the boobs, but nothing; the aroma had faded a long time ago.

She'd nailed deer antlers to another wall, hung a jacket and scarves on the points. There were cigarette burns in the flowered sheets. A crate for a side table. A fringed lampshade on a jade fish lamp with the tail broken off. A torn scarf tacked to the ceiling to cover a bare bulb.

This was the glory of Meghan, this madcap style. Even when I was little I knew she was different. The way she collected things: broken side tables, crates, lamps. She could combine two things and make something crazy and beautiful. In her childhood room, glass doorknobs on bedposts refracted light like jewels; massive rock sculptures in the corner dripped multihued beads like psychedelic water. The way she could see magic in trash.

Everybody wanted a piece of her even back then. They called her "different" and wouldn't let her in, but then they'd chase after her, chase her down. How they wanted her, how they desired the force of her, how they wanted her legend.

As she grew, so many boys. At fourteen, right before she left, old men in flatbed trucks stopped fast and hard to stare at her, spewing gravel and pheromones. How she'd lean into their truck windows, how desperate she was for attention. I'd stand nearby on Miss Universe, wary, tense, confused.

In her grown-up bedroom, I saw wads of cash spilling from pockets. On the floor, piles and piles of clothes. I rifled through, found twenties, tens, ones. A loose five-dollar bill floated in the corner. More in a jacket pocket. Hundreds of dollars like loose confetti in my fist. I took the wad, placed the edges of the bills beneath the lamp so she'd notice when she got home.

In the kitchen, the refrigerator had two beers and a quart of spoiled milk. There were no doors over the cupboards, and they were empty except for a couple of plates, two cups. A jacket was stuffed into one of the shelves. I went to the bathroom. The toilet had no seat, the shower no curtain. A bottle of Prell shampoo. A single cracked bar of Zest soap.

It was cold, and I couldn't find a thermostat, so I put on my wool plaid coat. I dug my fingernail into the sides of my thumbs.

I thought about how she'd throw herself in front of Father and take his wrath. How many times did she save me from a beating? Flashes of her and Father in epic jigs, grand ballets of rage, slow-motion waltzes; pirouetting on an unshakeable axis, spinning like mad tops over a magnetic point. The soundtrack a grunting, a slapping, a smashing, a wailing.

I thought of her like some peculiar tree outlined in a lone landscape, eccentric like the sassafras; nubby, pungent. A tree that hadn't gotten enough light but still grew, sideways, angled and twisted. The kind of tree you'd stop to take a picture of. The kind of tree that haunted your dreams. I roamed and roamed, touching her things. She was my sister. We were tangled together by story, bruised together in shape and texture. We were written up in each other's flesh.

She walked in at one p.m. She wove and stumbled like she was drunk again or still drunk from the night before. She looked at me and grimaced and went straight back to her bedroom. I followed. She curled sideways on the mattress.

When I sat on the mattress, she groaned and turned her back. "You gotta go. Go home." I thought of Father and his fiddle. I felt a despair so deep. How do you love, when everybody is always saying, *Go on, git.*

She wore a jacket with fake fur around the collar and knee-high boots. I stared at her back. I saw the wounded starlings and reached my hand flat and placed it between her shoulder blades. Maybe I could heal a broken sister. I focused and pushed and thought she had gone to sleep when I saw a white light glow up. Her whole body seemed to vibrate with it. She groaned, started to get up, moved her legs as if she were getting off the bed.

I changed my tactic. Put my finger on her jacket, and ran it in swirls and circles. I said, "What am I drawing?"

"What?"

I pressed harder, moved my finger with purpose.

"Guess what I'm drawing."

I saw her flash from light to dark, fast and firm. She turned with sudden force, grabbed my finger, held it hard enough to break. "Keep your fucking hands off me!" She got off the mattress, swayed above me.

"What are you doing here?" she screamed. "Some scrawny-ass kid I haven't seen in years. You going to 'save' me?"

She stood above me holding up her fist, just like Father. Just exactly like Father. I broke into sobs. Snot streamed from my nose. I put my face in my hands.

"You got your nice little mommy at home. Mommy Sarah, loves her little Pearlie." I got the hiccups and sobbed in abrupt spurts. "Now that he's dead, you got nothing to complain about." The stories she must've told herself about my life. The stories we all told ourselves about other people's lives. She grew cold. I felt the room ice up. "What the hell do you have to cry about?" She kicked a combat boot across the floor.

"I came to talk to you about …" I didn't know how to say it. With her fist raised like that, I didn't know how to tell her. I sounded so stupid. "I'm having these, these…visions," I wailed, but then I cried so hard I couldn't get the words out straight. "Everything's breaking apart…and you're in them, and I talked to Nadine …"

"Listen, I don't know what your story is, but I cannot deal with this shit. You are not my problem." She leaned over, took the cash from beneath the lamp, and stuffed it into the side pocket of my coat. "Get on a bus and go the fuck home to mommy!"

I ran out of the bedroom.

She screamed after me, "You're like sixteen years old now. You're not a kid anymore. Grow up! Grow the fuck up." I heard her bedroom door slam.

I sat on the damp sofa, bent forward toward the light of a tiny black-and-white television. *The Young and the Restless*. I fell into the stories of other families, other traumas. Bonnie and I had known these people our whole lives. *Guiding Light*. We'd hide out in Bonnie's air-conditioned house during the blazing heat of summer, play Hangman, and watch James and Barbara, Philip and Beth. How these fictitious lives wended their way into our history, our past and present, our future. The letter O in *As the World Turns* was a glowing earth that threw beams of reflecting light in all directions. I merged into the light. I blended and fused. I fell into lives I wasn't allowed into, whole families I had no part in.

Hours passed. I went to Meghan's door, knocked and called out. She didn't answer. I put my ear to the door, and she was snoring like a sailor. I was so hungry I went to the fridge and drank one beer and then another. To the echoing sound of my sister's sleeping breath, using my coat as a blanket, I fell into a hard sleep on the sofa.

I woke slowly to fingers in my hair. I looked up into Meghan's doe eyes. She'd showered and smelled like Zest. Lipstick had congealed into her cold sore; a crimson speck smeared a front tooth. She was looking at me almost softly.

"Your hair," she said, scrunching my hair in one hand and shaking her head. My hair had grown worse as I grew up—rougher, wilder. When we were kids, she used to pick twigs out of it at night. She'd root around in my hair like a monkey.

"You were always such a freak," she said. Her eyes were glassy. She coughed. "We'd be planting that stupid fucking garden. So stinking hot. I'd be in charge of watching you, and you'd wander off, and I'd find you talking to some fucking tree."

She shook her head, leaned to the table and took a cigarette, lit it, blew the smoke upward. I noticed craters in the sides of her thumbs. She picked them, too. For some reason that made me deeply happy.

"Listen." She turned her eyes from mine, looked like the words were being wrenched from her. "You got a chance to live a normal life. You got to go back and live your life like a normal person. You got no idea what other people live like. You got no idea."

I barked a laugh at the idea of my living a normal life. She stood, grabbed a short leather biker's jacket off a chair, put it on.

"You can't stay here." She headed toward the door. "Go to the top of the road and grab a cab to the bus station. Go home."

"My life's not normal, either," I yelled.

She turned, raged back to me and put a shaking finger in my face. "Listen, little sister, this isn't some kid's game." Her whole body shook. Her fear stank like Father's. "Go home to your mommy. I don't want you here." She raged back to the door and stormed out.

Meghan's way of walking got her a lot of attention from men. I ran out after her, stayed a block or so behind. I wore my heavy plaid coat, tried to hide behind greasy electricity poles. The wind was wicked, icy, and flat out in your face, like someone screaming against your flesh. I had to bend forward and trudge.

Meghan let the wind bluster her this way and that as she stumbled along. Men called out the car windows as she sashayed sideways and backward down the sidewalk. She waved them away with her cigarette. She popped something in her mouth, and as she walked she began swaying more, laughing more, being danced by the wind more. Night was coming on.

She turned the corner at the end of the road. When I turned the same corner, I saw her talking to a group of women. I ran through traffic to the other side of the street so I could watch her unnoticed. I squatted behind a pile of garbage in an abandoned lot. In front of me was a pile of filthy diapers, and my nose filled with baby shit as night darkened into scary echoes. I didn't have gloves and blew furiously on frozen fingers. I watched the other women—high heels, fish nets, fur-necked short jackets—get in and out of cars. I wasn't stupid. I knew what was going on. I saw Meghan get into a metallic green Mustang.

About forty minutes later, the Mustang dropped Meghan off. I jumped up and ran through honking, screeching traffic. By the time I got to the other side, she was already getting into another car. None of the other women had moved that fast. My sister apparently was a popular whore.

She started to close the car door. I reached in and grabbed the lapels of her leather jacket. I saw my pouch around her neck, and reached instinctively to my neck. My pearl, my arrowhead. She must've untied it while I slept. I remembered something else about Meghan. How she'd steal your stuff without a thank you. How even as a little girl, I would go through her room after she went out, searching for my lost things.

She slammed the door and it smashed my upper arm, but I still held on. She yanked hard back, said my name in sudden spurts, like she was shooting bullets, "Pearl-Pearl-Pearl!" I wedged the door open with my shoulder and pulled at her.

The driver was the guy at the apartment. He cursed, reached sideways and grabbed her other arm. The wind took the car door and swung it wide with an aching squeal. I yanked hard, and I must've had some adrenalin, because I was out of the car, and Meghan was coming out with me.

"Pearl, you don't know what you're doing," Meghan said so soft I could barely hear.

"Crazy little …" the man growled. He yanked back at her. We pulled her back and forth like a ragdoll. There was his will and my will. "Lila, goddamnit."

"Lila?" I asked. Meghan pulled out of my grasp, but I reached and got her wrist.

The driver put his hand inside the pocket of his rabbit fur coat. Meghan saw him and lifted her legs. She put the flat of her boots against my chest, kicked hard. I went flying and landed on my back, the wind knocked out of me.

The car door slammed. The car screamed off. The fight had jostled the cash loose in my coat pocket, the cash Meghan had stuffed there. The wind took the bills and whipped them up, danced them high. I watched from my back on the sidewalk as they floated silver like large fireflies. The women around me ran in high heels after the money, like children chasing lightning bugs, hands up and giddy. They ran in slow motion, with their spangles and bright colors, after the glowing money, laughing like little kids.

A woman with a red fro and a rainbow coat scrambled after a twenty spinning in little hurricanes near my feet, near the curb. She said without looking at me, "Lila must like you. Anybody else mess with her like that and she would've had Russell just beat the shit out of you. Or take that gun of his and just fucking shoot you between the goddamn eyes." She caught the twenty, danced it into her cleavage.

I pulled myself off the pavement. I watched the car do a screeching U-turn and speed back by, the man screaming at Meghan, who sat with her face buried in her hands, and my pouch with my most precious belongings still tied around her scrawny neck.

Who knew doors locked behind you in town? After Meghan sped away, I pulled myself up and stumbled back to her place to crash until morning. I didn't know how I'd get back home; I just knew I wanted to leave East St. Louis, just wanted to go back to the life I had before I knew so much.

I couldn't open the back metal door to Meghan's building. I tried jimmying windows but just couldn't get in. I sat on a crate in the back with the homeless man nearby and waited for an hour to see if anyone was coming in or going out, but it seemed like all the residents left and stayed gone all night.

It was too cold to sit any longer. Early November in Missouri could be like autumn or it could be sudden winter; you never knew what you were going to get. I reached in an inside pocket and found an old threadbare pair of gloves and a moth-eaten stocking cap and put them on. I had to keep moving. I wandered aimlessly through the neighborhood, dodging men in low-riding cars, drugged-out psychos on the sidewalks.

One guy in a Mustang kept slowing down to stare. I was getting scared and thought about how I looked in my plaid oversized wool coat, my torn-up hat. How much money would a guy pay for this, I thought to myself, and laughed. I didn't know if the guy in the car thought the laugh was an invitation, but he then stayed right beside me as I walked. I slipped down an alley and hid. There I came across a kid's bike. It had a white woven basket on front with blue and yellow plastic flowers painted on the seat. It glowed and reminded me of Miss Universe. I thought of the poor kid who lost the bike. It must have been stolen, because it was way too nice.

Knees and elbows squawking at awkward angles, my coat whipping from winter wind, I biked back through the devastation that was East St. Louis, made it across the bridge. I'd biked this way once. I could do it again. I just wanted to go home.

It was cold and hard going. It reminded me of running—how if you could get in the zone, just pay attention to the rhythmic motion of the body and to the breath, then all the thoughts, all the darknesses, all the truths you'd rather not know, would be pushed hard and fast right out of your head.

When I came upon the convenience store I'd visited years earlier, I biked up the ramp. I had to eat. I couldn't keep biking if I didn't eat. I had no money. I biked behind the store to the metal dumpster, dug up a half-eaten hot dog and devoured it. Next were the remains of a Slim Jim, some soggy potato chips, and half a Ho Ho.

Even pedaling hard, I made ridiculously slow headway against the wind. The chill made my fingers so numb it was if my hands weren't attached to my body. I worked the pedals gangly like a drunk person.

I rode through Hermann and thought about stopping at Nadine's, but couldn't. I was too exhausted. I didn't want to deal with seeing her have another vision, or with her calling my mother. Anyway, I had no idea how she was doing. I knew Mother had taken a liking to her after that Christmas visit. I could tell Mother was surprised by how much she liked Nadine, how the rumors and gossip had kept Nadine's light bundled up in a dark blanket. I could hear them laughing on the phone, and I thought maybe Nadine was Mother's replacement for her dead husband. I knew they kept in touch for a while, but then the calls fell off. I didn't find out why. But, that was the way of our family—nobody stayed in touch for long. There were too many stories you had to keep hidden, and there's only so much you can talk about when you spend so much time hiding.

I had to pass out. I had to sleep. The sky was black. Night clouds covered stars and moon. My face felt like a frozen mask. There were few lights on the highway. The only illumination was sudden shocks of speeding headlights.

It was so dark, so deeply black. So frigidly cold, so raw in the bone. I felt a bruise across my breasts where Meghan had kicked me. My right upper arm pulsed from the slammed car door. It was past midnight now, and it was as cold as it was going to get. I figured it was still just a touch above freezing. I hoped it stayed that way.

I looked around and recognized the patch of shadowy fields; the weeping willow was somewhere near. If I could find the willow and get beneath it, somehow I'd be warm.

I got off the bike and maneuvered it into the pitch-dark fields. My feet slurred the slick grass. It took a while of wandering, but I found the willow. The branches were bare, thin and black, hanging down like an old hag's thinned-out hair. I parted the limbs, lugged the bike beneath. I fell to the ground, exhausted.

My body shivered. There was no way I would sleep. I hugged my wool coat hard. My body felt as stone tough as the ground beneath. I didn't know if I slept, but later I opened my eyes and saw a glow. The Osage woman flew above me. I couldn't tell if it was a dream or a vision. I could no longer feel the frozen earth. She floated with Nadine in her arms, swirling and curling in smoky flush. They looked at me with such love. They glowed with such tint and hue. The brushed glow seemed to flow out of them and wash down over me. A brilliant phosphorescence of ruby, sapphire, amber and emerald swirled around me. It warmed my flesh. It set my heart with a warmth, entered my belly, wandered into my limbs.

I was dying. The Osage woman would now lift me up and carry me away. Part of me hoped she would. I found this world so exhausting, my way of seeing so shattering. If she could just lift me up and take me away, I could rest. Just rest.

But instead, as the colors and light washed through me, every horror seemed to leave me—the ghastly visions, Father's death, the bruises, what I'd learned about Meghan, the deep chill that fell across the land. I felt unburdened; the grief and anger sweating off me seemed to open up space for the love. All those dark thoughts and all the upset and anger were like a fat-assed dog sitting on top of all the gentleness. Now it was as if my self was revealed to me. A self I knew as a little girl.

The glow faded. The Osage woman and Nadine left me. I blew out tufts of cold air. The warmth still filled me, but I knew it wouldn't last. I wished I could live feeling that much love the rest of my life, but I didn't know how to make it stay. I lay huddled on the harsh earth, eyes opened, thinking about it all until dawn.

The sun came up, and I was clear-eyed. The ground was cold and my body cold; we were one and it was a good feeling. I lifted my head, and my hat and hair were stuck to leaves and forest debris; my head clung to the flesh of the earth. When I sat up, the detritus came with me. I took off my hat, ran my fingers through the frozen strands and pulled out the twigs.

The air was dry, a stubborn cold that made me feel alive. I knew most people felt the Missouri winter so hard they couldn't stand it, but for me, the cold was a fisted blessing. For me, the outside had always been safer than the inside.

The frost made the old willow grey. I parted her hair, walked the bike across the highway to the other side, wandered through a strip of forest until I reached the Missouri River. I sat upon the frozen bank and watched ice chunks in brown river water chug down the russet current, the water like sluggish morning blood. Hoarfrost clogged my nostrils.

Death. The crack of branches. Icicles dripping sharp points of light. I found myself in the cold air and it in me. Everything was so blessedly quiet. How winter came in and killed. What a relief that was. Death. What a profound relief, mortality. How the end was a healing. A wisdom of rock, of frozen dirt.

When you're in a car, the ponderous rivers of that place—the Osage, the Missouri, the Mississippi—were nothing but green signs, blurred metal. As I grew up, I was slowly forgetting how it was to be near the ground. Near the tug and haw. The Missouri was depth and flow, pull and current. It was sky reflections, exposed bank roots. It was a relish of frozen muck, of laboring fish and icy fowl. I was forgetting everything. The bitter relief of the frozen season. I was forgetting all that I loved. I sat on that frozen bank for hours, thinking about the Osage woman and Nadine and their love, thinking about how I used to love the dirt, willing myself always to remember.

I stayed outside all day. I would love to have lived my life always outdoors. Mother knew this; she could tell without me even saying. She'd told me once that her father had been that way, and it scared her to death. Scared her because she didn't know how anyone could survive in the real world that way. Her father didn't survive. He got drunk one night, fell asleep in the snow and froze to death.

By the time I reached home, it was past nine at night. I pulled up to the front yard and saw a glow from the kitchen window warming a patch of dead grass. I dropped the bike, went up and peered in. Mother sat at the kitchen table holding hands with a man I did not recognize. They talked close and intimate. A radiance bound them. Mother was crying. Mother rarely cried. I watched the man lean in and touch her hand. I felt horrible guilt.

I had done this to her by running off. I'd caused her this much pain. I'd only seen her cry this hard after Father's death. I rushed around the house to the back.

"I'm here," I said as I burst through the door. They looked up at once. "I'm back."

The man popped up and rushed across the kitchen toward me. He put his hands out flat like he was trying to tame a wild dog. He said, "Where have you been?"

"Mother?" I tried to get around him. He barred my way. He had silver hair cut in a crew. One eye was bigger than the other and pulsed sideways. Veins at his temple. Something was coiled in his body. His energy rattled me. "We called the police and reported you missing. Do you know what you put your mother through? That friend of yours wouldn't tell us anything." He shook his head.

I stared blankly at him. Who was he?

He looked me up and down with disgust and said, "Well, what happened to you?"

I smoothed down my shirt, put my hands up into wildly flying hair. I could smell the dark sweat of me.

When I didn't say anything, he sighed and said, "I'll go call the police and tell them she's been found." He left the room.

I ran to Mother and knelt at her chair.

She cried like her heart was breaking. It seemed to me one of the greatest tortures in life was to watch your mother cry. I didn't touch her. It wasn't done. "I didn't mean to scare you."

The man came back into the room and stood over me. He looked at Mother with such pained eyes and said to me in a whisper, "Right now, this isn't about you." I stood and moved back;

something about his energy made me uncomfortable kneeling below him. Anxiety twitched his too-big eye.

"We just got the call," Mother said, rubbing her red nose with a white kerchief. "It's my fault. I shoulda stayed in touch. I couldn't…"

The man patted her head like a dog.

"What?" I said, holding my breath. "What?"

The man said to the top of Mother's head, "Your Aunt Nadine is dead. She killed herself."

chapter 14

EVER WRACKED FLESH, coursed darkness through artery, ached bone, hollowed out heart. It started when I heard about Nadine's death, kept on day after day, spiked at night, filled my bedroom with dark visions, with childhood nightmares.

I sweated brutal stench. A cold sore grew in the center of my lip and spread up into my nose. My first cold sore, a gift from Meghan. I coughed phlegm.

Days passed. Mother came in with an armload of recipe magazines and put them at the bottom of the bed. "I was waiting to bring this in until you got a little better." She had dark circles beneath her eyes. She was in mourning. We were a sickly pair.

Even as ill as I was, I knew Mother's mourning wasn't just for Nadine. She'd been mourning for a few months now. Even sick as a dog, I knew she was witnessing the end. Something had been set in motion with the loss of Father, with this new man she was dating, with the ignoring of the earth. It was the end of her dependence on soil, of a life she'd lived with the seasons that went back generations, so many filthy past lives. She was about to get everything she ever wanted. It was a lot to mourn.

It was a full day before I reached for the magazines. When I was starving myself, I'd taken to looking at food in recipe magazines. The recipe sections of *Better Homes and Gardens* were better than the one in *Ladies' Home Journal*. The colors were brighter, the pictures deeper—crimson and burgundy and frothy eggshell. Since I'd started starving, I'd turned to staring. Cherry Delight, Queen Sheba Mousse; one cup raisins, a teaspoon of vanilla, two cups sugar, a quarter cup milk, one stick of margarine, two sticks of butter, four cups syrup, one can of cherries in sugar paste. Mars Bars Peanut Brittle, Luscious Lemon Layer Cake.

Food porn.

Mother didn't seem to notice I was eating again, that I no longer needed the pictures. I found a letter on top of the stack of magazines. Foggy and confused, I thought, *It's a letter from Meghan.* It'd been opened. I tried to focus on the return address. It was not from Meghan.

Written-down words had more power than anything. I stared at Nadine's slanted cursive on the envelope, sniffed the paper like a dog gnawing a bone. I took a long time to open it. I wanted to put off the verbs and nouns, put off the weight of words lodging in my flesh, weighing down my bones.

Dear Pearl. I don't know how to write such a letter as this. I guess I wanted to tell you how much I appreciated your visit. I can't really be around people because with my way of seeing I can pick up everything about them. I could see that your way of seeing is bigger than mine. I can see into the people around me, but I think your seeing goes further. I think you can see more than I ever did. It has been such a hard time for me, this life, and I don't want the same for you, but I don't know how to stop it. I can't even stop it for myself. How could I possibly help you?

I wanted to talk to you about the visions when I brought you the gift for Christmas, but with Sarah there, I couldn't.

Next to me on the bed was the copy of *Little Women* she'd given me. I'd never read it. How could I? How could the book possibly live up to my expectations? Instead I slept with it, carried it from room to room. Slowly, the binding was breaking. As I read the rest of Nadine's letter, I held the book against my chest.

When I was little, I always thought there was a reason for my way of seeing, that it was important and would mean something in my life. I don't know, maybe I was born in the wrong time, when folks were too scared of people like me and would rather electrocute them than listen to them. Maybe it belongs to your generation. Maybe there's some important reason for your gift, Pearl. I don't envy you that burden. I've been seeing for a long time how much worse the world is getting. We're living out some story that just has no end but a bad one. For me, it's too late.

That night you left here, I was out back staring at the stars. It was the first time in a long time I had some peace. It was the first time I thought maybe the world wasn't such a horrible place. I thought maybe there was hope. Talking to you seemed to open up something that had been closed in me. I was like a sleeping tied-up dog who just woke up for the first time. I never in my life had anyone listen real serious to me. I never had anyone talk to me in a way that didn't mark me as crazy. She scratched out the next sentence, and I could only read the words *your father. I don't want you to think anything I've done has anything to do with you.*

The thought had not occurred to me, that she might have killed herself because of something I'd said, something I'd dredged up, that my witnessing her had sent her gradually over the edge. Now that it was written, guilt seared into my heart. I coughed phlegm into a wad of toilet paper. Sometimes a person seeing you saved your life, but maybe sometimes a person seeing you could be the death of you.

When you open up the joy, you also open up the hurt. It's not anyone's fault—that's just the way it is. I seem to have an On switch and an Off switch. After your visit, I decided to stop taking the pills. I decided to try to see what it would be like to live inside the world again switched on instead of off.

The visions came back real hard. How can I live with that much joy, mixed with that much pain of knowing? How is a person supposed to live with feeling so much, all that love of every blade of grass, but all that fear? Does anybody have the answer? I wished we could have talked some more.

I hope you found Meghan and saw to it that she was OK. I hope your life leads you someplace special. I know mine is nothing to brag about, but I hope you'll do better. Then she scratched out an entire sentence and I couldn't make out the words. She then signed it *Sincerely,* scribbled over that, and wrote *Love,* and then *Aunt Nadine.*

I had no words for it all. I couldn't get my hands around it all. Some hate boiled inside the whole world. Or some love that couldn't fit inside this horrible "real" world.

Suicide wasn't new to our family. Grandpa Swinton, Mother's brothers. I wondered if they all had the gift. Mother didn't talk about her brothers. We never discussed Grandpa. We rarely visited our relatives. There were never any stories. I was starting to see why. It was so brutal. It was so painful. It was like a hunting knife slitting open your guts.

I was sixteen, and I lay in bed feeling one thousand years old. The letter settled hard inside my lungs, and I slept the days away like a person buried alive, beneath all that dirt and all those untold stories.

Jason and Bonnie glowed in fuddled morning apparition. They glittered like two angels, back-lit by light streaming in the window.

Bonnie gave me one of her looks, a hard stare, plopped herself Indian style on the hardwood. She wouldn't look at me after that, wouldn't talk to me, was still mad at me for getting her in trouble over the Caddy's hubcaps. She sat on my bedroom floor arranging and rearranging rocks and roots and jam jars full of earth.

Jason stood above my reeking bed and held up one of his paintings. The paper was textured like fabric. The window sun reflected in its weave. I reached up to run my finger along it. He'd titled it *Miss Universe*. The colored drawing was me on my bike. Huge wheels, tremendous spokes. Stars and streamers bled out into the sky, like meteors and shooting stars in a wide-open universe. He'd gone from drawing real things to forcing them into intangibles. It was a leap. He was growing so fast. I touched the paper and began to cry.

Jason saw me. I didn't know why it was, but being seen like that was going right into my flesh. I cried open force, my whole wretched sadness out there for all to see. I never showed so much of myself before, to anybody.

Jason put out a hand to touch me but stopped himself. He stood with his hand in awkward thrust, like he was fearful to go forward, to comfort, fearful to move back. I keened, broke open like a gutted catfish.

Bonnie looked over, her face affected by the sobbing like a Picasso—her eyes and mouth cracked and muddled, her regular self misplaced. I sobbed myself to hysteria. I sobbed myself into a coma.

When I awoke, they were gone. I saw they'd put the *Miss Universe* picture on the floor and ringed it all around with rocks and roots and such. A primal protection. A ritual. A sacred circle.

That night the fever broke.

I scotch-taped *Miss Universe* up next to *Time, Tide and Pearl.* I lay in bed and stared at those pictures for hours. I had no answers, only questions.

What happened when folks didn't like the way you saw, what you saw, how you saw? What happened when you saw them too clearly and they wanted to hurt you for seeing that much? What happened when what you saw was what the whole world was trying to avoid?

Life began picking up speed. When I thought about it, it had started going too fast way before. Its speed had something to do with the neglected farm, with the magnetism of town. Its velocity scared me. I wanted to shout, *Slow down! I need to figure things out. Stop! What brick wall are we barreling toward?*

We were having dinner with the silver-haired guy. Mother asked me to sit down with him, to get to know him, to try to like him. *I need time to think. Give me time to think.* It was all too soon.

His name was Jack. She told me some of his legend. He'd grown up an Army brat, moving every few years as a kid. He knew nothing about calling a patch of earth his own, about intimacies with bush and tree. He was raised only by his dad, and now his dad was dead. I knew what it meant to have a dead father. I could at least understand that. He'd never been married. He'd been in Vietnam, then gone back to work for the Army as a civilian, a recruiter. He worked a couple of towns away at Fort Leonard Wood.

earth

He sat in the easy chair in the living room and watched Mother in the kitchen as she prepared dinner. His grey hair had been cut and spiked harder and flatter. His left eye looked like it was starving. He looked like a hawk or vulture that was famished. Slight and wiry in a grey business suit, too much cologne. If Father was the bloody entrails of a freshly butchered mammal, Jack was a shoulder cut cradled on Styrofoam behind suction plastic beneath a glare of florescence.

He talked to Mother as she prepared the meal, wove his head this way and that to watch her pull plates from the cupboard and walk them to the dining table. He looked like a little boy. He was Father's age. Father had always looked like a caved-in old man.

I sat on the scratchy plaid sofa and wondered how much he could see. I always tried to figure out how much a person could see.

I saw that he spent all of his grown-up years, all those years alone in the military, building some fantasy of the family he'd have some day. Welcome to your new family, Jack. Me with my "gift," wearing a khaki dress Mother had sewn. My delicate mother with her all-encompassing need for town, a woman who was not even half there. The farm, so full of muck, so bloody and shitty, so abandoned.

Jack got off the chair and came up to me. His energy sent some mighty force through my gums. His vigor made my teeth jangle. I had the same effect on him. His face clenched and shivered. His hand twitched. Mother seemed to notice he wasn't watching her anymore and came to the living room doorway and wiped her hands on a dish towel. He put his face close, his too-big eye like a cartoon. He gave me a hard look in the eye, his back to Mother so she couldn't see.

"This is a fine daughter you got, Sarah. A fine daughter." He stared at me rigid, turned to her and smiled. He turned back to me, the pungent tang of his cologne screaming up my nose. He said as if it was an order, "There's a fine woman in there, a good woman." He gave me a stiff wink with his bulging eye.

I didn't notice the base of my skull screeching like a tree full of starlings. As the force slammed me in the gut, as I stood up from the sofa, as I arched on tiptoe, I saw Mother's face fall; caught Jack spinning to look at me right before my head flung up, my eyes rolled back and I lost what little control I had over my crazy world.

All spring, the sky was a wet blanket; clouds hung in an unwavering coffin lid low on the land. Rain flooded from the heavens, ran in streams down country lanes. The Missouri broke her banks, turned backyards into swimming pools. Whole fields lay drowned beneath standing stagnant water. It was the wettest spring in living memory. There was something wrong with the weather. It was the year the gods sobbed upon a sopping earth.

Through the windows in history class, the murk and tug of the sooty sky. The thumping beat of perpetual rain. The weather frizzed my hair wild. Bonnie was in the desk next to me. Mr. Crane was droning on about the Civil War, brother against brother, father against son. Students' heads bobbed in drowsy monotony.

The buzzing at the base of my skull went ignored, and I didn't know one was coming until I was already in it. I'd never had a vision at school. I'd always figured they were something to do with home. My body went rigid in the desk, my back arched, my stomach banged the edge of the desktop, my legs punted the desk in front of me.

Patent leather shoes and white socks morphed into broken leather boots, torn soles, socks drenched with rain and something else. My navy school uniform turned into a soldier's caked with dirt, with torn cuffs that didn't meet my long, skinny wrists. The noise was deafening; shots and cannons and the cries of men. I was in mud up to my kneecaps. I carried a rifle musket with a smoldering barrel. We were in a field, a Missouri field. Smoke like the dark fingers of shadow fog crept along the ground. Boys and men were dead all around me. It was nearly the same vision as I'd had in front of Jack. But this time I was the soldier.

I saw the Osage woman. She floated above the field and held up her arms over the scene as if to say, *See. We need you to see this.*

earth

I lay down flat in the mud. I had a rolled-up blanket, a haversack, a tin cup. I was starving. I closed my eyes. I pretended to be dead. I heard the suck and slop of boots in deep mud, voices.

These other people terrified me, and I knew to keep quiet. They spoke about taking our mules. Mud smeared my lips and chin and eyelids. My whole soul filled with the darkness of the muck. I peeked sideways. The dead guy next to me was my brother. My brother! Flesh of my flesh, blood of my blood. I looked at him and felt part of me die. I thought with deepest anguish, "All of this for some mules?"

I came to on the floor, books and notebooks spilled. Classmates gathered round, staring down. I looked at Bonnie. She looked down, helpless. One of the kids said, "All of this for some mules?" I guess I'd said some of what was happening to me out loud. The class roared.

"Settle down, class!" Mr. Crane yelled. "Get the nurse!" he screamed to Bonnie.

It wasn't just that the world was speeding up—my visions seemed to be speeding up, too. The heat was being turned up, the ante upped. The problem wasn't just the Civil War vision. The problem was that the Civil War vision was just like the Vietnam War vision I'd had with Jack at that first dinner.

With Jack, it had been the same grey devastation.

Blown-out huts on both sides of the road. It was a humble country, where the people still lived close to the earth. Dead bodies. Sickly trees that looked like petrified skeletons.

A ravaged landscape, blackened stubs of exotic trees, burning bushes. A lone solider walked through the smoking soil. At first I couldn't see, but the air cleared and it was Jack in an Army helmet, full fatigues. He mumbled something, mumbled and stumbled through the smoky death. The Native woman floated in rainbow colors above the entire scene, coming in and out of view when the black smoke cleared.

No longer were my visions just about the people I knew, about my own patch of earth; now they gave me lush details of bombs and guns—not just here, but in countries I'd never been to. Now I was privy to trauma all over the world. I lay on the cot in the nurse's office and thought of Nadine and was terrified.

Nurse Kathy had thick calves, Farrah Fawcett hair, a soft face, almond-shaped eyes. There was something about her—something light, deep, calm. She kept trying the house, but Mother was not home. I slept for a while. When I awoke, school was just about finishing for the day, and still Nurse Kathy couldn't get hold of Mother.

I swung my legs off the cot, still dizzy from the vision, but tried to pretend I was normal. I told her I'd go catch a ride with Bonnie. She looked at me sad and deep, but gave me a note anyway. I went out to the parking lot, lumbered into the orange truck. When I'd turned sixteen, the truck had become mine. Mother took over Father's old blue flatbed. I didn't want to find Bonnie, didn't want to have her ask any questions, or worse, look at me with that clear face and not say a word.

I drove home real slow, both hands on the wheel, inching my way down rural roads. I read and reread Nurse Kathy's note. I had to go to our family doctor, the note said.

Could I get a prescription for what I had? The note gave me the skeevies. The note grew in my vision, became a huge white scroll laid out upon the truck seat, the cursive dancing like letters of an ancient text. The note was some primal decree that would be my undoing. Still I inched homeward. I turned snail-like down Powwow, crawled toward the house. I just had to get home.

As I turned into the gravel driveway, I saw a woman. She was walking with her back to me down the gravel. She wore high heels. A short skirt. The rain pattered upon her coiffed hair. Nobody I knew dressed that nice. I couldn't make out who it was through the rain-spattered and smudged windshield.

The woman turned. She held up her arms like she was holding a shotgun at her shoulder. She was pretending to shoot me through the windshield. I couldn't see her face. She pretended there was a back-kick to the butt against her shoulder, danced backwards on high heels on the gravel. She lowered her arms and laughed. I could see her face.

"Holy shit." I threw the truck in park. I jumped out, slipping on the sopping gravel. I stood in the rain facing her. "Meghan." Her name left my lips like a small burst of air, like a final breath.

"Hello, sister of mine," she said, the rain streaking her mascara down her face like black tears.

I broke my arm when I was five. I didn't remember much, just Meghan and me using a plastic lid for a Frisbee, the purple nighttime sky, the damp humidity sticking my shirt to my belly, fireflies popping. The tall, wet grass was where I fell; the bone protruded from forearm. The excruciating pain.

Dr. Festus was drunk when Mother called, said he couldn't fix the arm until morning. It was rare for folk like us to go to a doctor. It just wasn't done. You didn't go to an emergency room unless you were near death. When Meghan was twelve, she lay for days on the plaid sofa moaning and clutching her stomach. Mother wouldn't believe her pain, or couldn't afford her pain, or both. They only took her to the hospital when she started screaming. They got her there in time for her appendix to burst.

That night, my broken arm cradled by an old cloth diaper for a sling, Mother lay in my bed with me. I never had her so close before, except when I was born to her. I cried and cried, it hurt so bad. In the middle of the night, she started to sing. She had no voice; the words were scratchy and off-key. *Amazing Grace, how sweet the sound.* It was the only song she seemed to know all through by heart, because she sang it over and over, soft just for me. *Amazing Grace* became my favorite song. After that, I spent a year getting hurt, just so she'd lie down with me, just so she'd sing to me, but then Father figured it out, gave me the belt, and I had no choice but to stop.

Meghan had to use the bathroom. I got her inside, too hyped to talk, showed her to the downstairs bathroom. Then it was my turn. I talked excitedly to her through the door, but she was just quiet. When I came out, she was gone, and Mother was standing in the kitchen.

"Who you talking to?" she asked.

"Bonnie. She must've left without me knowing."

I went outside to see if Meghan was just hiding behind a tree, but she was nowhere. I figured she'd parked at the bottom of Powwow, snuck out when she saw Mother coming.

When I came back in, Mother was reading the nurse's note. I'd dropped it on the counter in my excitement. She looked up at me, eyes inward, rigid with fear. I'd only seen that kind of fear on her a couple of times before: once when the crops failed and we didn't have money for food, and then when Father died. It was centuries old, that dread. It was about survival in the real world.

Doctor Festus read the nurse's note, looked me over. "You look healthy as a horse." He gave me the physical, hands shaking, the smell of him like the huge bottle of Jack Daniels Father had kept hidden beneath the sink. I couldn't stop thinking of Meghan, who I hoped was hiding somewhere in town. I prayed she hadn't left, prayed she didn't take off back to East St. Louis. Pasty shaking hands took blood pressure, listened to heart. All I could think was I had to find Meghan.

Mother stood in the corner of the doctor's office, stiff with the terror. She watched the doctor's every move, like she could control what he found, what he diagnosed, what future he was predicting. All I could do was think of my sister. Meghan was home.

Dr. Festus wrote a note to give to the school nurse. He said, "She's not got nothing wrong with her. Nurses," he scoffed.

earth

Mother looked so relieved on the drive home. "Pearl, you got to do better. I need you to do better. You can beat this." She made a white nubby fist at me. "You're strong." She took hold of one of my arms. "Look how strong you are." She was right. All that running, all that breathing had made me buff, had made my skin glow. Even the angles of my face were sharper. "You've always been the strongest person I ever knew." All I could think was, *Where was Meghan? How could I find Meghan?*

I awoke in the middle of the night to the smell of my sister. Musky, boozy, sour. She was lying with her back to me in bed. I raised my head and saw the window was open and figured she'd climbed up the oak and let herself in. The moonlight turned her shoulders molten. With her dark hair, her ivory back, she was like a black-and-white photo.

"You awake?" I whispered. I was careful not to touch her after what happened in East St. Louis.

She coughed and hacked, spoke groggy from sleep. "I'm so damned tired. Just sleep."

I tried a few more times, but nothing. She was like a fragile forest creature, and I had to put out some food, make no sudden movements, let her come to me. Or I'd have to just figure it all out myself, like I always had to, put the puzzle pieces out in front of me, fit them together, create some sense, figure out what to do. I was the one who told her to come home. Now she had come home. What was I supposed to do about it?

Later, I jolted awake from a nightmare and she was gone. I paced the bedroom, looked out the window again and again. Finally, exhausted, I went back to bed, tried to keep my eyes and ears open, but fell hard back into heavy sleep.

When I woke up at dawn, she was back. She smelled of sex, cigarettes, of pure grain hooch. I breathed a great sigh. I got up and went to the bathroom.

When I came back in, she was out of bed, standing by the dresser, using a flat Tab cola to down some pill. She was naked. She was all hide and marrow, a bulbous bruise around her left knee. In her dress-up clothes she hid her body. If you didn't get close enough, you could swear she was almost normal; you could swear she was fine.

I stood at the dresser beside her. I wore a tattered Mickey Mouse T-shirt. The mirror was old and grey, and it was hard to see in it. We looked so much alike, she and I. I loved how close our faces were. We both had dark hair and wild green eyes. I had Mother's alabaster skin and hers was more dark, even swarthy, like Father's. But still her face was my face. I felt with Meghan right then what I'd felt with her as a kid. I could not discern myself from her. Her soft, round brown eyes were my eyes, the thick pouty lips my lips, her long, stringy hair my hair.

When I was five I put up a wall with Mother and Father. *These people are not going to raise me right.* I blocked them out. I would only let them influence me so far. But Meghan was on my side. It was Meghan and me against the parents. So I never blocked Meghan out. Meghan could enter my skin and burrow into my soul and there was nothing I could do to stop her.

After Meghan ran off, Mother used to say to me, "There but for the grace of God, Pearl."

No, Mother, wherever Meghan was, *There go I. There go I. There go I.*

I was staring at her in that murky mirror for a while before I saw the bruises. Her cheeks were covered in mottled black and grey.

"Oh my God, Meghan, what happened?"

She mumbled and fumbled her words. The booze oozed off her like a field sopped by a chemical spill. I ran to the bathroom and wet a wash rag. I needed ice but didn't want to risk going down to the kitchen and running into Mother.

I ran back in. She was back in bed. I sat beside her, put the rag to her face. She cursed and squirmed. I tried to go soft. The black marks came off on the wash rag. It was mascara. Nobody had beaten her up. She'd had a crying jag and her mascara ran all over her face. A booze jag and then a sobbing jag. Angry with my own fear, I pushed the wash rag hard around her cheeks and chin until it all came off. She said something garbled.

"What? Repeat what you said. I didn't hear."

"What the fuck is a person supposed to do in this fucking one-horse town?" she repeated.

After that, she snuck in at night about three or four times a week. I'd wake up to her smoky smell beside me. I didn't dare ask her where she was sleeping on the nights she wasn't with me. I didn't want to scare her off. Every morning before dawn, I had to wake Meghan from a drunkard's sleep, sneak her back out the window before anyone saw her.

One night while she was sleeping, I got up and rifled through her bag. I didn't know what I was looking for. She had a huge carpet bag she carried around, red and fuzzy with a rope for a shoulder strap. She had so much random stuff in there. A fork and spoon, six twisty straws, tampons, a Barbie doll, three oranges. My hand settled upon something familiar in the dark recesses. I pulled it out. My pouch. I fumbled the string opening and poured out the pearl and the arrowhead. It was like I found a piece of me that was missing.

I made sure Meghan was sleeping and slipped it into my bottom drawer, behind the pillow cases. A couple of days later I went to get it, but she must've found it, because it was gone. I stole it from her purse again a few nights later and hid it in the back of the closet. She found it again, stole it back.

Finally, I took the pouch and hid it where I knew she'd never ever find it.

chapter 15

YOU LIVED THE rules and regulations of one man for years. You lived one story for decades, a man's story, and then some other man came along and changed the game plan. Mother believed we had to live this new man's vision to survive. Mother believed a woman could never live her own vision and survive.

Were there women who didn't think you had to live the man's story? I didn't see any in Missouri. Every woman I knew lived their life through a man. Every girl I knew wanted to grow up and live their life through a man. I always thought, even when I was little, *Why can't my story just be my story? Why can't my life be mine?*

Jack was slowly moving in. Schedules taped to the rusty refrigerator. New rules and regulations. A time to wake, a time to sleep. A time to cook, a time to clean. Jack lived life in small boxes, tried to force others neatly into small boxes. He rearranged cupboards, drawers, closets. You could never find anything you were looking for—batteries, bulbs, empty bread bags. He never said a word about the farm. I had hoped he'd want to resurrect it, but it was as if the farm were some faraway fairy tale that everyone was trying to pretend never existed.

He turned Mother's sewing room, Meghan's old room, into an office. I went in once when he was gone. An old desk I'd heard him say belonged to his grandfather was against the wall where Mother's sewing machine used to be. I ran my hand along the polished wood. I didn't know what it was like to have a grandparent who could read, and here was one with a desk. A couple of boxes of books sat on the hardwood floor next to store-bought bookshelves. I'd never seen so many books outside of school. I rifled through. Most were about recruiting or about war strategies. I found one called *The Art of War*, by some Chinese writer from thousands of years ago. I would have liked to read it. I didn't know if I could ask Jack if I could read it.

When you're forced into someone else's story, do they let you know your role in it? Do you piece together the myth, so you can guess who you'll be in the story? Can you change the ending?

I couldn't get Meghan out of the window. I pulled, pleaded, pampered. She squirmed, sputtered, spat. She wouldn't be budged. I thought if I could feed her something, she'd sober up enough to make the climb down. I went downstairs. As I turned the corner, I saw Jack and Mother in the kitchen. Something was up, so I hid behind the living room wall to watch and listen.

Jack had bought her another pair of shoes. The box pulsed gold on the table. He took her arm and sat her in one of the metal kitchen chairs, extracted a fuchsia sandal, kneeled, put the shoe on her right foot. He threaded the buckles around her ankles. Prince Charming. She smiled giddy down into his face. A glow lit them both. All I could think was, *Mother sure did find men who loved her.*

I waited until their love fest was over and went in. Jack looked me up and down. I smelled like Meghan, perfume and cigarettes, and it oozed like fragrant poison. He checked his watch so I would notice. The wall clock said past eleven. His Army training couldn't fathom such laziness.

I went to the fridge and took out the stuff I needed. I put mayonnaise on Wonder Bread for a ham sandwich. I was taking plastic off a piece of cheese when I heard Mother gasp, a chair screech back on the linoleum. I turned to see Meghan standing in the doorway to the kitchen.

She wore a fringed silk robe she'd had in her Mary Poppins bag. It was short. Very short. Along the glowing ruby fabric was a threadbare embroidered dragon. She had a Virginia Slim dangling from her lips, black circles beneath her eyes. Jack sat on the edge of his chair, tensed up, like he was ready for a fight.

Meghan plopped in one of the kitchen chairs. "What's a girl gotta do around here to get a cup of coffee."

"Here it is, Meghan. I'll get it for you," I said, rushing around.

"Meghan?" Mother looked from her to me several times, then stared at Jack with fear. She said polite as she could manage, "So, when did you get into town?" She stood up, one fuzzy slipper, one fuchsia sandal, and shuffled up to her, turned to Jack and said, "Jack, this here is Terry's girl."

"How do you do?" Jack said, holding out his hand. Meghan looked him up and down like he was some john. Her robe fell open. You could almost see her nipples. I ran up to block Jack's view, put the cup of Folgers in front of her. I leaned in and fixed her robe, hiked it up to her chin. I looked up into Meghan's eyes, and she was looking past me at Mother. She looked at Mother with such hopeless need. I gasped at the level of want in those eyes. I remembered how she'd done this as a child, looked at Mother with that gut desire, that black hole of need. How Mother had ignored her. How I'd tried to make it up to her by playing games with her, by running after her every need.

"Meghan showed up last night," I said. "I didn't want to bother you all. She's just staying for a day or so." She was holding up her burned-down Virginia Slim, looking for a place to smash it out, even contemplating the kitchen linoleum, so I took the cigarette from her fingers, went to the sink, poured water on it, and threw it in the trash.

Jack sidled up to me at the counter. His jeans were so clean. I was strong from the running but still felt fragile next to him. Around him, or anyone like him, energy drained out of me and left me feeling weak.

"Your mom don't need more trouble," he whispered. He looked slanting at me with his too-big eye and put his hand awkwardly on my shoulder. "We can make sure of that, right?"

I got Meghan to take the coffee and sandwich up to the room. I dug around and found a pair of fringed blue jean shorts and a rainbow-striped T-shirt with a peace sign on it. I got her to put it on, as well as a pair of my running shoes. She looked like me by the end of it all. I thought, *Getting Meghan to be like me, as if being me would assure her a better life.* I looked her up and down. *Was turning a person into me a way to keep them safe?*

After that, Meghan stayed in my room every night, and in the mornings, I ran interference with Mother and Jack. Mother ran her own interference by getting Jack out of the house as much as she could. She kept asking when Meghan was leaving and I kept saying soon.

Then I woke up one morning and Meghan was there, but this time the mascara on her face wasn't mascara and wouldn't wash off. I pulled back the covers and she was covered in bruises, and I knew I had to find a way to go with her on these nighttime jaunts and keep her safe.

All over rural, all over town, men hollered up from their groins, wolf-howled from their primal places. They slobbered scarlet syllables all over thin plaid shirts. They circled, sniffed, grunted. Meghan was a bitch in heat, and everywhere the dogs circled.

My sister and I cruised the boulevard. It was surprisingly easy to talk her into letting me go with her at night. She commandeered the orange truck. She'd found my old blue rosary—in a dusty velvet case in my dresser drawer—and hung it from the rearview mirror. She hung a string of tiny disco balls across the back window that caught the headlights and threw sparks across the cab.

Around her, the men gathered, snaked, slithered. They were sucked toward her from all corners. One by one, they leaned into her window, sniffed her like beasts. One by one, she left with them, worked herself upon them in old rusty trucks, dented Mustangs, orange Camaros. She returned disheveled. She returned with pockets full of cash. A cacophony of wolf howls, an orchestra of groans.

This evening she wore a rusty sequined top with bald patches that reflected murky light. She'd gone in my dresser and taken another pair of jean shorts. She found the pair I didn't wear because I'd cut them off too short, causing my butt to hang from the back. Sandals with thick cords that tied up her calves.

I was no innocent. I drank. I partied. I let myself be led by boys. But Meghan had some fierce pheromones born into her. She had some other force that bound her. I saw her sex force as akin to my visions. It was big. It was uncontrollable. It arched her body. It slammed her guts.

I tried to keep the men away. I was rabid, a witch, a shrew, a gruesome monster. None of it made any difference. Their libidos overswelled me. Off Meghan went, night after night, to work her body upon them, in parked cars in busy parking lots, in trucks on the edge of highways, on hoods in broad street light.

I started to hear Mother and Jack fighting in their bedroom below. Then it built to fighting in the living room and the kitchen below, then to fighting right in front of me. It wasn't just about Meghan. I was having visions in front of Jack. I couldn't control them. It was only a matter of time, and when that time was up, I wasn't sure it was just Meghan who was going to be tossed out on her nose.

I came home from cross country with my head befuddled by what I was supposed to do to help Meghan. I didn't know what the Osage woman wanted from me. It was a bad day of running. I couldn't get my breath. All the partying was wearing me down, and I'd started smoking Meghan's Virginia Slims. It was a day when the breath was short and the road too long.

earth

I came up to my bedroom and stood in the doorway. I looked around and didn't know where I was. Meghan usually slept the day away. She wasn't in the bed, and my room wasn't my room.

Meghan had transformed it. On the floor was a shaggy, bright-red, round rug I'd never seen before. It glowed up to the ceiling. On the wall, rag art, a weaving she'd made from the old socks and bits of fabric from Mother's scrap box. It threw echoes from the rag quilt on the bed. The biggest change, though, the biggest draw, was a shelf along the wall. It was huge, had hundreds of tiny cubbies. It'd been in the basement where Father had left it, and I had no idea how she hauled it up the stairs by herself.

I went up to it. She'd filled some cubbies with bits of earth, jam jars full of dirt, roots and rocks and such; others were more her style: glowing marbles and bits of blue broken glass and a kitschy collection of floral thimbles.

All his life, Father had collected stuff he found in the woods. Bits of other lives. The basement had always been overflowing with junk. Green glass circuit breakers, railway ties, a rusted sword, clocks, wrist watches, Army boots, an acoustic guitar with broken strings. In the corner, between the deep freeze and the bins of musty, scabby potatoes, the bric-a-brac sat for months and years. A country museum of forest garbage. Objects as stories fit together in a hundred ways.

He'd found the massive shelving unit of tiny boxes, each one not big enough for a salt shaker, in a ravine right before he died. He'd hauled it back in the flatbed, drove around to the garage and offloaded it.

I rubbed my fingers over scraped bark and knotted root, the broken glass—each cubby full of a Pearl treasure. It felt like Meghan was seeing me, really seeing me. *This is you, Pearl. This is who you are.* And I remembered this about her, too, how she could disarm you.

Maybe that was all any of us could do. Wake up and see another person, just one other person. To witness them. Maybe then all the blind people I knew, after someone had witnessed them, would open their eyes, and be able to really see a specific tree or a particular bird or the person sitting right next to them.

I heard hammering and followed the noise down one flight of stairs, then another, into the basement. Meghan stood at Father's work bench, in front of his wall of rusted, crusted tools, surrounded by forest junk. She looked so natural there, so human. She was holding the swirly lamp from my nightstand. What was left of the lamp. She was smashing the glass with a hammer.

I was never a big fan of Mother's store-bought things, so I didn't stop her. I stood back and watched. I wasn't sure she even knew I was there. She smashed the glass until she got to the innards. She extracted the metal pole, the wiring, the light bulb. Beside her was a chipped casing, like something used on the top of an electricity pole. She started putting the innards of the lamp inside the casing. She seemed to have some strong vision of the thing and worked feverishly.

A vision hit as I stood there. I arched and stumbled back against the deep freeze. The basement grew into some forest kingdom, some imaginary place of rough shod buildings perched on the branches of ancient trees. The Native woman was there. She whipped up all of the objects around Meghan and they flew off the walls, each object emanating some light. The stuff came together to create a man.

The man looked like Father. A makeshift father of found components. A forest garbage father, with a circuit breaker hat, a body of old lumber, a railway tie for a hand. He flailed his guitar arm. He waved his sword arm. He rocked his old clock face. He looked at me and laughed. I laughed back. He ran around in mock hysteria.

He stopped and came to stand in front of me. His mouth on the clock face was the number six. He shook his tick-tock head.

I'd been thinking a lot about him since he died. Did dying mean he was whole now, wherever he was? Did dying mean he was now a good soul, with good thoughts? Did dying mean he now loved me?

"Can't you see, Pearl, that we're all made up of parts of a million other things? Of course you and Nadine and I could see so much, because we ARE so much. You ARE that soldier there, that sister here. Every part of us is a part of something else."

He waved his sword arm, and all of his parts flew up in the air and resettled in different places. Now the sword was his spine, the clock his knee, and his face an old broken guitar.

He disappeared. The basement came back. No forest father. Just the echo of the closed-down father, a father with a crazy joy inside him that never had a chance to get out.

Meghan was staring at me. She was holding a crazy made-up lamp and staring at me. I was plopped on the basement concrete, my back against the frigid deep freeze. The buzz of the freezer, the stench of potato rot sending waves of Father's lost life up and down my spine.

"Jesus fucking Christ, Pearl. What the fuck was that?" Meghan said, still holding the lamp and not moving any closer to me. "What the fuck?"

It was a week later or three. All the nights with Meghan started to wash together as one eternal nightmare. I lost track of time. I was so tired sometimes I forgot cross country, and the coach was about to throw me off the team.

It was late. I came out of the McDonald's as a long-haired guy with a beaded vest was leading Meghan to his mud-splattered El Camino. I'd had enough. I was so sick of the destruction. So exhausted with the pummeling. I threw the cup I was holding, ran up and grabbed Meghan's arm.

"You're not taking her anywhere." The guy pulled. I pulled. Meghan was like a floppy doll between us and didn't resist. Her hair hung in her face.

I was so exhausted. They sucked Meghan dry, and she sucked me dry. It had to stop. I saw a different Meghan at Father's workbench, and maybe this was what the Osage woman wanted, for me to fight for her, for me to fight for her dear life. The long-haired guy turned a drunken dance on me.

"Whoa!" he said, weaving his head down to look in Meghan's hang-dog face. "Is she like in charge of you?"

"She's my shishtah," Meghan slurred.

"Well, she ain't my boss," he said. "Let her go," he spat.

"You let her go!" I screamed. I saw a classmate cruise by and stare at us. Kids at school were gossiping. *Slut. Whore.* Meghan's reputation was becoming my reputation.

"Yeah, what if I smashed up that sexy little body of yours?" The guy made a fist with his other hand.

"Go to the truck," Meghan slurred. She peeked between stringy pleading hair.

I threw up my hands. "Fine. Do whatever you want."

They stumbled to the El Camino.

I turned to see Anthony, the dry-hump guy I'd met with Bonnie, blowing into the parking lot in his truck. We hooked up every once in a while, although I still wouldn't have actual sex with him. He'd done something to the engine to make it roar. On his stereo, Bob Segar. *Trying to lose the awkward teenage blues. Working on our night moves.*

He parked and yelled out the window, some words I could barely make out. "… on over here. Git over here!" I hadn't seen him in a while. My energy was all taken up with Meghan.

I went over, without will, and leaned into the passenger window. His cowboy hat was pulled low, his eyes red wolf spots in the dark interior, his mouth stretched wide and long.

"Why don't you wear stuff like that when you're with me?" he said, looking at my halter top, cut-off shorts.

"What?" I looked down at my scuffed cowboy boots. Somehow I'd started dressing like Meghan without realizing it.

He reached over the passenger seat and grabbed my hand. "Get in. Come on." He pulled at me. "Get in."

For a moment, he looked like Father. When someone dies miserable, it sticks in your body like glue. I tried to clear my vision. There it was again. The resemblance was uncanny. He was surrounded by such a sadness, a mesh of barbed-wire grief. I felt so exhausted, so pulled into his pain, so without will against all the suffering. I never believed people who said the past was over. My past was the present and the future, and my future was my past.

The truck door screamed long and low as I opened it. As we tore out of the parking lot, the tires screeched like someone torturing a cat. I thought I heard Meghan yell from the El Camino, "You go, sistah," in her drunken, hacking way, but then I wasn't sure if I just imagined it.

A thicket of forest gorged with the primal thrum of night. We were down the Old Algoa Road, a road once linking country to town, a narrow winding path beneath thick overhanging branches, a potholed byway that disintegrated in great arcs at the road's edge. Anthony turned the truck into a field, pulled a brown paper bag from beneath his seat. I leaned my head out the open window. I tried to breathe. I couldn't seem to get enough air these days.

I wanted to get out of the truck, go into the forest, lie on my back and let mud seep into my bones. I wanted to dissolve into the fractal forest, bits of me speckled into bark, measurements of me absorbed in roots, breaths of me sparking kindling. I wanted to merge.

I thought if I could just bring Meghan into the woods, into the clearing, and have her sit on the earth. If I could just get Meghan to merge with the earth, maybe then she'd be healed. Maybe we could start the farm again, and Meghan and I could ride in the back of the truck as Mother jostled us over potholes down the dirt track, and I could show her how to let the branches brush your face. I could show her how to be of the earth, and we'd all be okay then.

Anthony wrapped his mouth around the thick lip of a Jack Daniel's bottle. He leaned, took a tin out of his glove compartment and popped some pill. He held one out to me. Like I needed drugs. I shook my head.

He leaned in and stuck his tongue hard in my mouth. I felt the energy of him enter me, a devouring. I was a drug to him. He sat back and laughed. He scrambled his hands rough over my body, dug a finger beneath my halter top. His breathing grew heavier.

"Damn, you got it fuckin' going on tonight."

I kept my eyes half open, watched through the windshield languid pinpoints of stars burn up the night. I was the smattering of glitter. I was the night. I let myself loose into it.

He pulled me down by the hips and got on top. He grunted and held himself aloft using the top of the back seat. He unzipped his jeans. My chin was raw from his whiskers.

"I gotta get inside you." I was terrified of getting pregnant, of ending up saddled with some kid. But I couldn't think; my jeans were around my knees. I put my hands down to guard myself.

"Come on, baby. You're so beautiful." I let out a whine he took as pleasure. He pushed himself toward my pubic bone. I covered down there with my hands.

Anthony's smooth-headed penis on the back of my hand. Him on top, his Wranglers around his ass, his whiskers rubbing my face raw. The muscle and slip of forest cry. The penis pushing again and again against the back of my hand.

chapter 16

I WALKED INTO the house, and something didn't smell right by the back door. Usually I smelled Father's old boots there, a greeting when you entered, of sweat and sod. Instead there was the aroma of lemon cleaner and new shoe leather. I looked around. All Father's coats and boots were gone, replaced with Jack's puffy neon coats, an Army jacket, Mother's faux fur. I walked into the living room in a fog. Glassy-eyed deer heads—gone. Rocks Father had collected and put on end tables, some still caked with dirt—gone.

On the fireplace mantel, an especially large hole where a stone had been, a grotesque boulder bigger than Father's foot. The rock was grey, blocky, ugly, hardened dirt wedged into fissures. I always thought he'd put it there to say, *See, the earth ain't pretty; it's ugly, monstrous. If you don't understand that, you don't understand nothin'. If you're looking for some pretty ramble through the countryside, go live in the city. We don't want you here.*

Now, the walls held department store art—paintings of exotic flowers and tropical fruit. The surfaces held knickknacks, coasters, and cheap plastic clocks.

It was Jack's kingdom now. It wasn't like Father was a bowl of cherries, but it felt like with his possessions gone, we were being yanked farther and farther from the soil.

I walked as if underwater down the stairs to the basement. The boat and trailer were gone, but I noticed that only in passing. I turned to the corner, his special corner, Meghan's special corner, and it was empty. Freshly scrubbed down, the concrete floor swept clean.

earth

Such emptiness. A massive extraction. Not a forest undergoing a natural disaster, but akin to a clear cutting. Not a death, but a black hole of nothingness. In a farm house in the middle of the middle, in a landlocked place, with muddy-bottomed rivers, we lost a story. We lost Father's legend. Jack or Mother or both burned his book.

I knew he was a mean father. I wasn't stupid. I knew he was a brute. But he was my father. Like me, the dirt was the blood in his veins. What happened when a person wasn't allowed to tell their side of things, because it was peculiar, crazy, or just too beaten up? What happened to the children, the ancestors, when they took one man's story? What would happen to Mother's story now? Meghan's story? To mine?

I thought of the Osage. What happened when a whole group of people weren't allowed their say? What happened when only the rich folks or the folks with education spoke up? What happened when we killed the story of even one man, neglected his truth just because he was nearly illiterate or just plain mean as a dog?

If nobody wanted to hear a poor man's story, a poor girl had no chance at all. A farm girl was expected to let them spoon-feed her story to her, and if she denied them, if she had her own wisdom, they beat her to a pulp.

I went upstairs to find Meghan. She was nowhere. She didn't come home that night, or the next. Or the next. Somehow in my mind, the extraction of Father from the house and Meghan's disappearance became intertwined, became all Jack's fault, as if Jack had extracted Meghan like another one of Father's messy leftovers.

I was running with Jason down dirt roads that looked like his painting. Simple. Lonely. Meghan had been gone a couple of months. It was Sunday. Jason had shown up at the back door asking for a race. I'd obliged.

He was keeping up with me, which bothered me. All the lack of food and the partying was taking its toll. But as I ran, as Jason and I matched our feet and our breath, I could feel the muscle memory deep inside. I could feel the strength down deep. The branches in autumn wind, the geese in flight, the cold smells worked together in some orchestral harmony.

We took a break and sat in the weeds at the edge of a field. Jason was so quiet. It looked like he was clenching his jaw to hold in the words, like he had something important to say.

"I'm glad you're back," he said.

"I wasn't gone," I said.

"Oh yes you were. You were nowhere to be found. Missing in action."

I plucked the grass, blade by blade.

He stood up, agitated. "I'm worried about you, Pearl. Really, really worried." He looked down at me. I saw real despair in his face. He seemed to be searching for something in my eyes.

"Run!" he yelled. He took off down the road. I got to my feet. "Goddamn it Pearl, run! I said run!" he yelled back at me.

I sprinted after him, but there was no way I'd catch him now. He thrust his body forward with all his might, fast, with a violence. I watched his blonde hair blow out like fire from the back of his head.

I hollered after him, "You're acting as if the world is going to end!"

He sped off hard and fast. I ran with everything in me, and I swore he slowed down so I could catch up.

Mother found Meghan three months after she went missing. Mother was up before dawn, opened the back door to get the milk. Meghan was passed out and leaning against it. The girl who wasn't her daughter splashed onto the linoleum like spilled milk.

I heard the noise and ran downstairs. Mother stood above Meghan. Mother and I looked down from a distance as Meghan tried to get off the floor, as she fell back again and again, drunk or drugged or both, out of her mind. Meghan's crushed face. Mother's crushed face.

We heard Jack moving around in the back bedroom. Mother leaned down and pulled Meghan by the arm off the floor. She handed the droopy package to me.

"I didn't sign up for this, Pearl." Those mesmer eyes. I fell into them. Nodded.

"Don't worry, I'll take care of her."

Mother deserved a normal life, didn't she? Didn't Mother deserve normal?

Jack opened the bedroom door. Mother rushed us to the living room. "I've done my time," she said in my ear. "You hear me? I've done my time." I pulled Meghan up the stairs, but not before Jack came into the living room and got an eyeful.

Before dawn every day, I'd wake up early to see if she was still in the bed. If she wasn't, I'd get up and go out hunting for her. I happened to have one of Father's crusted hunting coats in my closet when they cleared out all his stuff. I wore it over my pajamas.

Once I found her passed out in the cab of the orange truck. Another time I found her curled on the front doorstep, blood running from her ear. Another time, I found her back at Lady Luck's doghouse. I stared down at the two of them beneath the glow of a full moon for a long time. I guessed she'd squatted to pet the mutt. I guessed she'd fallen over in the dirt and passed out. Lady Luck leaned his fat belly up against her flesh. The two of them spooning. Lady Luck whimpered in a sort of otherworldly happiness. Meghan and that brutal snoring.

One time I couldn't find her. I came back to the bedroom just as the sun was rising. I opened the door, and she was sitting on the bed, just on the edge, like she was about to stand up. She stared at a spot on the floor. Her arms were bent, elbows on knees. Hands pulled into fists. She didn't move. I watched her for as long as I could bear. I stood and watched. She didn't shift once.

I thought of the Native woman and the bird again. I wanted to put my hands on her like before. I wanted so desperately to heal her.

I came in and sat beside her and didn't touch her. She put her face in her hands and rocked forward. She said in a deadpan voice, "What does it matter if Russell shows up?"

"Who? Who's Russell? Wait, the guy from St. Louis? The guy in your apartment? The guy in the car who was going to kill me? What are you talking about? Did you see him?" For the first time, I was really scared. For her. Of her. I looked around the room as if the creepy guy would pop out from the closet.

"What does it matter? They're all Russell. Every one of them is Russell."

I sat there a long while not touching her. Finally I got her into bed. I went to the bathroom, got a washrag, and once again cleaned off the bruise-like smudges from her swelled-up face.

Right foot, inhale, left foot, exhale. You've got to manage the anxiety or you can't run. If you start a long-distance run with your hands in fists, the tenseness radiates up your arms, enters your lungs, and you'll never get enough air to finish.

I preferred to run on dirt. I didn't like man-made surfaces. I liked the softness of the earth, the quirky unevenness of real soil, the potholes, the sudden inclines and declines. It was real. It made you focus.

I was running down the dirt road to the farm. Red berries marked blood drops against bark and snarl. Dawn fog, the pitter of dripping from crackling branches.

The coach used to say that I had this ability to take pain when I ran that most people couldn't take. He was right. As I ran, I'd feel the pain in joints or lungs, and I'd study it. Pain was just a sensation, right? I'd enter pain and study it, parse pain down to its components. In that way I managed it. In that way I kept running.

The farm wasn't that far, but I was getting so weak. The coach didn't have that much good to say anymore about me or my running.

These days, I had to divide up a mile, turn it into smaller blocks, make it through one block, and then run the next one like it was a whole new race. I had to cover my nipples with Band-Aids, or my breasts would bleed, because I was heavy-chested. Even skinny, they were big. I'd inherited Grandma Pearl's cleavage.

I'd missed too many cross country practices. Coach wouldn't let me run the meets. I had to find another way to run. I had to find a way to figure all this stuff out. When I ran, life seemed to fall back into its rightful place. Since Nadine's death, since Meghan's arrival, I worried that on this earth, there were things too big for running. That no matter how hard you worked, how carefully you paced yourself, no matter how you managed your breathing, no amount of running in the world could make what was happening fit into acceptable.

I made it to the farm, more out of breath than I had a right to be. I paced, panting and gasping, circling like a pained and chained-up dog. I picked up a long stick and poked around.

Overgrown weeds around the barn, whole sections of the roof missing. The coop was collapsing. Everything was so deadly quiet, long echoes across field and wood. The barbed-wire fence around the cow field had been trampled in a half-dozen places. I went to the garden, took the wire off the nail, entered. All overgrown and in disarray. I went and lay on my back on top of the dead plants and the soil.

My head filled with gritty soil. I felt myself sink deep. I was so tired. I could've rested there for years, for centuries. I could've lain full-bodied in the dirt for past, present and future. My whole body took in the fecund soil. I didn't know how long I lay this way—minutes, hours? It was like I was consuming the whole blessed earth. "I'm sorry. I'm sorry," I kept repeating. Deep in soul and gut, I just wanted every blade of grass to know that I was sorry.

I heard the sound of a car coming down the dirt road. The road only led to the farm. Who would be coming down here? Nobody ever came down here anymore.

I pulled myself limb by limb off the ground, lumbered into the forest and hid behind the burly base of an oak.

Car doors slammed, voices. Jack came into view. He wore pressed blue jeans, a puffy blue coat, glaring white Nikes. Another man was with him, a portly guy in a plaid coat. Despite the freezing weather, sweat poured from the chubby man's waxy face. He held a clipboard and took notes. He put the clipboard under his armpit, took out an Instamatic and took pictures.

"So the forest stretches back to the house?" the man with the clipboard asked.

"Yep. The acreage is on the deed." Jack leaned over, took the clipboard from beneath the guy's armpit, flipped through papers, showed him something. He pointed around the woods. "Some good trees here for harvesting."

"You'll have to demolish that shack back there and clear out some of the barbed-wire fencing, fix the barn up."

"No problemo," Jack said, leaning against a maple, his palm flat against the bark. "Can you believe Sarah held onto this place for so long? Sitting on a gold mine."

"Some folks got their own ideas, I guess," the guy said, making notes.

Jack took out a stark-white hankie and cleaned his palm of bark crumbs. "How long you think it'll all take to sell?"

"With the house and all this acreage attached? We got people from St. Louis and Kansas City snapping up agricultural land. Everybody wants a hobby farm. A parcel like this won't be on the market long."

"Don't do anything yet. Just get all the paperwork together. I'll let you know when it's time. I've got to get Sarah on board."

The man nodded. They went back to walk around the barn. I sat down at the base of the tree and waited.

earth

A young Native American man sat forlorn against the trunk next to me. It was a vision. I was in another place and another time. He clutched a bottle in a paper bag. He swayed drunkenly even as he sat. His hair was matted with forest debris. I looked at him. He was the Osage woman's son, all grown up. He looked up sideways with bloodshot eyes, slurred, "I ran from the reservation. I came here to remember. My name is Two Tree."

I said, "This is my farm. My name is Pearl."

He took a swig from the crumpled-up paper bag. His head wobbled on his shoulders like a dashboard dog, and he drooled on his dirty coat. He was young, in his twenties, but the skin on his hands looked like leather.

"I'm having daytime dreams again, because you are not there, but I hear you talk," he said.

I told him, "I'm in a vision too."

He said, "We're both in a dream now. Or we are both crazy. Or we are dreaming and we are crazy."

"The world is crazy. Maybe we're the sane ones."

He laughed and coughed and put his palm to his chest as he tried to breathe. He twitched his leathery hand over tattered trousers. "We sane people sure look like piles of shit." He coughed. "The world is a crazy dream."

I put my hand up in my hair and picked out sticks, rubbed clods of soil off my arm.

"Where are your mother and sister?" I asked.

"How would you know them?" He spoke so blurry I could barely understand.

"I met you all in a clearing not far from here—you were just kids. There was a bird with a broken wing and your sister was little. In a vision."

The Indian started to cry.

"Dead," he said. He held up his hands like a baby saying, *All gone. All gone.* He let the paper bag fall, and the bottle tipped over in the dirt, spewing liquid.

The rough slurp and puff of his breathing. I think he said, "Maybe they had to die. Maybe people like us could never live in such a place as this. Maybe we have to die and come back in the future when the people can tell themselves a different story."

I couldn't take the suck of despair again, and stood. "I'm sorry for you," I said.

He took a swig, looked at me from top to bottom. "I'm sorry for you, too."

chapter 17

TICKLE PINK CLENCHED between thighs. I was out cruising by myself. I had my own growing covey of boys, my own howlers. Not just Anthony, but Jude. Not just Jude, but Patrick. Not just Patrick, but…What did it matter? What did any of it matter?

I saw Bonnie's blue Caddy. She was idling at the McDonald's drive-through. She'd gained so much weight. She was obese. She was jelly welly, alright. In Bonnie's passenger seat sat Blake, face pulsing with acne.

She didn't see me watching her. My earlier life with Bonnie seemed like such a long time ago. I was so tired, so exhausted. I felt like I was losing my best friend. At school, the rumors were getting worse. I heard boys utter *slut*, mouth *whore* as I walked down the hall. I knew Bonnie must've heard the rumors. I knew.

Bonnie must've felt me looking, because she turned. I looked at her. We stared at each other a long time. Finally, she smiled.

I smiled back. I put up my hand. *How.* She put up her hand. *How, Pearl.* I smiled harder. *How, Bonnie, How.* She smiled big and hard. I wanted so desperately to run out of the truck, hop into the backseat of Bonnie's car. I wanted a game of Hangman. *How, Bonnie, How.* I wanted to fit letters into spaces to make words, and nothing more.

Somebody honked, and Bonnie had to move up.

In psych class with Jason. The teacher was Mrs. Friday. She never did anything to me, but I always sensed she had this deep dislike for me. I saw us as animals squaring off in a clearing. It was as if we were beasts in the forest, snarling and protecting our turf.

She was thin up top, heavy around the hips, wore black polyester bell bottoms and white sneakers.

She was always putting us to odd tasks, psychological tests. Once she had us draw names, told us to stand up and say the person's name and one kind word, an adjective, to describe the person. People were saying nice things to people they didn't even like. *Funny. Smart. Happy. Friendly.* I was dying for a compliment. I was desperate for a single kind word. I could survive on one compliment for years, horde and nurture it, let it fill me up. For years.

Kevin Stockman, football captain, held up his slip. "Pearl Swinton." I looked up at him hopefully, pleadingly. He was handsome but so dumb. He asked to borrow my history paper once so he could come up with some ideas, and copied it verbatim. He was that dumb. We were caught and of course the teacher knew I wasn't the one who cheated.

"Pearl is …" He paused for effect and scanned the class with his blonde movie-star handsomeness. "Different."

The class tittered. Mrs. Friday hadn't been paying attention and asked him to repeat it.

"Different," he yelled. "Pearl Swinton is different." The class went crazy. An explosion of energy. Desks thumped with fists in primal beat. *Different.* Thump. *Different.* Thump. *Different.* I stared straight ahead, dripping, red behind the eyes.

Today, in art class, we had mirrors and we were drawing our own faces. Jason was the best in the class. I was magnetized to his charcoal marks on white paper. It was like he was drawing his own soul. It was like he was exhaling light on the page. Watching him draw was how I felt lying on the earth, aligned with the tug and sway of popping bulbs, grounded with the yank and pull of roots.

Jason could feel me staring; he turned, smiled over his shoulder, but then his eyes grew wide and shocked. He saw it coming before I did. A cigar box full of charcoal sticks went flying as I arched. I felt like my flesh and bone were being shattered, thousands of multihued shards of me scattered in crimson, cobalt and gold, like a star bursting in some far-off galaxy.

I came to in the girls' bathroom, Jason behind me, his arms locked under my ribcage, my feet off the floor. His cheek was pressed against the back of my hair.

"I gotta sit," I croaked. He let go. I tumbled to the floor tiles. The visions were getting worse. The visions were coming more often. I was strung out from Meghan, from booze, from not eating, from the Anthonys, Judes and Patricks. I felt myself standing on the edge of some crevasse.

"That was so frickin' intense," Jason said, pacing, smearing his forehead with charcoal. "I grabbed you, yelled to Sister you were sick and that I had to get you to the bathroom before you puked. I carried you in front of me to block her view. You were like this rigid, petrified tree. Man, you're skinny. You got to eat *something*." He squatted, lifted my hair out of my face. "What was it this time?"

"Does it matter?" On the floor, a tampon lay on the tile, half-bloodied. I stared at it.

"Oh, it matters." He got up, paced. "It really matters. I mean you should be writing them down. Why'd they choose you if it wasn't important?" He looked down at me, squatted again, said quietly, "Listen, if anything at all in this world matters, those premonitions matter."

I groaned.

"They matter."

He kept playing with my hair. "I have a theory. Maybe the Osage woman is just trying to show you that there's another world than this one. Maybe all these visions are just trying to show you this other realm or reality or whatever."

"I think I'm losing it," I whispered. "I don't know how I can be like this and live like a normal person." Mother's words echoed in my head: *You got to be tough to survive. You can't live like this—you'll get crushed. Smashed right down.*

"Yeah, maybe you are going crazy." He said it almost absently. My head snapped up. He looked at me hard. "But maybe we all have to lose our minds to get to some other place of sanity. Maybe that's the only way." He twisted a strand of my hair around his finger. "Maybe these visions are saying there's another way of seeing the world. The way we're all seeing the world is not the right way. That how we're living is crazy right now! I'm not explaining it right."

I was trying to take in what he was saying when the bathroom door opened and Mrs. Friday said in her low voice, "Jason, get out of the girls' bathroom. Pearl, if you're throwing up, go see the nurse. Jason, back to class." He didn't move. "Now!"

I didn't go see the nurse. I kept my head down and tried to make it through the day.

But now the visions seemed to be happening every day.

The next day with Bonnie, at her locker, I felt myself flung upward like some storm-tossed tree. It was lunch break. Kids turned to stare. Again, I awoke in the girls' bathroom. Bonnie had plopped me on my back on the floor. She stood with her arms crossed, staring down.

"What's going on?" My jaw was so rigid I didn't even try to talk. "I mean it. I mean normally you scare me, but now you're really freaking me out. And I don't just mean the epileptic fit you just had."

I rolled sideways. The tampon was still there. *Will somebody please fucking clean this goddamn tampon off the floor!* Bonnie went into one of the stalls and sat on the toilet, didn't say a word, just held the space quiet and deep, while my body slowly and painfully uncoiled.

In the corridors, kids whispered. Kids giggled. Too many had witnessed what had happened in history, in art, and then at the lockers. Here and there someone would pass and murmur, "circus freak," "nutcase," "all of this for some mules."

It was the next week or the week after that, I couldn't be sure. Life was blurring into a jumble of sensations. I entered psych class and the vision hit on the way to my desk, in front of Mrs. Friday, in front of the entire class. I came to and fell hard to the floor. Some students ran up, stared from above. Mrs. Friday sent one of the kids to get the nurse. When Nurse Kathy came, I let my head loll against her. In my family, you never touched and you never got touched, unless it was being slapped. The feel of Nurse Kathy's flesh against me was like water to a person dying in the desert. She reminded me of the Osage woman touching the bird with the light. There was some of that light in her. I cradled myself against her armpit.

As we maneuvered across the classroom, Mrs. Friday clapped so loudly as we passed her that both of us jumped. "OK everybody, let's get back to normal," Mrs. Friday screamed and clapped. "Everybody back to your desks. Let's try to have a normal class today, OK?" If she used the word normal one more time, I was going to smack her.

In the nurse's office, I curled up on the cot while Nurse Kathy called Mother.

She showed up right away wearing a skirt and new lace-up sandals. The nurse told her what happened. She looked at me so heavy, like I was a weight around her ankles that would pull her under, drown any hope she had of normal.

She sat down in a plastic chair looking defeated. When she was nervous, she'd open and close the metal latch on her handbag. Receipts, tissues, and rubber bands would explode outward, and she'd smash them down and shut the purse again. Open, explode, smash, shut. Open, explode, smash, shut.

The sun came through the window and highlighted Nurse Kathy's dishwater hair. She must've recently gotten a perm, because her hair was wilder and bigger around her head. With that good-hearted look in her eyes as she stared at Mother, I thought, *Maybe someone like her could be a woman I could look up to.*

She sat down and said softly to Mother's downturned face, "Let's just start with another physical. Take her to a doctor at the hospital. We'll get to the bottom of all this." She started to put her hand on Mother's shoulder but sensed Mother didn't like to be touched and stopped herself.

Mrs. Friday popped her head in. "Just wanted to check on our little patient." She came in and looked me over, smiled, but it degenerated into a snarl. I must've looked like some wounded animal—so skinny, lifeless, purple below the eyes. She put her hand on her ample hip. "I hope you're sending her for a psych eval."

Mother flicked and re-flicked the purse latch rapidly. Nurse Kathy paused. "We like to start with a physical. See if it's not some kind of physical problem."

Mrs. Friday turned. "Mrs. Swinton, you got to get this girl to a psychiatrist. This is something serious." Mother hunched. She wasn't good with women like Mrs. Friday, women with an education. "The girl has some kind of disturbance."

I didn't say, *My disturbance is with people like you. Adults who think they got it all figured out and destroy everything that doesn't fit in their box.* Nothing terrified me more than to be defined by someone like Mrs. Friday, with all her dime-store, one-sided high school psychology.

Mrs. Friday stood over the nurse and made sure she wrote a note for a psychological evaluation. Mother sunk far down into herself. Like with Nadine, I felt I could put my hand down into her to pull her back up, and no matter how deep I reached, I wouldn't be able to find her.

Mother seemed to be putting off the psych eval. One week passed. Two. She never mentioned it. I spent much more time in the kitchen.

Baking. Two sticks margarine. One cup white sugar. A cup brown. A tablespoon of vanilla. Two cups oats. A bag of chocolate chips. I was making cookies. I was baking up a batch. Two batches. Three. I was obsessive. I still would not eat, but I baked. I sifted and mixed. I measured. I would disappear off the face of the earth.

I had to lean against the counter because I was tired from not eating. I dragged a chair over from the dining table so that between whipping the butter and mixing the egg, I could sit and catch my breath. Sometimes I went three whole days without eating. When I did eat, I took in only the smallest amount.

Mother came in the back door. She put two paper grocery bags on the counter. She looked at me. She looked at my body. She looked at me as if she hadn't seen me in years. I saw fear in her eyes. She came over, took my arm in both hands—it was a long, thin toothpick in her hard-knuckled grasp. She looked down at my knobby knees poking out beneath my shorts.

"You're killing yourself," she said more to herself than me; she looked around the kitchen madly. She stared at the mixing spoon I held in my hand. It was covered in cookie dough. She grabbed my wrist, held the spoon to my mouth.

"Lick the spoon," she screamed, her eyes wide and spinning like saucers. I looked with horror at the goo-covered wooden spoon, like it was a foreign thing somebody had picked up off the ground. It was more than I would eat in an entire day.

"Lick the spoon," she repeated. I tried to pull the spoon out of her grip. She pulled back. I held on. She pulled me upward from my sitting position. We struggled across the linoleum, daughter and mother in a terrible slow dance on the fresh-mopped floor. The smell of vanilla and lemon cleaner. I was so weak. I let go. She held the spoon at my mouth. She put a hand behind my head.

"Lick the spoon, Pearl." I turned my head this way and that. A smudge of batter landed on my lower lip. "Lick the spoon!"

"I can't!" I twisted away from her. "I can't," I sobbed. I ran from the kitchen, up the stairs to my room, curled into a ball in the corner on the hardwood. Mother came up to my bedroom and stood in the hall and talked through the door.

"Pearl, just come with me to see a priest. Something's wrong. Just come to confession. That's all I ask. Will you do that for me?"

I guess Mother thought I was more sinful than crazy.

The priest was young, maybe twenty-five, with a bald spot and milky white hands. Fresh little girl hands. No grease stains on the fingertips, no grime beneath the fingernails.

I sat across from him in a metal chair in the back room at Holy Cross Church.

The room was bare and white, uncomfortably hot. A rectangular window at the top of the wall glared into the room from halfway up. My head throbbed. The priest said the blessing under his breath. I scooted my chair, and the legs barked a hollow grunt against the concrete floor.

"It's hot as hell in here," I said and laughed, coughed, rubbed a palm over my forehead.

"In the name of the Father, and of the Son and of the Holy Spirit." He crossed himself, kept his eyes low.

"Bless me, Father, for I have sinned; my last confession was four years ago."

He stared at his hands. The stream of light rained a diffuse glare, like a white-out in a snowstorm. I felt sick. I leaned forward and put my elbows on my knees.

"I blew this guy in his truck," I said to the priest. It just came out. I couldn't control it. Sexual vomit. The young father kept his head down. I didn't really have that much sexual experience, but for some reason, I wanted to see this guy squirm, see if he could handle reality in his sugar-coated lie. "This other guy liked me blowing him while he was driving. Miles like that."

I went on, giving details, being as explicit as I could. I kept going. I couldn't stop. I regurgitated sex upon the young priest's head.

When I finished, when I had nothing filthy left in me, he whispered, still studying his hands, "Are there any other sins you want to confess?"

"Oh yeah," I said, leaning toward the top of his lowered head. "Sure. One more thing. I wish I was dead." Sweat dripped in my eyes, and I swiped at it. "That's a sin right?"

The priest slipped off his chair, knelt in front of me, took my hands. I straightened, rigid in the chair. Fine hairs grew from his bald spot. His thin shoulders moved beneath his vestments. I thought of Jason. Something about the sensitivity of his shoulders, the way he would spread himself open at your feet. I strained back.

He put his face to the back of my hands. He cried, and the moisture lit onto my skin. I scooted the chair, tugged at my hands to get them away. I grabbed my jacket off the chair. The priest still knelt on the floor.

"God, the father of mercies, through the death and resurrection of his son, has reconciled the world to himself and sent the Holy Spirit among us for the forgiveness of sins." He sat back on his haunches, his eyes closed, his hands folded. I ran around the partition toward the door. "Through the ministry of the church may God give you pardon and peace."

After the white glare of the confessional, the church was as dark as a cave. I couldn't see. I roamed the aisles like a blind girl looking for Mother, tripping and steadying myself. There were fewer than a dozen people in the pews, but still I couldn't find her. I was nearly desperate when I finally saw her kneeling in one of the back pews.

I lowered myself onto the wooden seat and stared at her back. Her handbag was on the pew, bloated as if it were ready to explode. A tissue was tangled in the clasp. I could see the side of her face and her lips moving in silent prayer. I reached out to touch her. My fingertips brushed polyester. I wanted to connect. Just one moment of connection.

Her mouth moved soundlessly. I read her lips. She was trying to figure out what to do with me. She was praying to God for some guidance on what to do with her crazy daughter. She was silently screaming to the stained glass windows, "I want my daughter back." I swear, she was saying, "I want my daughter back. You get my daughter back here."

Finally, a week or so later, Mother took me to the hospital for the psych eval. They probed and prodded. They picked and delved. I told them about the visions. What did I have to lose? They gave us a diagnosis. Something about anxiety. Something about a personality disorder. The word psychosis came up. I heard the phrase *anorexia nervosa*. I grew foggy with all the details.

I started seeing a therapist. She looked like a nun. She wore the same type of outfit every session: a buttoned-down blouse, a stern skirt, rational shoes. A yawning, etched frown. Her office was next to the hospital. Cork ceiling tiles, metal shelving, a handful of medical books stretching sideways, industrial carpet, slatted window blinds, an absence of anything that could be called light or life or joy.

I knew something had to be done about the visions. I knew I had to figure out how to eat food and not gag on every morsel as if someone were poisoning me. I knew if I was going to survive, I'd have to find my way back to what the crazy world I lived in called *normal*.

I was out cruising in the orange truck. Meghan had been missing again for more than a month. I stopped looking for her. I had my orange bottle of prescription pills. I popped one. From a paper cup, I was drinking Jack and Coke. I pulled into the McDonald's and stumbled in to use the restroom. I was so out of balance, I almost knocked a girl over on my way to the stall.

I stumbled outside. I didn't think I'd drunk that much but couldn't seem to function. I found myself outside in the parking lot. In front of me was Anthony's truck, and leaning against his driver's window was Meghan. I wove my way up to them.

Meghan's boobs were pressed against the metal of his driver-side door. She was arching her back, looking up at him. She pulsed with promise. Feeling ugly and awkward and dizzy, I opened my mouth to say something. Thought I did, but nobody paid any attention. I tried to focus on Anthony's face, but it jiggled and stuttered. For some reason, I was holding my pill bottle. The cap was off. Had I taken another one? Meghan reached over, put a finger in, chipped black nail polish, helped herself to two pills. She swallowed one, held the other up to Anthony.

"Why don't you girls jump into the truck, and we can go find a place to party properly," Anthony said. I reached over and held onto Meghan's wrist, felt I was falling off some cliff.

"Whoa there," Anthony said. Meghan pulled her wrist away, laughed, and ran around to the other side of the truck and got in.

He said, "You coming?"

I shook my head. I watched them drive off. I seemed to lose all track of myself, went into some liquid fugue where time warped, where a minute seemed like an hour, and hours like seconds. When I finally came awake, I found myself sitting in the orange truck. I was using makeup now, and my eyes were bleeding black in the rearview mirror. I found a napkin on the floor, used the bottle of Jack to clean my cheeks. I started the truck. I just needed to get home. Or maybe I could make it down the rutted road to the farm. I just needed to feel the earth again.

It was a long drive down rural roads. My head kept bobbing. The landscape danced. Streetlights streaked into moon, streaked into stars, streaked into electrical currents, spilled into colored lines across the night sky. The lines met in small flashes, like shooting stars. Even trees and farm houses pulsed a subtle light. Light filled the windshield. The great white light grew in volume and vigor.

Then something hit me. There was an awesome crunching, a smashing of metal, a spinning, a crushing, a thumping, a white-hot scream.

Then nothing.

chapter 18

I OPENED MY eyes. A room in white glow. Nadine and the Native woman hovered above my bed in multihued glory. I reached to them, but my fingers floated in air.

Blackness.

Jason glittered blue. I moved my mouth to smile, to speak.

Blackness.

Mother like a flash of red flame, a sudden spark. I tried to say, "Mother?" but no words came. I swore I heard her singing "Amazing Grace," her voice hoarse and off-key.

Blackness.

Meghan stood looking down at me as if she were floating near the ceiling. She spoke, but her words were garbled. Her syllables grew into puzzles in my brain, formulas I could not decipher.

Blackness.

"You're awake," Mother said in view, but then she was quickly gone. I tried to move my head to follow her across the room, but couldn't. Pain coursed from foot to fingernail.

"You broke your left arm." She came over and held a hand mirror to my face. "Sprained your right ankle. You got two black eyes." Purple bruises with yellow edges spread across the top of my face. I could see a massive bruise on my chest. "Some of your ribs got smashed. There's internal damage." She took the mirror away.

earth

She was there and not there as I passed out and woke again and again. At one point, she was holding my hand. She never held my hand. Her glowing face was close to mine.

"What happened? You used to be such a good girl." That pain in her eyes, that inward glance that went so far down. "You got to do better. I need you to do better."

Time warped. Nurses, doctors, poking, prodding. Bandages, blood, bedpans. IVs, injections, interns. Cherry Jell-O on green plastic platters.

Jack came with Mother. He held a file with my name on it—not a hospital file, but one he'd made himself. The story of my life written in bits of paper collected by the likes of Jack. Mother started folding some piece of cloth up, a towel or a robe I couldn't tell, folding and refolding, her knuckles moving fast and the corners fitting perfectly. She didn't look at me, said, "We got some news."

"Meghan?" I whispered. She hadn't been around. I was wondering if she was alright.

Mother glanced up, gave me a hard look, shook her head in exasperation, went back to her folding. "Jack talked to your therapist. She says you're a danger to yourself, and they got to keep you for observation. After you're healed up, they're moving you to the psych ward here at St. John's."

I knew Jack couldn't sign the papers to get me committed. We weren't related. I knew Mother had to do that. I started weeping. I tried to reach up to my face, but it hurt too bad.

"Don't cry to me," Mother said, flicking and turning the cloth she was folding. *You made your bed, now sleep in it.* All her life Mother had been put to work cleaning up other people's messes. "Count yourself lucky that you only hit a tree and didn't kill anybody else."

Jack pulled up a chair beside my head. His fit body, my bruised one. His energy sent me on a painful slow scoot toward the other side of the bed.

"Look, it's not so bad. They got a good operation here." He held the folder out and put his finger on a sheet of paper. "Look what they got to offer here: individual therapy, group therapy, occupational therapy."

My eyes caught a brochure clipped to the folder cover. *Fulton State Hospital.* Nadine's Fulton. *The* Fulton. The funny farm. The loony bin. I couldn't take my eyes off that brochure. A psych ward at this hospital was one thing, but Fulton was a whole other beast altogether. What was that brochure doing in the folder with my name on it, in the story Jack had created of my life? He kept reading the services at St. John's. I kept staring at that brochure. *Fulton: The oldest public mental health facility west of the Mississippi.* Four concrete half-columns framed a long sidewalk, a blocky building in the far-off distance. A snowless winter picture, limbs and branches bare, narrow, reaching out to nothing.

"They can even do some trial and error on your medications."

"Like a military base but a lot more fun," I said.

His face swelled red. He shut the folder, scooted his chair back.

Mother said, "You need to be grateful for what Jack's doing for you here. Most men would wash their hands of you."

I awoke to the bluest sky you've ever seen. A shimmering, a cobalt, a rosy billow. I felt myself float up from the bed, up and up, losing myself in that sky.

"I've never seen anyone sleep so long." It was Jason. He was holding a canvas over my bed. It was a painting of the bluest sky I'd ever witnessed, wispy white clouds gliding forward as if by a blissful wind.

"How long you been holding it like that?"

"Too long." He put the canvas on top of the table in the corner so that it was easy to see from the bed. "It's yours. Make sure you take it home with you."

"Home," I said.

He sat on the edge of the bed. "How you feelin'?"

"Like a train wreck."

"You look gorgeous."

I started laughing. The purple bruises on my face were now yellow and green. I looked like an emaciated Hulk. "Oh man, don't make me laugh; it hurts my face."

I kept staring at his painting. He followed my eyes, said, "When you get better, I want to take you there. I'll show you the sky like you've never seen it before."

I moved my head to the side. "They're moving me to the psych ward. I'm not going home."

His face grew dark as a storm cloud. He pulled up a chair and sat and held my one hand in both of his. For once, I didn't pull back. "Listen, I know you can figure this out. If anyone can figure this out, you can."

"Do you think I'm crazy?" I clenched his fingers so hard he grimaced.

"I don't think your visions are crazy. I think you got a lot to be upset about. Maybe it's a mixture? Maybe because you have this special way of seeing you have to figure out how to manage it all. Just don't check out on me, OK?"

I stared at the wall. I felt bloated with rage or grief or both.

"You need some kind of miracle," he said low and depressed.

I said bitterly, "Did the Osage get a miracle?" I looked back at him. He looked hopeless.

I said more softly, thinking again that Jason had his own troubles, "I guess the whole world needs some kind of miracle."

Jason said, "That's what I'm trying to say about the visions. Maybe there's some miracle in those visions of yours."

I could see why Jack loved St. John's psych ward. So many regulations, life scheduled to the second. Wake at seven a.m. Drugs at noon and eight p.m. Therapy, therapy, therapy.

The hospital used to be run by the Catholic Church, and there were still plenty of nuns around. The nuns and nurses walked bent with tiredness. The whole place was dingy. Scratched wall paint, floors raw with bald spots. On the windows, something black that wouldn't even come off if you scraped it with your fingernail. Plastic chairs around plastic tables in the rec room. All around the feeling of too many crazies, not enough money. The sounds of the ward were a shuffle, a grind, a chomp, a snivel. A slumping, a screaming, a subduing.

Fifteen people on the ward. A Native American guy about Jack's age. Scars on his face like cracked dirt on a dry river bed. I saw him mostly in crafts. When we made dream catchers, I thought it would insult him, but instead he took to it. After that, he sat around all day in the rec room twisting circles, threading string and wire into tight webs. Twisting, tying, meshing. Intricate stories told in thin wires. Stacks of the dream catchers piled up and up. Once I came up to him, tried to talk to him. He turned and barked, scared me to my bones. After that, I steered clear.

Later, after he watched me for a while, he came up and handed me one of the dream catchers. It had a tiny soft blue feather and blue beads and was so light I could barely feel it in the palm of my hand. I hung it above my metal-framed bed. After that, I swore the native guy was not just watching me, but watching out for me.

Some middle-aged white guy kept saying he was going to kill President Reagan. He was the only one who smoked my brand, so I had to listen to his stories of Reagan as the Antichrist for hours on end to be able to bum smokes.

There was a nympho on the ward, a teenage girl who'd stand by the window at night, hum under her breath and do a striptease. She'd strip to whoever was supposed to be standing outside that tall window. As far as I could tell, it was just a parking lot and a line of birches. Every other night, she'd come up to that window and do her striptease. I'd stand half-hidden with Reagan's assassin, smoking and watching her. The nurses would run up, grab her clothes off the floor, try to cover her up.

earth

It turned winter. They kept the thermostat on the ward at 55°. A nun with bottle glasses brought out the lost-and-found box and let us dig into it for whatever we could find to keep warm. I found a striped Rasta hat, orange fingerless gloves, a high school letterman's jacket without the letter.

Like Nadine, the pills sent my visions to the dream world, twisted them into nightmares. Dreams of the other inmates, earthquakes grumbling up the soil; each one of the people I met on the ward became tree, hill, river. Each shuddered like tectonic plates smashing into each other below the earth's surface. Each splintered and exploded into a thousand pieces.

All my life, I had issues with picking up other people's energies. Their vibes entered me, vibrated me, stayed inside me, until I couldn't tell what was me and what was them. I could just barely manage such forces in the real world, around people who were thought of as ordinary. It'd been worse with Father, of course, because nobody could call him normal. On the psych ward, there was no way to get away and go to a clearing to decompress, and the currents veered and ricocheted in all directions, landed in my shoulder, heart, womb, lodged there. On the ward, my whole body became the vibrations of other people's madness. How could being around other people's craziness possibly heal me?

The medications made me edgy and groggy, high-strung and sleepy at the same time. I shuffled and held onto the walls and couldn't seem to sit.

Of all the people, two obsessed me. One was an anorexic in her twenties, nothing but angled bones and elbows from beneath hospital sheets. She looked more like a cardboard cutout than a real person. Every day, a woman visited her to talk about eating. She'd try to coax her to take a bite. Grilled cheese. French onion soup. Mango sherbet.

My therapist told me, to scare me, that if this anorexic girl didn't eat soon, they were taking her someplace to force feed her, or worse. She didn't have to say "electroshock"; I knew what she meant. The threat of it was all around us all the time. Fulton. Pulsing behind every threat, every plea, every breakdown, was the echoing refrain. Fulton. Fulton. Fulton.

I swore I could hear a wail rise up from the anorexic's room. The coaxing woman sounded small and humming, like a fan blowing inadequate air into a boiling hot space. Above and beyond was that wretched high-pitched wail. The anorexic scared me to death. I couldn't seem to stay away. I'd hover at her door and stare in.

Across the ward was the water-head baby. Her head was ten times the size of her body. Hydrocephalus. Inflammation of the brain. We'd had some relatives who'd had water-head babies, but they all died as infants. I was told this girl was in her twenties. The rumor around the ward was that she was left at the hospital when it was run by nuns, and they took her in, and she'd been here all her life.

Her room was across from the nurse's station and right next to the padded cell where they put the real crazies. I'd shuffle by the water-head baby's room and stare in. The nun with the bottle-thick glasses would be inside spoon-feeding her. Below the head was a tiny, frail body.

The nun had seen me watching. One day, she said, "Have you met Lulu? Come on up. Introduce yourself. Don't be shy. She won't bite. Promise not to bite her, Lulu!" The old nun giggled.

I'd never talked to the old nun. I didn't much like nuns. I'd had my fill of them at Holy Cross and then at St. Francis. They were almost as bad as Father, as Jack, with their hatred of anything different, anything they couldn't understand.

Still, I felt pulled forward. I came up and stood beside her.

"Lulu has lived her whole life here. Haven't you, Lulu?" The nun used the spoon to scoop the dribble off Lulu's balloon-stretched cheek. "Twenty years ago, someone left this miracle on our doorstep." She offered me the bowl and spoon. "You want to feed her?"

I looked at her with horror but took the bowl anyway. Water-head baby seemed to be mentally retarded and unable to speak or hear. The nun stood to give me her chair. She was a full head shorter than me, had cartoon facial features, bug eyes, globular nose, pouty lips. Her lower teeth were a crooked mess, and she spoke with a lisp. She played Monopoly a lot with the Native American dream catcher guy. The energy of her, though, reminded me of Nurse Kathy, like you just wanted to stay there and lean against her a while.

"I'm Sister Alice," she said.

"Pearl." I nodded nervously, sat down, and started spooning pudding into Lulu's mouth.

"Lulu, this here is Pearl. We're going to get Pearl to feed you dinner from now on. You'll like that, right?" Feed her every night? My hand shook, and a glob of pudding fell from her mouth to the sheets, left a brown mark like poo there.

I didn't want to do it, but despite myself I found that every evening at dinner, I made my way across the ward to Lulu's room. I spoon-fed her tapioca, pea soup, cream of mushroom. I talked to her, too. I couldn't talk to the therapist, but it all flowed out with Lulu. I found Sister Alice standing at the door listening sometimes, and still I talked and talked. I told my whole story to Lulu that way.

I learned to stop asking about Meghan. Every time I mentioned her name, inquired how she was doing, everyone got tight-lipped. I asked the shrink where she was, if she was OK, and she gave me a hard look. I'd told her all about Meghan, of course. Even Sister Alice looked upset when I cornered her to see if she had any information on Meghan. Finally, I gave up asking.

The anorexic disappeared for a few days. There was such a holding of breath around her disappearance that I knew something bad was happening. Some of us were watching *Bewitched* when they brought her back in. She was in a wheelchair and her head teetered. The wail was gone. It was the missing wrench of her that worried me the most. That missing wail would truly be the death of her, I thought. I stood up. I felt like someone should do something, say something, go up and offer her something. If this was the anorexic's home, then we were her family, and we needed to at least greet her.

The moment I was on my feet, the energy hit me like a shock wave. I cried out with it. It'd been months. I thought the medication had forced them down into my dreams. I was so damned tired. My body arched, my head flew back. I stood on tiptoe.

Hail, fire, oceans destroyed, rivers poisoned, skies darkened, whole hemispheres lost beneath water, scorched land. The world as we knew it was coming to a bitter end right before my eyes, right behind my eyes. With every revelation my body convulsed. Never had a vision been so rapid-firing or felt so physical. The vision lasted for seconds or hours. I couldn't know. I couldn't tell. I stood on tiptoe as wave after wave wracked my body for all to see.

I folded hopeless, helpless to the couch. Sister Alice was there, her arms around me. I looked into her face, and she looked down at me with awe. Her eyes glowed iridescent light. I lifted my hand to touch her cheek. She was so beautiful, so gorgeous. Before I could reach her flesh, two of the orderlies wrenched me away, stuck something in my mouth, threw a white jacket over my front, tied it so my arms crossed my body.

"Be gentle," I heard Sister Alice say. "Oh, you misunderstand. Oh, there's no need …"

One picked me up and carried me. He brought me to the padded room and put me on the floor. I lay on my side in the straightjacket. I heard the eyehole open and close several times. Hugging myself against my will, I fell into an exhausted sleep.

I awoke to Sister Alice untying the jacket. She was visibly upset. Her hands shook. We both knew that the padded room was only good for one thing: bringing you closer to a stay at Fulton.

I sat against the wall, stared at her. Her eyes bugged out so much that her eyelids brushed against the inside of her thick glasses. She had a perpetual blink because of it, and sometimes she'd hold her eyes wide open, which made her look confused or shocked. Curly grey hair escaped from the edges of her habit. On her feet were flat sneakers like Mother used to wear. She still had that shimmer of a glow I'd seen right after the vision.

She said shyly, "I brought you something." She handed me a book. "I had to get permission to bring it in here, but I convinced them you couldn't hurt yourself or anyone else with it." The cover was a brown paper bag. In grade school and high school, we were required to make book sleeves for all of our textbooks out of brown paper grocery sacks. Sister Alice had covered the book in the same way. She stood me up. I was wobbly.

"I got you a get out of prison free card," she said. "I called in a favor. You get to go back to your room at the end of the day. They're insisting they need to watch you for a few more hours." She tapped the book, said quietly, "Read it, but let's keep this just between us."

There was a single bed in the room. I went over to it, sat and opened the book. It was about Saint Teresa. I was so sick of the whole Catholic religion. I put it to the side after just a couple of pages and fell into a dreamless sleep.

Back in my room the next day, I opened the book again. Teresa was a nun in the Italian Church in the 1800s. Not far in, I realized why Sister Alice gave me the book. Teresa had visions. I sat up hard and straight on the edge of the bed and cradled the book in my lap. I couldn't believe what I was reading. She was a Catholic mystic. It was the first time I'd heard those two words put together: Catholic and mystic.

She saw Christ's ravishing hands, then she saw his face. There were other visions, some in flavor close to mine.

There was a story of how it was her turn to cook. How it was taking her such a long time, one of the other nuns came to look. She stood at the stove, hand clenched around the ladle, head thrown back. She was having one of her "ecstasies." I couldn't imagine calling what I had an ecstasy, but when I read it I laughed so loud, dream catcher guy came to my doorway to make sure I was OK.

Some people believed her visions were from the devil, and for a while she thought so too, and flagellated herself trying to get the devil out of her. I understood. I knew how to beat myself up. I was as good as anyone at hitting myself with sticks and stones and hating thoughts. Teresa wrote she was more afraid of people who were scared of the devil than she was scared of the devil himself.

For the rest of the night, I devoured that book. I inhaled, feasted, gorged. I hadn't read anything like it since *Black Elk Speaks*.

The nurse who did rounds tried to get me to go to bed, but she looked at my fierce eyes and backed off like a mouse.

In the morning, I grabbed the book and ran to find Sister Alice. I was about to turn a corner when I heard her talking. I heard my therapist's voice. I stopped to listen. Their voices were strained, rough, angry.

"How could you think that was a good idea, Sister? A book like that will just end up confusing her."

"What can possibly be confusing about a book about a saint?" Sister Alice asked.

"You know what I'm talking about. You fill her head with grandiose ideas. She'll think she's some kind of saint with special powers. She won't focus on getting better."

"You know how I feel about all this," Sister Alice said. "You can't just define everyone as sick. Not everything is sick. The soul has its messages. Sometimes those messages don't come out in a nice, cleaned-up package."

"Some people have obvious psychological illness. Even you must be able to see that. Anyway, I need you to stay out of this. You're not a therapist. You shouldn't be interfering in this."

"No, you're right. I'm not a therapist. I'm a nun." Sister Alice said it strong and clear, with surprising pride. "I'm a woman of God."

"You'll make it worse."

"I'm not the one making things worse."

chapter 19

AT CHRISTMAS ON St. John's psych ward they fed us processed turkey loaf and boxed potatoes.

The Saturday after Christmas, Jack and Mother came for a visit. I sat most of the morning in the game room in my fingerless gloves, Rasta hat and letterless letterman's jacket waiting for them.

Mother wore a pair of fancy leather boots. She'd wrapped up a couple of black notebooks for me and handed me a tub of Christmas cookies that looked like stars and ornaments and trees, symbols of a fairy-tale life.

"Pearl, your hair looks real nice. Real clean," Mother said. Something was strange about her. Something was different. She didn't look well. She looked green around the gills.

Jack said, "Real clean-cut. Good for you." On the table in front of us was his Pearl file. It was so cold in the room that they'd kept their coats on.

"I hope you'll keep working real hard," Mother said, her breath coming out in a puff in the cold room. "Dr. Gold says you're doing OK. You look better."

Ever since that book on St. Teresa, I felt better. Stronger. For the first time, I felt maybe there wasn't something wrong with me, maybe the way I saw things wasn't completely wrong. I was talking a lot to Sister Alice about it, informal chats that were better for me than the therapy.

earth

"Dr. Gold says you're strong enough for her to take the therapy to the next level. If you listen to her real close, I bet you'll be home by Easter."

She looked at Jack and, like she'd been waiting to say it all along and was just talking to me to be polite, blurted, "We got something important to tell you."

I saw Sister Alice staring at me from across the room. I smiled at her, and Mother thought it was for her and smiled back at me and even reached for my hand.

"Jack and I got married." She put her other hand on Jack's, and I saw the ring. He smiled like a little boy. I looked at his buffed fingernails. I wanted to stab a fork in the back of his hand.

"We kept it real simple. Only a dozen people were there. I have some pictures." She reached into her crazy nest of a purse, took out an envelope of 3x5s, scooted them across the table. I ignored them.

"Did you put the house and farm up for sale?" A rage as big as an ice storm welled up. I gave Jack a frigid look. He clenched up hard, like he was ready for a fight.

Mother wiggled in her chair. "How'd you know? We're looking for a place in town. We go driving around on Sundays after Mass."

"What about Lady Luck?" I screamed. I saw the orderlies stand.

Mother looked confused. "Lady Luck? That old dog?" She looked from me to Jack.

"What's happening to Lady Luck when you move?" I screamed at Jack. I was out of my mind with rage. For some reason all I could think about was that tied-up mutt in the back yard. The orderly headed toward us. "I need to know what's going to happen to our family dog."

"Oh, grow up," Jack said with disgust. He half-stood up, hands resting on the table. Mother put her hand on his arm to calm him. "No, Sarah, that's enough. You can't coddle your daughter anymore. She's sick. She's got to hear a few home truths."

"What would you know about truth?" I spat.

He had fire in his twitching too-large eye. "You think that dog, that two-bit piece of shit land you called a farm are so damned special. You think you're something special because your daddy knew how to gut a deer? Or you think you're so special because you see crazy shit that doesn't even exist. You got no idea what I'm doing for you and your mother here. You got no idea how hard I'm working to give you and your mother a proper life."

I snorted. He pointed a finger in my face. "You got some fantasy about life, about that two-bit farm. Even compared to other farms around here, it's nothing but a scrubby piece of shit. This is the real world. Try fucking living in it."

I felt the last of the ground beneath my feet ripped away. I felt the groundlessness of all of the residents on the psych ward, the homelessness of their souls, swell up and fill my head to bursting. I screamed, "What is it you want from me?" *From all of us? What do people like you want?*

"Respect." He looked at Mother, said clear and straight, "Respect."

I snorted. I felt like pulling a knife and gutting him. I felt like nicking him from crotch to throat and pulling out his innards. I lunged, shoving the table into Mother. Jack grunted low and profound, shoved it back with a force that sent me and my chair flying. The other residents started screaming high-pitched, crazy whines. I scrambled up, circled the table and threw myself, both fists flying at Jack's head.

"You—*smack*—fucking—*smack*—thief!" I yelled as I hit him in the head. "You take, you take and you take. You turn trees into merchandise. How do you expect any fucking person to survive in your fucked-up world? Nobody can be sane in your screwed-up, arrogant world." My fist caught nose, eye, lip, temple.

He tried to push my hands back, but I kept at him. I saw the native guy out of the corner of my eye coming toward us.

"I'm not the one who's fucked up," he yelled. He gripped my upper arms, lifted me off him and pinned me to the floor. Not Jack, Father. Not Father, Anthony. I was losing touch with reality. Jack's face morphed into every man I'd ever known. I flung fists against flesh and tissue. Jack/Father/Anthony/Russell slapped me. Father was screaming down at me. Not Father, Jack. Not Jack, Anthony.

Somebody grabbed my shoulders, pulled me backward. The native guy wrapped his beefy arms around Jack. An orderly behind him was trying to pull him off. Jack had a bloody lip, a mark on his left cheek. His nose was oozing blood. He looked helpless and confused. He said, "This can't happen again." He swiped blood from his face to the back of his hand. He tried to put his arm around Mother, but she looked sick. He said to her, "I'm not this man. Sarah, I'm not this person. She's making me look bad. You can see that, right?"

The orderly lifted me off my feet, backed me out of the room. Mother was bent over holding her stomach. When she did look up, she stared at me with a low, fallen face, a goodbye face, a face that said I was dangerous and she could not trust me ever again, a look that gave me one of the worst hollowed-out feelings I'd ever known.

They tied me to a bed in the padded room. Three-point restraints, one leg free. They allowed a free limb to keep you from losing circulation. I'd asked once when I saw Reagan's assassin in here. They put him in the padded room at least once a week. He'd go in full of spit, ready to take down a president, and come out looking like a zombie. The bed had a moveable side, like a baby's crib. I tried to move my arms, but the straps were too tight. An hour passed. Two. Three. Four. A nurse came in to feed me, but I spat the food down my chin. She left after thirty minutes of trying. Every once in a while a pair of eyes would appear in a slot on the door.

The next morning, the nurse opened the door with the breakfast, and someone at the desk said, "I heard they're moving her to Fulton." The nurse tried to feed me. I kept moving my head, and the spoon kept hitting my chin.

"Why're they sending me to Fulton?" I asked, straining up against the leather ties.

"You've gone from being a danger to yourself to a danger to others," she said in monotone, like a robot. I screamed for her to get out. I screamed and hollered until she had no choice but to leave.

A rage grew to a hot red fist in my gut. I bellowed. I cursed. I dropped my free foot to the floor and used it to rock the flimsy bed. The padding cushioned all sound, which made me more enraged. I put all my disgust into that free foot. Adrenalin rushed as I heaved myself into a shaky standing position, mattress and bed frame coming to a standing position with me, the heft on my back like a grotesque growth, or the weight of the world bending me in half. The whole mess remained strapped to me as I hopped across the room. When I got to the far wall, I turned and slammed the bed frame against the door. Slam. Slam. Slam.

The eye slot shot open. "Oh, for God's sake. Mary Beth. Mary Beth!" It was Sister Alice.

The door opened. I tried to hop but fell on my stomach. The bed crashed on my back. The nurse and Sister Alice grabbed hold of the metal frame and tried to turn it right side up. They couldn't.

"Orderlies!" Mary Beth yelled. "Get some orderlies. Orderlies!"

Sister Alice leaned and looked in my eye as I lay squished beneath the thin mattress and the metal frame. She looked at me long, hard, deep. I looked back with a fire to burn her up. She reached a hand in and touched my cheek. "Your face is a mess." The left jaw hurt where Jack got a few punches in.

"You oughta see the other guy."

She laughed and caught herself. She untied the wrist restraints, scooted around the bed and undid my leg.

The orderlies rushed in and took the bed off. It hadn't really hurt. I had a high pain threshold anyway. "Don't move until I check you," Sister Alice said. She turned to the orderlies. "Take the bed out of here, please."

They hauled it up and out, and she shut the door. She felt my body with her puffy hands. It'd been so long since I'd been touched, and I felt almost human as her fingers touched my calves, the back sides of my knees, my ribcage and my neck.

"OK, nothing's broken."

I scooted up against the wall and rubbed my wrists and ankle. "Did you hear they're sending me to Fulton? You know what they're going to do!"

Sister Alice sat with her back against the wall next to me. "You're going to need all the strength you've got. You got a lot of strength inside, but you're going to have to build yourself back up." She had a rotund stomach and kept trying to find a way for her legs to be comfortable: up in front, stretched out, sideways. "You have a powerful gift, Pearl. I've been blessed to witness it. The Lord has blessed you, and He wants something from you."

I shuddered. I wanted to scream, *God is not a He!* but kept quiet. She turned toward me.

"With the world the way it is, and with you being so open, it'll be easy to get thrown off your strength, to be thrown off your truth. You always have to come back. Can you do that? Can you always find your way back to your truth?"

She took off her thick glasses and used a white tissue from her sleeve to clean them. Her eyes were buggy but surprisingly small without the magnified glass. I noticed for the first time that she smelled like Juicy Fruit.

"What if the truth is horrific?" I asked. I couldn't get that last vision on the ward out of my head, seeing the world end like that. Why me? Why'd I have to hold those images lodged in my head?

"Real truth is blissful," she said with surprising misery. "I know you know joy. I can see it shining off you."

I didn't want to talk about joy. Not in this place. "What *is* truth, anyway? How does anybody really know what the truth is, what reality really is? Are the Catholics right? The Native Americans? The Russians?"

"People spend their lives figuring truth out. It's a lifetime thing." She shifted her chubby legs. "But sometimes we get too far away from reality. Do you understand?" She looked at me, started to say something, stopped herself. "You're not the only one who sees things differently, Pearl."

She went somewhere else, somewhere deep in her own self. There was that glow again. "Do you know how many times I've been told I'm wrong?" She was quiet for a while, rested her chin on her chest.

She looked back up. "I'm not sure all the madness is wrong. I think some of how we're all feeling is spiritual. I think if you're not feeling bad about the world, you're not paying attention. I think some of the people who end up here are the barometers of how the world's doing. I think some of them are actually philosophers or geniuses or, like you, seers. But we can't listen to them if we drug them all up." She looked at me scared and worried. "I've said too much. My views aren't very popular."

She scooted next to me until our sides were touching.

"I don't know if you think some miracle is going to save you." She took off her glasses again, cleaned them. "Some divine intervention, some vision. But I'm not sure this world works that way. I know there are miracles, but sometimes I don't think it's a miracle we need. Sometimes I think it's just a decision." She blinked her eyes a dozen times. "I think it's just about shifting your mind. What you love, not what you hate. What do you love, Pearl? Maybe it's not a miracle, it's a decision."

As I looked at Sister Alice, I saw myself reflected there. Who would've thought I would see myself in a nun?

I heard the door rattling as someone was opening it. I scooted away from it, buried my head on folded arms. "If they give me the shock, I won't have any head left for anything, not truth, not strength, not decision making, nothing."

"I know. I know." She awkwardly pulled herself off the floor. "Let me see what I can do." She walked toward the door. "Meanwhile, don't do anything else to upset people."

I kept my head bowed. She left the room.

earth

It was a couple of days later. They'd let me out of solitary confinement for good behavior. Good behavior meant complete apathy. Good behavior meant drugs that kept you mindless. Good behavior meant fitting in and not causing a stir. I slumped against a wall. They told me it'd take about another few days to get all the paperwork together for the transfer to Fulton. Sister Alice told me she was doing everything she could to stop them. She was talking to Jack, to the therapist, to the powers that be. I felt hopeless, felt like the Sister Alices of the world had no real power anyway.

It was outdoors time. Through the window I could see some of the residents playing with an orange ball. The nurse hollered that I had a phone call. I went into a booth, waited for the phone to ring through. I picked up the receiver.

"Hello."

"Hey, sister."

"Meghan?"

"Your one and only."

She waited for me to say something. When I didn't, she said, "So, how's the funny farm?"

"Not a farm and not so funny," I whispered. Out the window, the residents were holding hands in a circle around the single tree in the yard. The branches were cracked like old lady fingers. I wondered if the tree was sleeping for the winter, or just dead.

"I need your help," she said, her voice like a scared little girl's.

"You need *my* help?"

"I got to get out of here, blow this pop stand. I got to get some money to get out of here. I got sick and couldn't, um, work, you know. Russell's trying to find me. I got to get hold of some cash. Pearl, he wants to kill me."

"You need me to get you some money." I said it flatly. I was stuck on a psych ward, and my sister wanted money.

She started crying, "I didn't know nobody else I could call."

I looked around the ward, at the locked doors, and burst out laughing. I laughed, bent over with the receiver to my ear. I laughed until I was crying. The nurse at the nurse's station kept looking over. I remembered the rubber room and took the laugh to a whisper.

"Sure," I said quietly, protecting the mouthpiece with my hand. "Sure, Meghan, I'll help."

"Great. Thank you, Pearl. Thank you." I heard her drag on her cigarette. "OK. Meet me tomorrow at like five at the Montgomery Ward, OK?"

I kept nodding with the receiver, saying nothing. I knew what I had to do.

"OK?" Meghan said. "Alright. See you there."

The next afternoon, I was at Jason's door, standing on his crooked porch. The sky was light blue, bright. A surprisingly warm winter day, as if we'd entered a January spring. As if the transition season, the thawing, had come way earlier than expected. I stood catching my breath, staring over my shoulder, knocking anxiously.

The door opened and behind the screen stood Jason's mother, Mrs. Paulson. She wore a painting smock and had her hair back. She stood steady like she was sober. I'd never seen her sober.

"Is Jason here?"

"He isn't back from school."

"Do you mind if I wait for him inside?" I didn't linger for her to answer; opened the screen, took another look over my shoulder and edged myself past her.

It'd been so easy. I'd gone out with the others for outdoors time. A couple of the patients were throwing that damned orange ball, and I grabbed it, tossed it back and forth with them for a while, then threw it too hard toward the tree line. I yelled that I'd get it and just took off. It wasn't like the place was maximum security. St. John's was in town, and I ran the back roads to Jason's.

I'd been off the drugs for twenty-four hours. I figured out a way to hold the pill in my mouth next to my teeth instead of swallowing. I hadn't taken the sleeping pill the night before, either.

Before I left, I took Jason's sky painting to Lulu's room and hung it in her line of vision. I touched her big head and said goodbye. She and Sister Alice were the only two I'd miss. I'd have to write Sister a letter later and explain. I had to leave books and notebooks behind. It seemed I was always having to leave my stories behind.

I sat on the sofa while Mrs. Paulson flitted, touching every object she passed. Fringed lamp shade, turtle-shaped ashtray, wall clock. She seemed spacey but alright. I'd never seen her anything but drunk. I realized watching her, I'd never really *seen* her at all. She didn't seem to know that I had been in a psych ward. I wasn't surprised that Jason hadn't told her. I assumed he rarely told her anything.

"When does Jason usually get back?"

"Any time now. He'll be back any time."

I needed his car to get to the house. I knew Jack kept money stashed in the closet. I wrung my hands. This was one place they were sure to look for me. I saw his mom staring. I didn't want her to ask questions and said, "You don't need to hang out here because of me, if you've got some painting to do."

She came over to the sofa. I looked up at her. She had the same faraway blue eyes as Jason. The booze had burst capillaries on her cheeks and nose, but sober you could see some of the past beauty in her. She said, "I know you been real good for Jason, and I always wanted to thank you."

I sat back. Me? Good for Jason? I was the best Jason had? Dear Lord.

She must've taken my reaction for judgment. "I know I ain't been much of a mother. I know. I knew he was beatin' up on him." She must've been talking about her boyfriend. So that's where the bruises on Jason's face came from. I was so absorbed in my life I knew nothing of Jason's. I felt red-hot shame.

"I know I let him come back even though Jason begged me not to." I stared at my hands. She said, "But I threw him out." She waited for me to say something. "For good." She looked down at my head, maybe waiting for absolution. I certainly had none to give. People were always opening up to me like that, always expecting some wisdom from me. Who was I to judge any other person's life, to forgive any other person?

All I could think to say was, "You got a real gift with the art, Mrs. Paulson. The way you have with light and color. It has a strong effect on a person."

She looked like I'd slapped her. I guess she didn't expect it. Tears sprung to her eyes and she left the room, on the way touching a framed picture of her as a new mother holding Jason as a baby.

I went to the front windows and looked nervously out, paced the living room, picking and sucking on my thumb. Jason kept his easel and paints in one corner. I picked my way around the drop cloth and tubes of paint scattered on the hardwood.

The massive canvas on the easel was yet another painting of the sky. He was so obsessed with the damned sky. But this time, it wasn't him looking up from the ground—it was as if he were floating. Along the bottom edge of the canvas, patchwork land. The sky itself was royal, navy, indigo. Iridescent, glimmering, flickering. His colors were symbols. His strokes were a language that came before words ruined everything.

Jason came through the door. I leapt up, ran and hugged him. I'd never hugged him before, and he stood stock still as if he were shocked. He'd grown so tall. How had he grown so much in just a few short months? His face was square, masculine. His arms and torso were thicker. I stared up at him.

"What are you doing here? What's going on? I didn't know you were getting out." He put his hand in the back of my hair.

"I need your car. Can I borrow your car?"

He put his backpack down. "What do you need my car for?" He still had the keys in his hand. I reached out and took them. He held my arm. "You're not going anywhere until you tell me what's going on."

He led me to the couch. I explained how they were sending me to Fulton, how Meghan had called needing money.

earth

Jason had his head down like he was deep in thought. He reached over, took the keys out of my hand, said, "I know I can't stop you, so I'm going to drive you."

"I need to do this on my own…"

"I'm driving you," he said, jaw set.

We parked at the bottom of Powwow. Mother was out. Jack was at work. I knew St. John's would be searching for me, and we had to hurry. I didn't know what I was going to do after I got the money, after I gave it to Meghan. Maybe I'd run away with her.

We walked in and half the kitchen had been packed into boxes. A grief came over me, but I pushed it down deep, as far down as it would go. I left Jason in the kitchen and ran back to the master bedroom. I knew where Jack kept his money. When he'd first started staying, he'd showed me a can he dumped his money into every night, then made sure to tell me not to touch it. It was just the perverse way Jack worked. He'd pointed to the can and then to me. *No touch, understand?* he'd said, like I was some retarded kid.

I opened the closet. On the back of the door hung a plastic shoe holder with dozens of Mother's glittering shoes. The whole closet stank of Jack's cologne.

I reached to the top shelf, shoved a pile of books out onto the floor, and grabbed the can. It was heavy with coin, and I could barely haul it down. I sat cross-legged on the floor and emptied it, coins and bills tumbling into a mound on the carpet. I counted more than four hundred in bills, probably another seventy in coins.

"You owe me, Jack," I said out loud as I stuffed the bills into my pockets. "Somebody certainly owes Meghan." Probably it was Father who owed both of us, who'd smashed our lives down, cracked our lives open, but he was dead, and now there was Jack to blame. I started loading my pockets with the coins, but they jangled and were too heavy so I put them back.

As I hauled the can back up, I smelled something hard and yellowed. A rush of gamey memories. I dug to the back of the closet. Beneath boxes and old shirts, I unearthed a pair of Father's boots. What were Mother and Jack doing with a pair of Father's boots? That Mother had kept them gave me a sudden crazy rush, something like hope. I took the boots out. They were steel-toed, the leather worn from years of tramping from barn to field to forest. The toes were darkened with the blood of wild beasts. The stench threatened to pull me backward. I hauled the can back down and poured the coins into the opening of the boots. I ran upstairs into my bedroom and took a jam jar full of earth.

In the kitchen, I saw the Pearl file on the kitchen table. I grabbed it. I would not be defined by the likes of Jack. I would not have my story told by the likes of men like him. Under the sink, I grabbed a garbage bag and stuck the boots and the file in. I ran upstairs to my room and snatched up a pile of black notebooks. I remembered where I'd hid the pouch from Meghan. It was like I was leaving a piece of me to be sold to the highest bidder—I couldn't just leave it. I heard a car outside, ran back to the kitchen and grabbed Jason's arm. "Let's go."

We ran out the back door, down the slope of the backyard.

"Where are we going?" Jason yelled behind me. Lady Luck whined as we passed his dog house, and I felt a pang deep in my gut for him, but we had no time.

We entered the forest line. I couldn't believe Jack was selling this forest. I'd known these trees all my life. I'd climbed them, spoken to them. I was intimate with their mulch. Every tree had a story. Every branch a plot, theme, character. What happened when you rid the land of forests? You destroyed its tales, its chronicles of root and bark. The loss took me out of my body; some part of me flew up and out.

We made it to the sassafras. Seeing it was like taking in a big gulp of air after holding my breath for months. I put the garbage bag down.

earth

There was something about my feet sunk into the muddy ice of the clearing, about the gritty cold winter smells, about the far-off echoes of crows in the leafless wood. It was as if the ground was shifting beneath my feet. I went over and pushed back the log, grabbed the mud-smeared pouch.

The base of my skull buzzed. I arched. The vision felt like a rape. The Osage woman whipped down, picked me up, flew me up into the trees.

From above, I looked down at the scene in the clearing. I was on my knees, back arched and head thrown back as if I was pleading toward the heavens. Jason stood over me, distraught, but he turned as if he'd heard a noise, and Jack ran into the clearing.

Jack screamed something, looked around him on the ground, leaned down and picked something up. It was a sopping dollar bill. There were bills in the mud all over the clearing. The money must've fallen out of my pocket. Jack picked more off the ground, wiped them against the grass.

He shouted something at Jason and ran toward where I was kneeling.

Jason lunged at him, shoving him hard in the chest. Jack fell back, righted himself, put his shoulders down like a football player, and rammed Jason in the gut. I felt rather than saw Jason growl. I felt a rage vibrate his body, a frenzy that had nothing to do with Jack or me; a fuming that had built in his own life. Jack and Jason went into an elemental dance of rage, both hitting the ground hard, clashing, smashing like great forest beasts, flesh and muscle contracting, expanding, pummeling. They picked up the earth with their backs, turned brown and muddy, swelled and cursed like a broken-open earth.

Mother leaned sideways at the edge of the clearing, one hand to her face, the other on her stomach. From above, they looked like a tableau of some dark fairy tale family: broken, muddied, pleading, sick.

Through the trees, I could even see Lady Luck, brought low by his chains, head down on the frozen soil, that whine piercing the soul.

The Native woman turned me until I was gazing into her face, made more of light and color than form. Her dark eyes expanded until I felt swallowed within them.

Her hand reached out toward the pouch. She took hold of it, opened it and pulled out the arrowhead. She tied the arrowhead to a spear she held, took leather strips from her belt and wrapped it until the arrowhead was tightly affixed.

She backed up. She held the spear aloft, aiming straight toward me. She lunged at me, drove the arrowhead directly into my heart.

I arched with excruciating pain, with piercing joy, unrelenting despair mixed with merciless bliss. She turned my flesh inside out. In primal shock, I stared at her, the spear protruding from my chest. She'd ripped my heart full open. The pain of it was nearly unbearable.

I was suddenly slammed back into my body. Knees icy against frozen mud, I wobbled with exhaustion. My fleshy heart was gutted animal flesh, ripped into chunks. In my imagination, I forced the flesh back together with barbed wire. My torn-up barbed-wire heart.

Jack and Jason still grunted and grinded across the clearing.

"No," I said, but it coughed out of me in a throaty whisper. "NO!" I wailed, a deep cry for a broken me, for a bruised Jason, for all of our brutalized selves.

Jack and Jason pulled apart. Panting and stumbling, they turned to look at me.

"This can't be the way. There's got to be another way," I said.

Jack grabbed Jason's arm, but he pulled away and ran to me. He kneeled in front of me, wiping a muddy sleeve across his forehead. Already his right eye was swelling up. He hugged me hard against him. I was like a ragdoll in his arms. Mother stood to the side, simmering with a sickly mustard tint.

Jack spit blood into the mud. "Another way…There's only one *way*." He leaned, holding his gut, and picked up a bill out of the mud. He held it up. "A one-way ticket to Fulton." He was panting. Jason must've gotten in a few good licks. "Go on, get up. And if you don't come peacefully, I'm going to go to the police to add a theft charge to your problems."

Jason scrambled up and started to lunge at him again. I leaned forward and grabbed his leg with what little strength I had. "No, this just isn't the way." I knew when I was a little girl that somehow people had gotten it all wrong, and I knew right then that this moment in the clearing we were the result of generations of people who had gotten it wrong for years and years on end.

I grabbed a sloppy wad of cash next to me, stood up, came up to Jack. "If this is what you want, you can have it. All of it." I crammed the muddy money into Jack's hands. "It's not worth it." I looked him hard in the eye, and he looked like he wanted to kill me. I swear he wanted me dead.

"Jack, just let me go," I said. I put my hand to my chest. My heart hurt. "I'll go live with Jason or something. Just let me go."

"You have got to be kidding. You escaped a psych ward!" He pointed, sputtering to where I'd been kneeling moments before. "You are clearly out of your mind."

I didn't know if my visions were insanity, or what they were, but my worst fear was someone like Jack defining me, people like Jack putting me into a box and nailing it shut.

"Jack," Mother finally spoke. She rubbed her belly and looked at him with plaintive eyes. "Maybe she's right. Maybe we don't need all this trouble."

I stared at Mother. Something was different—the way she held her stomach, that sickly hue to her flesh. Of course! Why hadn't I seen it sooner? She was pregnant. All those years she'd tried to have another baby with Father, and just like that, she and Jack were starting a whole new family.

A peace came deep into me. I saw a glow in the alders and thought it was the Native woman. Mother was pregnant, and Jack thought I was crazy, and I was due to be transferred to a mental hospital. I saw it so clearly. And still a tranquility engulfed me, a moment of grace. I knew it wouldn't last forever. I knew it was a temporary reprieve, like the one beneath the willow in the dead of winter.

I said calmly, "I'm seventeen. I can figure someplace to stay for the next year. I'll be in college by the fall."

"What kind of game is everyone playing here? Pearl is sick!" Jack barked.

"I'll take care of her," Jason said.

"You?" Jack scoffed. I knew he didn't think much of Jason; Jack thought all real men carried guns.

Jason tensed and fisted up. I put my hand on his arm. "OK, so Jack, are you going to come with Mother and visit me at the nuthouse? Is that what you're going to do on Sundays? You going to tell that kid you're having," I pointed to Mother's stomach, "where their big sister lives?"

"How did you know?" Jack asked.

"I figured it out."

The bulging eye, the perfect cropped hair, the twitching hands that kept making fists…I saw Jack clearly, too. He wanted to make everything safe, just wanted everything to be ordered so that everyone would be safe. I stared at the wad of muddy money in his shirt pocket. Our definitions of safe were vastly different. Our definition of what was safe for me, for the whole blessed world, was at epic extremes on some profound continuum.

Mother said without looking at me, "We'll let you go."

"Sarah!" Jack exclaimed.

"Jack," she said sternly. He looked helplessly at her like a small boy. She looked at me. "Pearl, you can't ever come back and live at home. Understand?"

I nodded. Really this was between my mother and me. It'd always been between us. I said, "You have to get me out of the psych ward, and Jack has to drop all the paperwork or charges or whatever that was getting me sent to Fulton. You have to tell them you take full responsibility for my care. Say you're signing me up with another therapist or something. Lie and say I'm safe and living at home. Go to St. Francis and make them let me come back to school."

earth

"OK," Mother said. Her shoulders slumped like she was so exhausted she could barely stand. Jack rubbed his crew cut furiously with his palm.

Mother came up to me, leaned in and gave me a loose hug. We didn't hug. It wasn't done. She whispered in my ear, "You got to work real hard. Harder than you ever worked. Your life ain't going to be easy."

She moved back. She raised her hand, those knobby knuckles, and for the briefest moment, placed her rough palm against my cheek. I closed my eyes. When I opened them, she was already heading out of the clearing.

Jack held back. She called, "Jack, come on. Let's go home."

Jack came up and stood in front of me. Still his energy rattled my very foundation. His jaw worked despite his efforts to control it. "There's just one thing you gotta get before I go. I was never 'out to get you.' I was trying to get you some help. I'm not the evil stepfather here."

I was about to say something, something I hoped would clear all this up, but I had no words.

"I'm not!" He turned and thrust himself out of the clearing.

Jason and I stayed in the clearing for a while. I needed to say my goodbyes to that frozen patch of earth. I looked around for a long time, ran my hand over rough bark, mulched log, icy stones. It was like leaving a long-lost friend.

As we came out of the woods, we passed Lady Luck whining at his dog house. I didn't think, just handed Jason the garbage bag with Father's boots inside, bent and undid the chain around the dog's neck. I picked him up, stuck my face in his matted, filthy fur, carried him up the hill, beside the house, and down the middle of Powwow, and put him in the backseat of Jason's car.

We went to Jason's house first; Jason got out and took Lady Luck. I got in the driver's seat. I was late and had to drive fast. When

I pulled into Montgomery Ward, Meghan was there, pacing. She didn't recognize Jason's car, so I had a moment or two to study her.

She wore a long black coat with torn tassels at the chest, some second-hand coat from a high school's marching band. Combat boots laced up to her knees. Black hair pulled back. White makeup and lipstick so red she looked like a wacked-out modern geisha. I knew it sounded crazy, I knew Meghan was trouble, but deep down I really loved her.

A beat-up blue truck was parked nearby, and she kept going to the passenger side. I could just make out the woman sitting in the seat. She was the one with the red afro, the one I'd met while lying on the sidewalk in East St. Louis.

I pulled up some more. Meghan looked hard toward the car and ran up.

"Shit, you're late!" she said. "You escaped OK from the funny farm, huh." Her arm moved toward my pouch. I'd cleaned it up as best I could and tied it back around my neck. I reached up and took her fingers off it.

"See that truck?" she said, smiling. "That's my new truck." She'd lost another tooth on the same side, leaving a gaping hole that made her look like white trash. "Aphrodite and I are heading out west. Road trip." She looked at me serious. "Hey, why don't you come with us?"

I laughed and shook my head. Her face fell like I'd slapped her. She said, "Forget it then. You got the cash?"

I rummaged in the garbage bag in the floorboard on the passenger side. I'd already decided what I was going to give her, but I was nervous about not having cash, so dug around to stall her.

She said, "When you came to visit me in East St. Louis, you really saved my life." I looked up hard and fast.

"What?" She was taking a deep drag on her cigarette and didn't answer. "What'd you say?"

"When you came to visit. I'd be dead right now if it weren't for that visit. Russell or somebody would've killed me. I'd felt it coming for a couple of years. That if something didn't change, I was going to die."

I stared at her wide-eyed. Both of her hands rested on the edge of my window, and I looked down at her fingers. She wore six rings, crazy vintage stuff, old pieces of metal.

"I know you hate me," Meghan continued. I started to say something, to say, *I love you so much it hurts*, but she batted me away. "But when you showed up, for the first time I thought maybe, just maybe, somebody somewhere gave a shit about me. When I left home when I was a kid, nobody even tried to find me." She tried to hide the tears. "Did you know that? Nobody even came looking for me."

Aphrodite honked the horn. She hollered out the window. "Lila, we gotta book. We're late."

Meghan wiped her snot on the back of her hand. "Anyway, who cares, right? Poor little fucked-up Meghan."

I leaned over and felt around in the garbage bag on the floorboard. I didn't know how to tell her I didn't have the money. I took the jam jar out of the bag, handed it to her. She held it up, stared at it. When she didn't speak, I said, "You're an artist. You know that, right? You have a gift. You know that, right? "

"Fuck. Goddamn. Fuck. Shit." She paced around the truck, her face twisted like she was in physical pain, holding up the jar in her fist. "I ask you one fucking thing. One goddamn motherfucking thing in my whole fucking sorry life. You bring me dirt? Dirt? Is this what you think of me?"

She leaned in the window with the jar and looked like she would hit me in the head with it. "Jack caught me," I whispered frantically. "I tried to get you the money. I got caught. It's from the farm. The earth…" I looked into her blue cracked eyes and saw Father's violence in them, a brokenness and rage that went back generations. She drew her arm back and I closed my eyes, held my breath and waited. Instead I heard a crash, opened my eyes with trepidation and saw the jar broken on the pavement.

She put her face in mine. She smelled like menthol cigarettes and sweat. Those eyes. Shattered windows to a broken soul. I knew then how careful I would need to be. I would become like Meghan if I didn't watch out. I'd need to be real careful.

"Maybe it's not your fault. Maybe you're just like me." She narrowed her eyes. "Jack," she said in a hard whisper. "Russell. They're all Jacks. They're all Russells."

All the fight seemed to go out of her. She hung her head, hangdog depressed, wiped a runny nose with her cigarette hand. A flood of grief seemed to well behind her face. Aphrodite honked again. Meghan put her hand on mine where it rested on the open window. The pressure was hard on my fingers, painful, and I was scared. But she released me suddenly. Looked like she wanted to say more but couldn't.

I watched her walk to the truck, shoulders hunched like a little girl. It was as if she was moving in slow motion, in a poetic unfolding of murky grief. I had no idea when I would see her again. My sister. Flesh of my flesh. I felt a pulling in my belly. *There go I. There go I. There go I.*

Just as she reached the truck, it registered what she'd said about when she ran away. I yelled after her, "Father went crazy after you disappeared. He drove all over looking for you."

She paused but she didn't turn to look at me. She held up her hand and waved me away.

"He went crazy, looking," I yelled. I knew even as I was screaming this at her how twisted it all was, a sick and mean father had gone looking for his runaway daughter and that was somehow a good thing. This was the consequence of a hard childhood, the love and hate all mixed up in your blood.

She put up both of her hands in surrender, still not turning around. I yelled, "He never got over you leaving. I swear I'm telling you the truth."

She got in the truck, backed up and pulled around Montgomery Ward and out of the lot.

chapter 20

JASON AND I were on the highway heading toward St. Louis.

"I wish you'd tell me where we're going," I said.

"It's not a surprise if I tell you." Jason laughed and played with the radio. Prince was singing "Kiss," and his voice kept fading in and out. Jason had told me that morning he had an early college graduation gift for me, if I'd accept it. We'd already been driving an hour.

"Does it have something to do with art?" I asked. In the backseat was an easel and a tool box covered in oil paint smudges.

"Yes and no."

"Thanks, that clears things up." Prince's voice had faded to static, and I tuned to a country station. Willie Nelson sang, "*Until there was no room at all, no place to run, and no place to fall.*"

"So, I'm assuming Bonnie couldn't make it," I said.

"Yeah, I guess that's what happens when you have a four-year-old," Jason said. "You become an adult overnight." Bonnie had gotten pregnant when we were still in high school. When we went up to collect our diplomas, her belly was out to there. I didn't see much of her anymore. The kid thing really freaked me out.

"I don't think it was just about the kid. When I told her it was a college graduation gift, she looked so uncomfortable. I think it has something to do with the fact that she didn't go."

earth

I thought of Bonnie all those years ago, how she'd hold her hand out flat, saying "How" like a Native American. How she'd say, "You smart. Me dumb."

I wish I could've told her life had nothing to do with how smart you were, not really. Deep down, I felt guilty about Bonnie, about not seeing her so much anymore, about moving on. I looked up at Jason and for some reason felt the same guilt. He was working part-time on a farm bailing hay, and he'd gotten so buff and tanned; his eyes were clear, his jaw square. Being outdoors was good for him. Girls chased him now, but he never seemed to have a girlfriend.

He looked over at me and smiled. "So what are you going to do with that fancy degree of yours, anyway?"

"I don't know." I turned up Willie Nelson loud to drown out my thoughts and said under my breath, "I have no frickin' idea."

A lot had happened in the past four years. I moved in with Jason and his mother. Lady Luck died. He only lasted a year, but it was a good year. He and Mrs. Paulson fell in love. She'd sit in the torn recliner in the living room, and Lady Luck would rub his loose belly flesh along the warp and weft of the rag rug at her feet, smile up at her. The two became inseparable. He spread himself out in the bed with her, hobbled through that old house with her, ate when she ate.

Sister Alice and I wrote letters back and forth every few weeks. She had answered all kinds of questions about visions, spirit, faith, things like that. She gave me a reading list. Some of the Catholic doctrine left me cold, but I read all the books anyway. One talked about people who'd done healing with their hands. A lot of it was too much to take in. Sister Alice wrote in one of her letters that figuring out the purpose of the visions could be a lifetime journey. After a while, I stopped going through the reading list. I stopped writing Sister Alice. I wanted a normal life, a normal career. I just wanted to be normal.

I had to give Mother some credit. She did what I'd asked. She got the orders dropped to send me to Fulton, and I never went back to the psych ward. She got me back in high school. I had to work to catch up, but it wasn't that hard. I ended up winning a big journalism scholarship. That scholarship was one of the few times I had some real hope, like the universe didn't hate me after all, that someone like me could possibly make it in the real world.

I helped Jason find a local art college. We filled out the application together. We created his portfolio. I drove him to the college to drop it off. He was shaking with nerves when we got there. I had to wrench it from his clenched fist and hand it in for him.

So, while Jason went to art school, I went to college for journalism. While he painted and his canvases took over the entire living room with the subtle smudge of oil and the clinging scent of turpentine, and while his mother had her week-long binges, I drove forty minutes up the road to another world.

The University of Missouri was a good college with an internationally renowned journalism school. The teachers had been editors at the likes of *Time* and *Newsweek*. The student body came from around the globe. The first few weeks, I thought I'd died and gone to heaven. Who knew heaven was forty minutes up the road?

While Jason painted, I sat cross-legged on the mattress and studied late into the night. Visions or no visions, I was going to have a career. I was going to make something of myself. No matter what it took. One thing I could always count on was my brain. I had a good brain. If it weren't for my unrelenting soul, I'd have been just fine.

No one I'd known had gone to college. I had no connection with my mother whatsoever, not that she knew anything about college. That was the problem with being poor—you had nowhere to go for advice. People thought that the poor lacked motivation, but really it was information. Such floundering passed down through the generations.

Journalism school proved to be my saving grace. It was a study in separating the self, in analyzing details, refusing emotions, keeping oneself outside the world's story. We learned to disconnect. We studied how to feel nothing, how to eradicate hearts. I needed that distance.

It was a schizophrenic time at Jason's house, with his explosions of color and texture, and my desperate desire for perspective.

In class, we read newspapers and studied earthquakes, tornados, fires and floods. They sent us out to cover local events. I learned to interview the soaked and the scorched with ice-cold detachment. We moved on to global catastrophes, third-world mudslides, Asian hurricanes, Middle Eastern wars, tsunamis in the Orient.

The world's trauma wasn't that far from my visions. It felt familiar. Maybe this was what I was called to do, to go out into the world and make sense of the clutter, to clean up the messes. From a distance.

I'd stopped smoking, started running again.

There were two things I had to work at. Jason thought we were a couple. We didn't kiss or cuddle or sleep together, but he treated me like a girlfriend. I picked my thumbs bloody over it every day. I didn't want to hurt him, but I knew marrying him would ruin my life.

Second, his mother drank in her bedroom, but nearly as often, I drank too, at night, in the living room. I had to watch the boozing. I would end up like Meghan or Mrs. Paulson if I didn't watch it. Alcoholism went back generations. I came from a long line of self-medicators. I knew I was skating on thin ice there.

I had stopped taking the medication. I'd always been sensitive to medicine, but those pills wacked me out. There was no way I could live anything close to normal with that in my system.

Some of the best advice Sister Alice gave me was practical. She kept talking about balance, how I had to keep the balance. She wrote a list in one of her letters. No alcohol. No drugs. No smoking. No bars. No boys (for a while). No cruising. No Meghan. The last one wasn't difficult. She wasn't around, anyway. I'd gotten one postcard a month after she left for California, but then over the past three years, nothing. I didn't even know if my sister was still alive.

Meanwhile, during all of this, Mother had a new life. Mother had all she'd ever hoped for—a new house, boy and girl twins. The kids were five years old. Every now and then she invited me to their birthday parties and such, but I didn't go. I couldn't bear it. I saw her with the kids in town sometimes, far-off echoes of her, floating, pulsing like a mirage. Or maybe it was the other way around—maybe I was the far-off echo in her life; maybe I was the ghost who haunted her.

I was gaining some weight back. Jason said I was now "ten pounds short of normal skinny."

In my notebooks, I wrote my stories. I scribbled pages about Meghan. I wanted to tell her story. I didn't want anyone killing her with their versions. I wanted to tell Father's, to finish it. Mother's. To make it all better. No. To simply tell the truth. Whatever that was.

To tell the stories for the sake of tales left untold. For the sake of a bruised patch of Missouri land. For the sake of bruised parents, a bruised Meghan, a bruised me.

I looked up to see that we had turned off the highway and were driving down a gravel road beside manicured fields. In the distance, I could make out a large metal building, alone and isolated in the flat land.

"Is this my surprise?"

Jason smiled and nodded. "If it's too much, you don't have to do it," he said.

"My surprise requires I DO something?"

"Oh yeah. Yes. You must DO something."

We pulled off onto a dirt road and drove up to the building. It was a hangar. A single-engine Cessna was parked out front. My heart beat in frantic rhythm.

"This is a drop zone," Jason said. "I've been coming here for months on Sundays." I thought he worked on Sundays. "I've been skydiving. And when I'm not diving, I set up my easel and paint." He pointed at the backseat, then stared at me and waited for me to say something, but I had no words. "I signed you up," he said. When I still didn't say anything, he held up both arms. "Surprise!"

I looked around, terrified. This was where Jason had learned to love the sky. He'd been coming here for years, learning and learning to love the sky.

"So, this is why you have so many paintings of clouds."

He nodded. "Now it's your turn. If you're up for it."

I spent the afternoon practicing falling to earth. I stood shaky on a ladder over a patch of grass, the top metal rung biting into my calves. I learned to jump, tuck, roll. Jump, tuck, roll. The jumpmaster looked up at me and said he didn't know about the wind, whether it would cooperate, whether we would jump that day, or sleep in the hangar beneath the wing of the Cessna and wait for the sun to rise.

"I see," I said, through gritted teeth. "It's not just about the decision to fly—the elements have to be in some agreement."

He nodded.

I jumped.

I tucked.

I rolled.

We learned commands that we were to follow as we prepared to plunge.

Get your feet out and stop.

Get all the way out.

Go.

I was made to repeat these over and over: a spell, a prayer, a mantra to save a life.

Toward the end of the day, Jason ran out of the hangar where he'd been listening to the weather on the radio. Wild-eyed, arms flailing, he yelled, "The wind's crazy! We're not jumping today. We're not jumping!"

Oh the relief, the air blown out from clenched teeth, the sudden exhaustion. To lie down, to sleep, to not have to give oneself over to the elements. To hold on, to cling, to remain rooted to this brutal earth.

We curled in sleeping bags in the hangar beneath the wing of the Cessna. Jason's sleeping bag was royal blue, and his blonde hair stood in strong contrast. Behind him, the splayed wheels of the plane. Above us, the cold metal underside of the plane. Instead of the soft underbelly of mother, Jason and I got a cold concrete floor, glass, rubber and metal.

Jason was telling me about skydiving. "The first time I jumped, I came floating down after the chute opened, and I looked down and thought, wow, my feet are useless. I just couldn't stop staring at them, and thinking how useless they were. When are your feet ever useless?"

I pulled my hands out of my bag, reached over, took his face and kissed him full on the mouth. All I could think of was leaving the earth behind. He hugged me tight against him through the sleeping bag, so tight I couldn't move.

He said in muffled voice, "Pearls are so rare. You can look through a thousand oysters and not find one. Against all odds this beautiful thing grows from this speck." It sounded like something he'd said to himself a hundred times.

I yanked myself out of his grasp, kissed his mouth again.

He pulled his head back, clung to me through the sleeping bags.

"Pearl Elizabeth Swinton, I've been in love with you my whole life."

I didn't want to hear it. Since I'd moved into his house, I'd given up boys completely until I could figure myself out. I knew my path couldn't be with Jason, or with any guy. I said, "All I want is just this moment. Nothing tomorrow, nothing next week. Just right now."

We were making love. I'd had sex before, but this was different. He was a musical note, a tone. I found myself falling. I lost myself, mislaid the ground beneath my feet. I'd never felt anything like it. I started inside him, in his guts, his veins, his muscles, his innards. Then I flew up into the universe and I met Jason there. We were in a deep and quiet blackness, joined among the stars. We were a glowing ball of light. It was so quiet, so silent; we danced among each other's constellations.

The next morning, a kick in my side jolted me. The jumpmaster, grisly beard and eyes red, leaned over and said, "Dear Lord, I never heard anyone snore like that!" I groaned. He kicked again. "Get up. The conditions are good. It's time." I raised my head, and the large hangar door was open. The pilot had already backed the plane out. Frigid air hit my face. I found my underwear in the bottom of the bag and slipped them on.

"It's time," I repeated and looked over at Jason. I'd felt something the night before. Feeling was dangerous. The way love, real love, can be the most terrifying thing of all. I tried to smile but couldn't.

His eyes were full of such deep sadness, a specific misery. I wanted to find out why he was so sad, but there wasn't any time.

Jumpsuits hung on coat hooks along the side of the hangar. I put one on. My hands shook so badly. The jumpsuit hung on me like a potato sack. I grabbed a helmet. Fully clothed, I was burning up. *Oh, Jesus, the heat. The burning sweat in the scalp beneath the helmet itching underneath the canvas jumpsuit.*

Jason said, "I'm not going on the first run. I'm sitting this one out." I looked at him frantically. There were other jumpers there, ready to go, strangers.

He said, "It's your turn, Pearl. I'm sitting this one out. This is about you, okay?"

"Fine," the jumpmaster said. He put a parachute on my back. "You'd better get on out to the plane."

As we loaded, I was the last to get on, because I would be the first to get off. I'd begged to go first. I couldn't abide bearing witness to any other diver, watching the fear, the obedience, the surrender, the giving oneself over to the sky. Jason straightened my jumpsuit. That grief again.

"Take care of yourself," he said.

"Don't be so intense. I'm seeing you in like thirty minutes."

He straightened the helmet. "Time, tide and Pearl," he said. Again, that confusing sadness in him that I could not decipher.

I sat knees to chest on the cold metal floor, on the edge of the open Cessna door. We taxied down the brown field, put-a-put-put. I swore the oak trees at the edge of the runway nodded in the dry wind, laughing for what we were about to know, them with their roots. Jason stood back, kicked the dirt with the tips of his boots, watched me go.

We flew up to two thousand five hundred feet. I stared helplessly into expansive dawn sky, at the Tinker Toy buildings, at the birds flying below us. Before me, the artwork that Jason had been painting for the past few years.

We were told to cup the red plastic pull cords attached to our jumpsuits to ensure our chutes were not deployed unexpectedly, like airbags in a moving car, cloth ballooning out, surrounding our pilot, sending us into a tailspin. Oh, there were so many ways to die here.

"Get your feet out and stop," the jumpmaster said over the rumbled screams of the engine, over the howl of the seventy-mile-an-hour wind. The three strangers in the plane's dark belly watched me with deer eyes.

Skydiving by static line was nothing like you saw in the movies. You didn't just stand up and jump out. During training, we'd been given step-by-step instructions. I would put my feet out of the plane when the jumpmaster told me to. I would sit on the edge. I would put my hand out and grab the strut, my foot on a small step. I'd swing my body out and climb the strut, hand over hand until I reached the end, where the strut met the tip of the wing. During the process, I'd release my foot from the step. They assured me the wind would take me, hold my body aloft as I climbed the strut. Any divergence from the path could lead to death. This learning to fly was not going to be easy.

"Get your feet out and stop, I said," the jumpmaster shouted again. In slow motion, I swung my legs out. The wind took my boots like they were misfit toys, flew them hard backward until my heels slammed the outside metal. I pulled them back up, tried again, kept my boots close to the plane's body. I sat with my legs out of the plane and waited.

"Get all the way out," the course man yelled above the sound of the grumbling engine, the mumbling engine, the chugging engine. Like I was little in the lake and flailing for the dock after Father threw me in, I pushed my hand out, pushed the wind until I got that strut in my palm. Boots on tiptoe on tiny metal step. Funny air patterns like hieroglyphics written upon cheeks by blustery winds. I heaved my butt out of the plane—it felt like a thousand-pound boulder or apathy deep-rooted in soil. Anyway, I made it outside. I grabbed the strut with both hands like a security blanket, leaned in and wrapped my arms around it.

The base of my skull buzzed. My body arched. A vision. Now? Now?

The Native woman whipped down, plucked me off the strut, and flew me skyward. I faced the earth as we ascended, saw the farm where I grew up as a tiny speck on the horizon, flew up until I was seeing all of mid-Missouri, and farther until the whole of the Midwest lay below us. Still we rose, until the North American continent was in view, higher still, until I saw the ocean and faraway lands I'd only read about in books.

I grew terrified of what was happening to me and flailed my arms and legs. I felt like the Osage woman was tearing up my roots. I wanted to go back—not just to the wing of that plane, but farther, back to the ground. I so desperately wanted the Missouri soil beneath my feet.

The Osage woman still yanked me upward. Suddenly we stopped. Around us, abiding blackness. In front of us, the earth was a small sphere, glowing like a gem, glittering like a precious object. I imagined plucking it out of the sky and placing it in the pouch around my neck where I could keep it safe.

Even though I could not make out details, I understood others around the world felt like I did, like the little girl who'd loved the earth as herself and like the grown-up version now who felt she had lost herself, felt like she had to lose her real self to survive.

The Native woman was a swirl of dancing light floating beside me. *Others around the world felt this same love for the earth, felt this same brutalization*, she said without words.

I knew then what I had to do. It came to me as both a deep grief and a profound relief. I had to leave Missouri, say goodbye to the only land I'd ever loved. But more than that, I had to leave America. I had to go see the world for myself. It would be the only way to get the perspective I sorely needed. I was being thrust out of my twisted Eden. Forced to roam. Some crazy, heart-wrenching, gut-wrenching universal plan.

That was why Jason was so sad. He knew. This was why he'd brought me to skydive in the first place. He knew I needed to leave. This was the gift Jason was giving me. He was letting me go.

I fell back into my body. I was miraculously still clinging to the strut. I had both arms wrapped around it, and my cheek was pressed against the chipped metal.

I was so exhausted. The vision had left me tired—not just for the long life I'd already lived, but for the unknown I was now going to be forced to face.

I turned my head to look into the plane. The jumpmaster stood in the open doorway screaming at me, motioning with his arm. His face was red with fear. The wind roared in my ears and I could not hear him. I looked blankly down at high-rises and busy highways. The Cessna was circling over St. Louis, over roofs and telephone poles, bridges and rivers. In training, they'd told us that skydiving into a city offered too many ways to die, power lines and buildings, trains and trucks and such.

How long had the plane been flying in circles with me attached to its wing? How long had Jason been watching from below, the Cessna circling like a confused raptor? How long had he been waiting for his friend to fly?

earth

So tired. With the vicious wind tearing at me like a dog, the burden of the fifty-pound chute, the weight of my indifference, why not just let go now? Why not just take my chances falling?

I let go of my hold on the strut. I let my body fall backward.

Something caught me. Stopped me. The roar and slap of wind, me dangling. I was hooked on something. I looked over my shoulder, my obstructing helmet. The jumpmaster. He twisted in awkward, dangerous pose. He had a handful of my pack. He clung to the metal doorway of the plane. He grunted and yanked. He twisted and pulled. He hauled me back inside the belly of the plane. I sat on the metal floor. The others, crouched in the belly of the plane, looked terrified beneath their sweating helmets.

"I've never had anyone die on me, and you're not going to be the first!" the jumpmaster screamed. He cursed. He growled. He turned to the pilot. "Get the fucking plane back in position."

Crouching by that open door, I looked down at the rag-quilt earth thousands of feet below. The liquid loam earth, flesh of my flesh, the stuttered roots and brambles of this particular patch of scrub. I thought of how much I loved this earth. The most significant relationship in my life had not been with Father, Mother, Jason, Bonnie or Meghan. My biggest relationship had been with the land.

We were in position. The jumpmaster turned to me. "The only way you can fly is if you let go." Sudden tears sprung to my eyes. "Now get your ass up, and get out." His teeth tobacco-stained, his thumbnail cracked.

This time so numb, eyes as wide as headlights, feet out, drumming against metal. Hand on strut, climbing it fist over fist down the wing. Surviving on automatic, no thoughts, simple, simple. The force of air was enough to resuscitate an army, and me not even capable of breathing. As I held the strut, I had to let go of my foothold on the step. We were taught that as we let go of the step, as we held the end of the strut, the wind would carry us. Now was the time to step away, to hang on, to hope against hope that my feet flew out behind me like a flag in strong wind. With the strut in my palms, my feet slipped off their mooring. The wind took me. It took me. It held my belly and thighs and lifted me up, held me like Superwoman, like Miss Universe. I noticed for the first time how thin-boned my wrists were, how starved my arms amid so much cloud and sky.

I turned to look back toward the open door of the Cessna. At the jumpmaster. He stared back. Craggy face. As I was taught, I waited for his sign.

He pursed his lips and yelled, "Go!" like throwing an ugly wet kiss.

I.

Let.

Go.

more by caroline

PEARL'S JOURNEY CONTINUES *in Air, the second of the four books in the Elemental Journey series.*

Uprooted from the only land she has ever known, Pearl finds herself alone in the middle of Tokyo, a city so distant from her Missouri reality, it triggers no memories; a country so foreign, even the language cannot interfere. Here she hopes she can float above and find some perspective. Still, how will she manage the visions in this place where she doesn't know the rules?

an excerpt of air

HE 737 HIT a pocket of bad air and the plane jolted, did a stomach-clenching plunge. I flailed like I was falling off some cliff.

"Your first time flying?" the wiry man next to me asked, the seats bucking like some wild bull.

"No, not my first time." I yanked myself back from the visual precipice. Miles below, the Missouri earth reared up, a jarring patchwork of inlets and winding paths etched like frantic pencil drawings. The receding land seemed to wail a song of loss. "It *is* my first time on a commercial jet." I didn't tell him the only other time I'd flown, I'd jumped out of the plane. The plane hit a pocket of bad air and plunged. I clenched the armrests and felt like I'd vomit.

"It takes some getting used to, flying." The man worked his jaw like something was caught in his teeth, his face bone and angle, whiskers gone awry. From his armpits flowered a smell of musky deodorant and pit bull sweat.

Again a thump, a jolt. "Turbulence," the man said. A bit of something was wedged in his whiskers. "It's getting worse, you know."

In front and around us, the waft of large-boned perfume. A Baptist women's choir was on board, sixteen blooming women filling and refilling six rows. They began a whispered "Amazing Grace."

Through many dangers, toils and snares, I have already—

We jolted again. The man asked through clenched jaw, "Where you headed?"

"I'm moving to Tokyo." We bucked and buckled.

That saved a wretch like me. I once was lost, but now—

.   "That'll take some getting used to, too." He hacked an involuntary cough. The plane jerked again, and someone in the back screamed an involuntary scream. We jerked, plummeted again, righted ourselves, jerked again. A collective whimpering filled the cabin.

When we've been there ten thousand years, bright shining—

"So, what's your story?" the man asked.

Something was rumbling up from the depths. I clenched the armrests harder, squished my face up. Dear God, not now.

"I know. I know," the man said, patting my clenched fist, "Talk and maybe it'll take your mind off the turbulence."

He didn't understand. This wasn't about turbulence. This was something far worse that turbulence—a turmoil of the soul, but worse still. I'd had it all my life. It showed up like an epileptic fit, and I had no control over it. I clenched hard down upon it, did everything in my power to smash it down for dear life.

The plane joggled again and the nose veered downward. One of the Baptist women screeched, "We gonna die! We all gonna die!"

A bell went off; the pilot's voice. "Sorry, folks, freak winds. We're doing the best we can. Stay in your seats and keep your seatbelts fastened."

Unexpected air pockets. Inexplicable winds. Unfathomable air.

The plane chunked hard left, down, right. Then the plane fell down, way down. There was no doubt now that the nose was aimed not skyward, but earth-ward. Everything seemed to be going in slow motion. Seatbelts strained against flesh. An overhead compartment exploded. Roller luggage, coats and handbags crashed down. Oceanic waves of despair floated; the smell of vomit rode the waves. My hand came down hard on top of the wiry man's, clenched and twisted, knuckles and nails.

Oh to come this far, to have left that landlocked place, to have sold everything that connected me to that gnarly patch of earth, to have kicked and fought my way into flight, to suddenly go down in that spit, that whistle of fire, water and earth.

"I don't want to die," a Baptist woman yelled.

The woman next to her cried in harmony, "Lord, take me gently."

And another, "Heaven make a place for me."

The leveling was abrupt. The plane went horizontal. A mass holding of breath. We waited. And waited. The leveling held. The balance remained. An eruption of applause. Oh the relief. My jaw was so tight I could hardly take in air and made little gasps like a panting Lady Luck. That dog was the only thing I'd really miss.

"Freak winds," the man whispered, as if to himself. I still held his hand on the armrest. I couldn't seem to will myself to move it. "I was a pilot." He extracted his hand. "I…" He punched a thumb in his chest. "Was…a…pilot."

I felt like I was going to vomit.

"Do you hear me? Are you listening to me?" He looked left and right, twitched in his seat. "I told them it was getting worse."

The Baptist women started humming, low and rhythmic.

"Oh, I used to be like you." He said it bitterly, pointed to my lap. I'd forgotten about the poetry book now smashed between my thighs. I had an intention to move my arm to grab it, but my white-knuckled hands wouldn't do my bidding.

"I used to think air had poetry." He spat out the last word. "When I was a kid, I always wanted to fly. Some teacher said the Greeks used to think wind was the earth breathing in and out. I got hooked." He tried to snap his fingers but couldn't. He reeked of ham hock and beans left cold on the stove too long. "Years I studied it, westerlies, trade winds, air pressure." He said *air pressure* slow and hard like the very phrase would make his head explode.

The Baptist women flowered into a low song. *Go tell it on the mountain, over the hills and everywhere; go tell it on the mountain …*

"I saw it changing. I saw it. I was a regional pilot. I saw it, and nobody would listen."

We were interrupted by a flight attendant handing out water. I still couldn't move my hands, and the guy grabbed the cup for me, put down my tray table. He put his face in mine. His mouth stretched wide over distraught teeth. I could feel my skin stretched too, the fleshy consequence of troubled winds. Another flight attendant, green in face, held a garbage bag and people were throwing in their vomit bags. The smell of it bled up into the face.

"What is it you do for a living?"

"Journalist," I managed. I hadn't actually worked as a journalist yet, just earned my degree. I didn't want to talk to this man. He was disturbing me almost as much as the turbulence. I turned my head to the window and pretended to watch the sky. The sight of all that defiant air sickened me, so I had to turn back.

"Don't even try to write about this, these winds. Hear me? I tried. I started saying there's something wrong, years ago. It was like the winds were slowly going insane. I tried to make people listen. Nobody listened. At first. Then they said I was crazy, and it was the stress, and they fired me. They will think you are crazy," he spat, sweating. "Well?"

"Okay." I pried my hand loose from the armrest, used the claw to grab at my water cup. I spilled it on the way to my mouth. "Okay, I promise," I said, dribbling water from the corners of my mouth like a handicapped child. Again I felt the peril in my gut, energy rumbling up, a fit threatening to outdo me. "I won't ever discuss the wind."

To continue reading, please look for a copy of *Air* by Caroline Allen on your favorite online retailer.

book group guide

THE FOLLOWING QUESTIONS are designed to spark dynamic discussion around the plot, characters, setting and themes in *Earth* for book groups and for individual readers.

To investigate further, readers can find an Enhanced Book Group Guide, including additional discussion questions and writing exercises, as well as recommended reading on subjects like mysticism, visual art and animal rights, at www.carolineallen.com.

1. Pearl's visions play a significant role in the novel. Pearl resists them, saying, "I don't wish my way of seeing on my worst enemy." How is the metaphysical perceived by Pearl, her parents, and the rural Missouri community? What roles do the metaphysical and organized religion play in the book? Are they at odds? In what ways might they be similar? Nadine was "in and out of the nuthouse" because of her visions. Were Nadine's and Pearl's visions a form of mental illness? A prophetic gift? Both?

2. In *Earth*, Pearl does not feel herself as separate from the land. "When I was little, I could not discern myself from other living beings. Everything was me. Dog, deer, calf. Sassafras, cottonweed, elm. Stream, lake, river. Every boot entering dog flesh entered my flesh, every knife worrying a joint, worried my joint." How does the butchering of animals affect her? If she feels this close to animals, why, then, does Pearl decide she wants to go hunting? Why does she want to kill a deer? Is

there any significance to the fact that the deer she kills is a doe? Is there significance to the way she kills the deer? Later, Pearl's father says with disgust when he asks her to go hunting a second time, "You can eat it, but you can't kill it." What does he mean by this?

3. Pearl's family never tells stories about their ancestors and, as a result, very little family history is passed down from generation to generation. "The shut-down silence of my kin grew up my legs and thighs and torso. I seemed to become swollen with their quiet. It filled up my head with air. It brought my limbs to a place heavier than a plow." How does the lack of storytelling affect Pearl's understanding of herself and her family? How does it compel her forward in her own desire to read books, write stories, tell the truth of her family?

4. What role do books play for Pearl's family? What role do books play in Pearl's life? Her teacher opens a closet and reveals a wall of books. "I ran my sweaty palm over the rough spines of the paperbacks like a blind person reading in quick succession. Whole universes to explore. Whole universes that were there the whole time." How might the power of these books be likened to Pearl's visions? Nadine gives Pearl the gift of a book. Why do you think that Nadine gives her a copy of *Little Women*? Why do you think she didn't read it? What do you think she would think of *Little Women*? What other books are named in the novel, and why are they important?

5. Visual art plays a key role in the novel. Jason gives Pearl a sketch of herself riding her bike, and she is moved almost to fear. "All I really was thinking about was that sketch. It was the first time I realized art could tell so much truth it could scare the pants off a person." Pearl's father plays the fiddle and invokes the muddy rivers with his music. Pearl tells

Meghan she's an artist even though she doesn't know it. What role does art play in this book? Could art be compared to the visions? In what ways?

6. Pearl stops eating after her father's death. "I refused to eat. Hunger strike. I would desire nothing. *You cannot take from me that which I do not desire.* I would not desire the earth. I would not crave the soil. I would not want its food. I would not want *anything.*" Is Pearl's refusal to eat about the pain over the trauma in her life, or is she making a point by going on a "hunger strike"? What is her point? Desire is key to both Pearl and her mother. What does Pearl truly desire? What does her mother desire? What role does thwarted or realized desire play for the women in the book?

7. There is a strong dichotomy between farm and town in *Earth*. What does Pearl think of the two? What is her mother's view on "town"? What did Pearl mean by this: "Life began picking up speed. When I thought about it, it had started going too fast way before. Its speed had something to do with the neglected farm, with the magnetism of town. Its velocity scared me. I wanted to shout, *Slow down! I need to figure things out. Stop! What brick wall are we barreling toward?*"

8. There are several objects that hold importance in the novel: a fresh water pearl and an arrowhead in a leather pouch around Pearl's neck; the stones that Pearl's father collects; the shoes Jack gives to her mother. "The morning light glittered off them like stars. She put her leg up and jiggled her foot, throwing sparks across the kitchen…On her feet, the power of one told story." What stories do all of these objects tell about each character, their hopes and dreams and their journeys through the novel?

9. When Pearl is in the hospital, Sister Alice says, "I know there are miracles, but sometimes I don't think it's a miracle we need. Sometimes I think it's just a decision." What does Sister Alice mean? Do you think that Pearl takes Sister Alice's advice? What decisions does Pearl make at the end of the book? Why are these decisions important?

10. Why does the novel end with skydiving? While Pearl is practicing falling to earth at the drop zone, she says, "It's not just about the decision to fly—the elements have to be in some agreement." What does she mean by this? How does skydiving help her realize she needs to leave the only land she's ever known?

Layout & Formatting

Print layout and design by E-BookBuilders;
digital division of The Book Connection